Fae
Hunter

Book One: Soulstealer Trilogy

NICOLETTE REED

ISBN: 0985640103
ISBN-13: 978-0-9856401-0-1

To my husband, my lover, my best friend, and the one I credit with giving me the strength to make this all possible

ACKNOWLEDGMENTS

I wrote this book in solitary, but it would not have been published if I didn't have the help of others. I received a lot of feedback early on from my revision group at Bellevue College headed by Lois Brandt and from my friends and family who read this story in its infancy. To all those who have gone through this journey with me I thank you.

Thank you to my mother, who first put a pen in my hand and taught me how to make things up.

I want to give a special thank you to my co-worker and friend Brandy Welch, whose enthusiasm for this story and daily words of encouragement meant more to me than she could ever know.

Thanks to my editor, Sally Berneathy, who reviewed this manuscript in painstaking detail multiple times to make sure everything was right. After her rave review I really knew I had something worth publishing.

Thanks to my cover artist, Kim Killion, who took everything I said about my world and translated into a perfect picture.

Thank you to the RWA and PNWA for providing support to all your writers big and small and for giving me the tools I needed to get this far.

CHAPTER ONE

I inched along the narrow ledge that led to the gaping maw ripped from the side of the rock face which provided shelter for the dragon and a hiding place for the Soulstealer. Frigid winds blew up the side of the mountain mixing with the unnaturally warm air that emanated from the mouth of the cave. Each of my steps grew heavier as the thick mist clung to my ankles and the weight of my mission bore down on me.

"Goddess, I don't know how he can stand that heat." I paused before the entrance, pulled several full breaths of the cool outside air into my lungs and flattened my wings against my back, preparing to traverse the remainder of the unstable berm.

A thump against my back threatened to knock me off balance. "I can take lead. If you think you can't handle it, Valora." Orris's rotund stomach prodded me forward.

"You can put your wings away, Orris. Kali's orders are that I am first Hunter on this mission. So if you can't handle it then you can just fall back." I closed my eyes to regain my focus and tried to push the image of Orris's greasy-haired face out of my mind. He wasn't the only one who thought I couldn't handle this or any other assignment, but he was the only one alone with me on this ledge. Kali sent Orris to shadow me because she had to. She was the only one who believed in me.

Another bump from Orris, and the rock beneath my right foot crumbled. Heart pounding wildly as I stumbled, my hands flew forward in search of something to grab onto. My wings tried desperately to keep me from sliding down the side of the mountain. As my other foot lost its grip with the ledge and I felt myself slipping, a hand shot out and slung me back into the wall of rock, knocking the air from my lungs.

Orris tucked his muddy brown wings back behind him, making a point of extending them to their full span before doing so. "Yep, good you have me here to help you handle things." A smarmy grin washed across his bloated face. His stomach wasn't the only victim of his love of butter breads.

"If you hadn't bumped me." I clenched my teeth and struggled to regain my breath as I turned my face back towards the mouth of the cave. Orris always made sure to point out that I was not like the other fae, but I couldn't allow him to best me today. I had a Soulstealer to catch.

At least Orris and I could agree on one thing, if you were a fae accused by the King of being a Soulstealer then not even the Goddess could help you. The Hunters would make sure of it.

"I'm going in."

I pulled my sword from its scabbard and swept it back and forth in front of me. The silver blade was light but strong, hopefully strong enough to pierce a dragon's hide. It was hard to know for sure since this was the first time I had ever come up against a dragon, and a sword was not the fae's usual weapon of choice.

"I won't have long inside. If I am not back in two minutes, head back to the Peixes," I said.

From our vantage point atop Mount Elbrus, I could barely make out the shape of the airship tethered below. The combination of the natural fog layer and the smoke that emptied out of the dragon's cave obscured my vision.

I didn't wait for a response from Orris before entering the cave. I immediately slammed into an invisible barrier which froze me in place – a fly caught in the spider's web. I looked down, surprised to see a faint glow coming from the red jewel set into the amulet around the copper chain on my neck. The sticky strings of magic that surrounded me released their hold one by one, and I fell forward into the cave. Something had counteracted the spell the dragon put in place to ward off intruders. *Did every creature in the Realms use magic but me?* If it was my amulet's doing, it was something I had no idea it could do.

But I didn't have time to contemplate that now. Despite triggering the dragon's defenses there was no sign of it as I crept into the darkened cavern. The magic had released me, but the heat inside the cave took hold of me immediately. Fae were not used to this kind of heat, and I knew I didn't have time to take in the scenery.

I took the first of three tunnels, searching for the inner cave where my King said we would find the Soulstealer. The heat seemed to grow more intense with each step I took, wrapping around me and pressing into my very soul. I rounded a tight curve, and the tunnel opened up into a small hollow. A few feet ahead, the Soulstealer sat on the ground, head bowed as if in prayer.

The once-white wings of the Soulstealer were thick with the mire of his surroundings. They drooped heavily against his shoulders as if he didn't have the strength to lift them. He didn't move; he hadn't heard me come in. I stepped forward and pressed the tip of my blade into the small of his back.

"Get up slowly and turn around. No one needs to get hurt."

He turned his gaunt face to me. "It's too late for that, isn't it, Valora Delos? Too late for that."

I grabbed the fae by the arm and pulled him with me towards the mouth of the cave. Beads of sweat trickled down my forehead. I knew I was running out of time before the heat would get to me like it had this Soulstealer who had taken refuge here rather than answer for his crimes. He stumbled along behind me as we came to the grand entrance of the dragon's cave, its lair.

Unfortunately the dragon was there to greet me this time. Smoke filled the room. Between the legs of the scaly black beast, I could see the entrance of the cave fog over. Soon it would be completely concealed.

A clatter of metal from behind me broke my concentration. I turned to see several dwarves shooting forth from one of the other tunnels, brandishing their short, tough and blunt warhammers fitted with spikes. Their squat bodies were covered in dwarven plate mail made of black iron, earning them their nickname, "the waddling cauldrons." Soot stained their skin, providing them excellent camouflage in the darkened cave. I doubted the dragon would pay them much attention since they smelled exactly like the fires that burned deep within this mountain, the fires that were currently causing me to become faint. I had to settle this soon, or I'd pass out and become the dragon's next meal.

"I am here to take your squatter away. I have no quarrel with you," I said.

A female dwarf with thick yellow braids came from behind the two facing me, pushing them aside. She looked at the Soulstealer and back to me. "I will instruct my fellow dwarves to let you go, but I cannot speak for the dragon."

She waved her hammer in a signal, and the dwarves turned and ran back down the corridor they had come from. The fae and dwarves had been feuding for centuries, but this was one quarrel they likely figured I would lose anyway.

"I don't know what kind of deal you struck with this thing, but now would be a good time to ask him to move, or we'll both be dinner," I said to the Soulstealer hanging on my arm as if I was his only chance of survival.

I crouched into a battle-ready stance and kept my eyes trained upwards to the wavering head of the dragon. It had not yet taken notice of us, but it was only a matter of time. The amount of smoke it exhaled trying to catch our scent made my eyes water.

"The deal I made was that I would let him eat whatever fae came after me," said the Soulstealer.

I whipped around to face him. My hands twisted into the front of his shirt, and I pulled him closer to my face. I spit out each word. "What did you say?"

"I'm sorry, Valora. I had no idea the King would send you." His eyes softened. A glimmer of recognition tickled the back of my mind as the Soulstealer said my name a second time. All of the fae I was sent to hunt down were from Dell'Aria, but since I had spent my years growing up within the walls of the Court, I didn't recognize most of them. Made my job easier. Until now.

I released the Soulstealer's gown. Intricate cording was woven in three sections down the front. The creases around his golden eyes were much the same as they were the last time I saw him when I was a child.

"Pryn?" The name came out of my mouth barely above a whisper.

The once deft temple leader stared back at me with weary eyes. Whatever power he formerly had was gone. He scarcely had enough energy to stand up straight. It was hard to believe he was accused of being a Soulstealer, a fae with the power to steal the magic of another fae. These Soulstealers weren't accused of just stealing the magic from a single fae, but from all of Dell'Aria and its inhabitants, causing the Blight which sent shockwaves of death and destruction through my home.

A rise in the level of heat brought my attention back to the dragon, its long neck lowering towards the ground. The crackle of fire echoed against the enclosed space.

"No time to catch up now, Pryn. We need to get out of here." I pulled on Pryn's arm and he collapsed against me like a child's rag doll. The mouth of the cave was swallowed in shadow, but it had to be through the legs of the dragon. If only I could get underneath it, we could make it outside.

I gripped my sword and gathered what strength the terrible heat hadn't drained from me. I broke into a labored run, pulling the dead weight of Pryn behind me. As I reached the golden belly of the dragon, the ceiling closed in on me as the dragon sat back on its haunches. I wrenched my arm around and threw Pryn in front of me, both of us sliding along the ground toward the opening of the cave. Gravel dug into my bare legs. My teeth gritted together in an attempt to squelch a cry of pain.

Suddenly we were out, but still sliding. I reached down and grabbed the edge of Pryn's robe with one hand and jabbed my sword into the ground with the other to slow our forward momentum. We stopped short of the cliff's edge. There was no sign of Orris. "Damn coward."

The dragon's head dipped low to pass through the open archway, searching for us. My grip on Pryn's robe slipped, and I turned back to see Orris hovering with Pryn in his arms. Our airship, the Peixes, had taken flight. A slight humming filled the air as the crew turned the massive arms on deck that controlled the rudders at its rear. It was circling. I breathed a sigh of relief. Kali was waiting for me.

"Are you coming or not?" Orris held Pryn in one arm and motioned for me to jump into his other. "Kali will have my head if I let this lizard roast you."

"Tell Kali that I don't want your help." Most of that was true, but I also knew that if I accepted Orris's help it was only going to cause the dragon to follow us back to the Peixes. A dragon's flame and the delicate skin of the airship would not be a good combination.

As I figured, Orris flew off without argument. I turned to face the dragon making its way out of the cave. Its wings shivered as they stretched to their full length, twice the span of the mountain's peak. I gripped the hilt of my sword so tightly my hands began to ache. Transfixed by the glittering surface of the beast's golden belly, my brain scrambled to remember my training as to which area of the dragon was most vulnerable. Before I could pull the needle of knowledge from my mind, the vice-like talons of the dragon seized me around the middle, and he took to the sky, letting loose a deafening roar.

Cold air whipped past me at an incredible speed, burning my eyes. The makeshift cage tightened and forced the last warm breath from my lungs. With the remainder of my strength, I pulled the silver sword upwards, dragging its sharp blade against the inside of the dragon's fist. The beast lurched and cried out in pain, releasing me from its grip. I tumbled head over heels through the air. My small black wings did nothing to slow my descent.

My thoughts were as jumbled as the images of the ground racing towards me. *So this was how I was going to die? Exactly as I had always feared, my inability to fly would be my ultimate undoing, proving to the others that putting fae born like me to death was the kindest option.*

A flash of white blinked in and out of the corner of my vision before I was jerked to a stop mid-air. I looked again into the golden eyes of Pryn, his white face a stark contrast with the darkened sky behind him. The Soulstealer pulled me into his chest and set his mouth to my ear. "I save you because I know in the end you will save us all."

Before I could respond I was ripped from Pryn's grip. I recognized Orris's smell before I saw his face. Two more Hunters from the Peixes had taken hold of Pryn. The Peixes circled around and we all landed on its deck.

"Looks like you scared it off." Kali Mirch, Captain of the Peixes and the Hunters, and my best friend, hobbled up towards me leaning heavily to one side as she grasped the handle of her gnarled cane. I turned to see a faint glint of gold tearing through the sky away from us. "Gave us quite a scare, too." She threw her free arm around my shoulder, her jagged wings prodding at my side.

"Oh, did I get you? Blame it on the damn trolls." The frame of Kali's wings spread askew at an odd angle. Her wings were as useless as mine, but for very different reasons.

I scanned the deck and saw no sign of the old priest. "Where is Pryn?"

"Taken below. You know the drill, Valora."

The belly of the Peixes held an iron-lined cage used to transport the Soulstealers back to Dell'Aria. What once was a ship that transported supplies from the outlying colonies of Overworld to Dell'Aria was now in the business of transporting the only thing that might keep us all alive: a Soulstealer with the knowledge of who was doing this to us and why. So far none of the King's interrogations had yielded the information we were after.

Kali gave a flick of her wrist and sent the other Hunters away to attend to their duties.

"The King has been in touch with me," she said.

"What is it?" I clutched at the amulet at my neck that had got me through the dragon's defenses, a gift from the King many cycles ago at a time when I had to grow up much faster than I was ready for.

"He wants you to report directly to his chambers when we return to Dell'Aria." A flush spread through my cheeks betraying the feelings I had held in for my many cycles.

CHAPTER TWO

I had been in King Aric's throne room before, but I had never been in it with him alone. It was rare that the Royal Guard would allow him to be alone with anyone else even at his direct bidding. I pulled at the edges of the straps on my leather skirt as it nettled the pebbled wounds on my leg. My weight shifted from one boot to the other as I watched him pace back and forth. My chest felt more constricted within the tight leather bodice of my armor than it had been within the grips of the dragon.

He paused to look out the window onto the city of Dell'Aria and spoke with his back to me.

"It is getting worse, Valora. The Soulstealers must be stopped." He paced some more then paused again. Over his shoulder I could see the majestic spires of the temple – copper sheeting covered its surface in a blue-green patchwork pattern in an attempt to hold it together. The once sparkling white sanctuary was now diseased.

I tugged at the pin that held the corners of my cloak around my small wings which fluttered slightly as did my heart at seeing the King in such pain. "You know I will do your bidding. Whatever you wish." Missions were growing desperate, but it was something I knew I had signed up for when I answered the King's call to become a Hunter.

He turned to look at me then. Although I had grown up within the walls of the Court and had often seen King Aric, his attention always caused a surge of energy into my stomach, and I had to reach for the back of the chair in front of me to keep myself steady. His long, white blond hair fell to his shoulders and blended right into the soft blue feathers that cascaded down his back like a cloak, stopping at the waistline of his supple white leather pants. I had only seen him take flight a few times when we were both younger. One of the many memories of him that I had burned into my mind. There were very few reasons that the King of the fae of Dell'Aria ever had to leave his throne.

Multiple bands of thin white silk wrapped around his torso outlining the muscles of his chest and arms. It was perfect save for one strap of silk which was missing, allowing a bit more skin to show through than would be considered modest for the King. But his wardrobe was likely the least of his worries. The softness of his hair and wings were contrasted by his eyebrows, the shape of lightning bolts, and his dark blue eyes. A storm always seemed to be brewing behind them, and his intensity was felt across the city by the fae of Dell'Aria who looked to him for salvation in this troubling time. He appeared wearier than the last time I saw him speak to the people.

King Aric stepped out from behind his desk and crossed the space between us. "Please sit down. I have to explain to you what your next mission is." He gestured to the chair I was holding onto.

"Oh, please, I don't wish to take up your time. Kali can certainly tell me what I need to do." I backed up slightly, hoping he would dismiss me before I fainted. I still could not figure out what I had done right or wrong to warrant such attention from the King, and I was afraid to find out either way.

He reached over and pulled the chair from my hand, turning it around and placing his hands atop the finials. "Sit down."

I think I let out a small squeak. I tucked my cloak underneath me as I sat down and tried to position my scabbard so it would not stick out at an awkward angle. I already felt less than graceful. I certainly didn't need to accidentally stab the King.

I could feel his heat recede as he walked silently away from me. I faced the door to his throne room and didn't dare turn around to see what he was doing. I heard a drawer open and shut.

"Close your eyes."

The blood rushed to my head all at once, and I was all too happy to be sitting down because if I had not, I would certainly have fainted then. Facing down a real dragon was easier than facing *The Dragon* – which was what many called King Aric after he took the dragon as his royal symbol. A symbol that adorned the clasp holding my cloak together.

I jolted in my seat as a brush of cool wet cotton swept across the angry wounds on my upper thigh. The heady scent of fresh rain and morning dew surrounded me as the King knelt before me. A strange scent for a King not allowed outside the walls, but then again this was the first time I had been close enough to catch his scent. I could feel the press of his chest against my bare knees, the warmth of his breath as he placed his face inches from mine.

"Do not speak. I need you to listen to me."

I was all too happy to let him speak because there was

nothing I could say in that moment. My voice caught in my throat, and my lips froze an inch apart. All the daydreams I had about a moment such as this flooded back, and I clutched the edges of the chair to stop my hands from trembling.

"There is another fae that I need you to collect. It is very important that this fae return to Dell'Aria." I bit back a wince as he pulled the cloth across my wounds a second time. "I know he has information that we need to stop this Blight that is destroying our city. He is a Soulstealer. If you do not bring him back then there will be nothing more I can do to stop Dell'Aria from falling down into Underworld."

My better judgment gave in to the yearning within me. I reached out with my free hand and stroked the silken strands of his hair.

He stood all at once, and my eyes flew open, horrified at what I'd just done. "I'm sorry, I..."

In the King's hands was a sealed scroll. He thrust it towards me as the door to his throne room flew open.

Siam, Head of the Royal Guard, barged in. "Sir, this is highly unusual. I must insist that you have one of the Guard with you at all times. We never know what the Soulstealers will do and who they are."

Behind him were the two Guardsmen that King Aric had dismissed when he escorted me into his chambers. Hot on their heels was the bug-eyed face of Siam's pet pikaki named Pika. He was supposed to be Siam's vicious attack animal, but he always ended up looking silly. He was covered in reddish-brown fur and bounced around the ankles of Siam. His large bottom jaw jutted out, and lines of orange drool fell from the elongated teeth that covered his upper lips. He was an animal of the Underworld who had taken a ride on one of the airships that had gone down for supplies.

The creature had immediately and unaccountably attached itself to Siam, giving him his only redeemable quality in my mind since he was one of the two Zeera brothers – Orris and Siam.

"You think this Hunter is going to do me harm? You insult me, Siam. And get that thing out of here. It is making a mess."

"Sorry, Sir, I was taken off guard. Sir, you know I have no choice." Siam scooped up Pika and deposited him into the arms of one of the Guardsmen.

The Queen, King Aric's wife, had disappeared many years ago, and the Guard were left in her place. As she had never returned, the Guard were in charge. The Fae Court had never been run by a King in all the years of its existence, and the Guard kept up the pretense that someday she would return. I didn't think anyone in Dell'Aria believed that anymore. Soon the Guard would choose a new Queen for King Aric. His marriage to the Queen had been arranged and would be again. There was no care of feelings of love where the King and Queen were concerned.

"Valora was just leaving. Were you not?" The King's steely demeanor replaced the softness I had sensed only moments before, as if what had just transpired between us had not actually happened.

"Yes, of course." I rose from my chair, clutching the King's orders to my chest.

He caught my arm as I was about to reach the door. "The final choice in this matter has to be yours," he said softly. "Please tell Kali your decision before nightfall."

I flew out of the room and down the stones of the spiral staircase to the courtyard below. As I jumped off the bottom two steps I almost toppled over my father who was carrying a stack of books. His dark eyes barely peeked up over the top. Those eyes were the only similarity between my father and me.

"Valora, watch where you are going." He teetered back and forth to regain his balance and keep the stack from falling to the ground, his white wings spreading in an effort to keep him upright. "What has you in such a hurry?"

"Sorry, Dad, can't talk. I have to get these orders to Kali. King Aric is sending me on another mission."

My father just shook his head and wandered into the stairwell. Being second in command to several Kings, my father had always taken his role seriously and sometimes found my youthful enthusiasm a bit more than he could handle. My mother would have laughed.

I ran through the courtyard and stopped to look up at the window of the keep. King Aric was again looking out across the land, and I was determined not to let him down. No matter what it was that he wanted, I would make sure that he had it. I was being given a chance to prove myself to him again, and I would not let him down.

⤜⚬⤛

I raced through the crowds in town towards the ice fruit fields on the outskirts of Dell'Aria. The sun was high in the sky as I passed the carts carrying sheets of shiny copper crafted from the malachite that our floating city was made of. Fae were bustling back and forth to take what they needed. It didn't seem to matter how much of the copper sheeting was placed on the buildings, the Blight seeped through the seams and entered into the homes of every fae. An invisible enemy. It was slowly killing us all, some faster than others.

I dipped my head to avoid the low hanging branch of one of the ice fruit trees listing dangerously over the path.

The parched bark burst forth from the limbs, littering the ground with ashen skin. Every day I had to help Kali clear more dead wood than the fruit they were supposed to bear. Another victim of the Blight.

Clutching the King's orders to my breast, I pushed my shoulder into the wooden door of the one-room hut I shared with the only other fae who would associate with me.

Kali jumped up, her wings knocking over a saucer of butter-cream and a bowl of ice fruits from the table. She quickly tucked them back in and gave me a stern look. "Well, since you just ruined my lunch, do you want to tell me what is so important?" Her frown quickly faded as I thrust the scroll in her direction.

The beaded braids in Kali's hair clicked together as she flipped them over her shoulders. She perched on the edge of the table sitting in the middle of the room and examined the seal holding the scroll together. "Is this what I think it is? Hey, watch where you put that scabbard."

"Oh, sorry." I unclipped it from my waist and threw it on one of the two small beds that sat against the wall of our hut, then sidled up next to her on the edge of the table. "The King just gave this to me."

"Himself? He usually gives these directly to me or goes through Siam." Kali gave me a puzzled look as she handed the scroll back to me and set to work on cleaning up the mess I had just caused her to make.

I reached down, picked an ice fruit off the floor and shined it against my cloak, barely taking my eyes off the parchment in my hand.

"Yes, I just came from his throne room. He bid me there himself. I thought maybe he found out that I was using some of the copper to hold my motorcycle together." I bit down into the cool flesh of the ice fruit, letting the blue juices run down the sides of my cheeks. The chilled pulp reached my belly and calmed the heat that had grown there from my encounter with the King.

"Enjoy that, and don't waste it. I think it is the last batch I will be able to get without being noticed. The demand has increased, and the Temple Magistrate has sent a message to the Court that he thinks the fields should be under his control because the fruit is said to be a gift from Mother Varuna." Kali rolled her eyes. "Damn priest just can't live without his ice wine."

The ice fruit trees had been farmed by her family for generations. She often told me the story of her mother birthing her in the fields and going straight back to work after placing Kali in the basket beside the glowing blue fruit. She would be working those fields now if her family hadn't been taken by the Blight and the King had not made a call for the Hunters.

It was the rousing speech of King Aric that made me decide I wanted to be a Hunter five cycles ago.

"There are Usurpers and Traitors in our midst. They call themselves champions for their cause, whatever that may be, but I call them Soulstealers. They are killing our beloved Dell'Aria. Somehow they are leaching the copper blood —- our magic -- from our very veins. You can see the copper plating we need to shore up the great temple and the copper piping we use to pump magic up from the surface of Underworld. These solutions are only temporary. My fellow fae, we are dying. Our only hope is the Hunters, those who will risk their lives to bring the Soulstealers back so we can find out how they are doing this. The Royal Guard protects the Court of Dell'Aria. The Hunters protect its people."

Kali paused as she placed the empty saucer on the table. "Just how much of that copper are you using for your bike?"

I wiped the juice from my face with the back of my

bracer. "Don't forget it was your idea. The Soulstealers are getting farther out in the realms of Underworld. Without my motorcycle, it would take me twice as long to catch them. And since it runs on magic, I need to protect it somehow. You know, since I'm not like the rest of the Hunters."

Kali rested her hands on her hips and tilted her chin down, staring at me with her pale green eyes. "You know better than to talk like that around me."

We had this conversation many times before. "Look, no matter what you say, I will always be the one fae in all of Dell'Aria, heck, most likely all of Overworld, who cannot fly because I was born with small useless wings. Your wings were rendered useless in battle. Dell'Aria considers you a hero and me a cripple." As if they could hear me the black wings on my back gave an indignant flutter.

Kali laughed. "Not even your wings agree with you." Her hands went to the ties on her braids as she loosened them and allowed her long brown hair to flow freely around her shoulders. I envied her long locks – I had always kept my black hair short for fear of covering my stunted wings, making them appear even smaller than they were.

"Are you going to tell me about this mission of yours or not?" she asked.

I studied the scroll, the King's seal pressed firmly to the paper. I remembered the press of his chest on my bare knees and a delicious shiver ran down my spine. That was something I could not share with Kali.

The sharp lines of a dragon's wings travelled down the sides of the design and ended in a lightning bolt forming the tail of the beast. King Aric had commissioned the emblem and declared it his own at his coronation ceremony.

I ran my finger over the seal. "I don't know what the mission is, he just told me it was important and handed me this."

Kali walked over to her bed and reached underneath it, bringing out a small locked box covered in copper sheeting and setting it on the table.

"Looks like I'm not the only one using the copper."

Kali brought her fingers to her lips in a shushing motion. "The walls have ears around here, keep it down. Besides, I felt it my duty since I am charged with holding onto this thing." She muttered the words "Destrave Segredo Dentro," and the lid to the box popped open.

"That wasn't an unlocking incantation, was it?"

"No, it is specific to this chest. My mother gave it to me."

I reined back childhood memories that threatened to overtake me as Kali pulled wads of rags from the box and felt along the inside. Kali knew why I refused to use magic, but she didn't agree with me. I heard a click, and the false bottom retracted. Inside were a number of items, but on top was a small black obsidian blade which gleamed even in the dim light of the hut. The tip of the blade had been dipped in pure iron.

"A seal breaker?" I reached in and took the blade in my hands. Iron was toxic to fae, but as long as we did not touch it, it would not affect us. I tried to hand it to Kali.

"No, you go ahead and do the honors." She waved me off.

I put the scroll on the table, placed the tip of the blade down upon the center of the blood red seal and watched as it slowly dissolved. The lightning bolt design reminded me again of the King's stormy eyes, and I wondered why he had given this mission to me in the manner he did.

Kali gasped. As I stared down at the paper – unable to speak – part of my question was answered.

CHAPTER THREE

"How can he send you Earthside? No one has ever been sent there. We are forbidden from going there, yet he is going to send you there on a mission alone?" Kali paced back and forth in front of the door. Her brow was set in a deep furrow, and her fingers had taken to worrying at her lips. She stopped to look at me. "The King said nothing of this to you when he called you in for this assignment?"

I couldn't tell Kali what had transpired in the King's chambers. I couldn't tell her that he had all but told me that what I was about to do was going to be dangerous. I understood that much now. The King's actions were highly unusual, and so was this mission. "Only that I was going after another Soulstealer, and that this one is important. But then we were interrupted by Siam before he could tell me more."

Kali threw her hands up in the air. "Is Siam still trying to push his weight around? Doesn't he know that no one cares anymore? The Queen abandoned us when the first wave of the Blight hit. The King didn't. He is the only one who is trying to do anything to help us."

The scroll clearly stated that the Soulstealer who had been located had been hiding Earthside for the last few cycles.

It seemed only a few cycles ago that I held another piece of paper that would forever change the direction of my life. Siam had handed that one to me, I had no say in that. I could still see the smug look on his face – it was then that I realized he had always known what the result of all my hard work would be. I spent ten cycles at the academy training to become one of the Royal Guard, and even though I had completed my training along with every other recruit, I was rejected because I was unable to perform a basic duty of the Guard. I could not fly.

"You know how I feel about Siam. But King Aric told me that I needed to bring this fae back alive, or he would not be able to stop the Blight. He said the final decision was mine."

"Well good, then you can tell him it is too dangerous, and we have already lost too many Hunters in the last cycle."

Ignoring her, I read the brief description of the fae listed on the scroll. "It says that his name is Brokk. Do you remember anyone by that name?"

She turned her back to me and shrugged. She knew my decision was made. "I could ask around." Kali blew her nose and wiped a few stray tears away before turning to face me again.

I nodded and tucked the paper into the inner pocket of my cloak. "I don't think I will be getting much sleep tonight. Kali, I have to do this. And I need to go back to Court and see my mother before I go."

"Okay." Kali straightened her back and took a deep breath, a sign she didn't want me to acknowledge her momentary breakdown. "I'll meet up with you tomorrow morning at the docks. Are you going to stay the night?" Kali knew the routine when I visited my mother.

"Most likely."

Kali reached back into the copper box on the table and pulled out a small silver band with a flat black stone set into the top. "Open your hand." She placed the ring in my upturned palm.

"What is this for?" I turned the ring over to inspect it from all sides. There was nothing unusual about it at first glance, but I could feel a small tingling sensation in my fingers that told me it was a magic item. "Not another one. Look, Kali, you know my feelings about magic. I'm already stuck with one piece of magic jewelry. I don't want another one."

"What are you talking about?"

I told her about my amulet and how I thought whatever it had done had freed me from the dragon's intrusion spell. "Isn't that the amulet King Aric gave you fifteen cycles ago as a gift after—"

"Yes." I cut her off before she could finish her sentence – before she could finish reminding me of a time I was constantly trying to forget, but no one would let me.

"What does the ring do?" I asked.

"It will allow you to communicate with me from the other side of the Portal. All you need to do is set the stone to any mirrored surface, and we will be able to talk to each other." She walked over to the corner of the room where we set all the weapons that we trained with as Hunters and started to pull everything aside. "It would be easier to teach you a spell," she said.

"I don't use spells."

"I know. That's exactly why you need the ring." By this time, the floor was strewn with weapons. The last thing left in the corner was propped up against the wall and covered with brown sack cloth. She pulled away the cloth, and underneath was a mirror with heavily gilded edges.

I walked over and took a quick glance at myself. "You didn't tell me I looked like crap." I fussed with my wiry black curls.

Kali pushed me aside. "I didn't throw everything around just so you could do your hair. This was my mother's talking mirror. They used to use them all the time when we spent more time in the other colonies of Overworld."

Since the Blight hit Dell'Aria there had been little to no communication with the other parts of Overworld. It was as if they were afraid that they might catch it, and I didn't blame them. If we didn't stop the Blight, it would be the first time one of the colonies of Overworld would fall into Underworld.

"You know I'm not going to need this. The Portal should put me right on target. I'll just bag him and bring him back. No delays."

"You never know."

Kali was right, of course. You never did know what was going to happen. It was an argument my father had used again and again to try to get me to finally learn some of the spells my mother had used. I could usually win the arguments with my father, but Kali was another story – I had to live with her. I slipped the ring over the first finger of my left hand.

"I'll see you at the docks tomorrow morning." I gave Kali a quick hug and turned to avoid the pointed gaze I could feel on my back as I left our hut. I knew that she was holding back what she wanted to say, but she also knew she would not be able to stop me from seeing my mother no matter how hard we both knew it was going to be.

჻

I waved up at one of the Court's Guard sitting in the tower, dressed in his bright white uniform. They all treated me like they would treat any offspring of the second hand to the King. It was hard not to notice that most of the fae avoided me in the same way they avoided the Blight — as if they were afraid that the condition of my wings was contagious even though I had been born this way.

The guard waved back, and then pulled the lever to allow me entrance to see my mother. The heavy stone door slowly crept open, and my gaze drifted across the great expanse of sky before me. The Court sat on the outer edge of Dell'Aria.

I settled into the alcove tucked at the base of the castle walls as I had many times before. Cool blades of grass fell through my fingertips. Brilliant shades of purple and orange swept across the sky, and in the distance I could see the faint outlines of the floating islands that made up the other colonies of Overworld. We had been closed off from them for so long I had forgotten the names taught to me in school. Things were different once, that much I knew, and I wished for the return of those times.

"All ready for you, Valora," the guard shouted down from his perch above.

I hopped up and waved again to the guard as I entered the narrow stairwell that descended into the bowels of the Court, the air cooler with each step. I came to the bottom of the stairwell and the chamber opened up in a large expanse. My boots barely made a sound as they shuffled across the floor inlaid with copper tiles – the metal which was so important to our survival. Here, in the depths below the Court, the floors were many feet thick with it. Faint blue-green light shimmered off the walls in the candlelight, bouncing off the malachite mineral they were made from. Copper was a conductor of magic and said to be one of the things that had once made Dell'Aria the strongest colony in Overworld. No other colony was as rich with the metal, but it was not enough to save us now.

I walked to the doorway marked Delos – my family name. My father's family had always served the Court and was given a place amongst the royalty for their final rest.

"Mother, I am here."

⁂

I wasn't sure how long I had been lying on my mother's tomb when I heard the noise of someone else descending into the crypt. The floor below my face was still moist from my tears. I turned to see my father in the doorway, my scabbard in his hand.

"Dawn is coming. Kali dropped your weapon off for you at the gates. She thought you would want to have it with you when you report to the docks this morning."

I pushed myself off the floor and hurried over to my father to collect the scabbard. My muscles ached in protest, and I cursed under my breath.

"Sleeping on the floor all night was probably not the best thing to do in preparation for a visit Earthside," he said.

"I didn't sleep. Who told you I was going Earthside?"

My father and I had always and only communicated on the terms of business. We all had a job to do. I think he was glad I was finally made a Hunter so that someone else was technically responsible for me.

"Kali told me when she delivered your scabbard. Are you certain you are ready for a mission of this magnitude?"

"King Aric thinks that I am. He specifically asked that I be sent on this mission."

Although he was past midlife, the lines on my father's face were only subtle. Such was the case with most of the fae. My father had spent all of his life within the walls of the Court. My mother had told me the story of them meeting in the kitchen dozens of times. After she died fifteen cycles ago I ceased to know my father, to have her eyes to see him with. What she saw as deep and caring, I could only see as cold. As cold as all of the other fae that wished to keep their distance from me. I had come to believe that all those stories were born only of my mother's imagination and the longing she must have felt for a man she never had.

My father shuffled his feet and then met my gaze at eye level, pausing for a moment longer than was comfortable for either of us.

"I am not here to stop you, but I should remind you that your mother would not have wanted you to throw your life away on a mission that is bound to be as fruitless as the rest." He stretched out his arm and dropped a book into my hands.

It only took seconds to register what it was. My fingers rubbed against the familiar brown leather cover, worn in places from constant use. The thick parchment had soaked in the scent of my mother and the ingredients of the many spells she cast. Notes of sea moss, amber and ginger-grass played upon my senses, key ingredients in the recipes contained within her grimoire which now lay in my hands.

He turned to walk out the doorway but turned back once more. "Dawn is approaching." And then he was gone.

Fruitless. Of course that is what he thought of what I did. I had no use for the spells contained within my mother's grimoire and had refused it many times before, but somehow this was different. Dawn was approaching, and I was not certain how many more I would see. There was a time I thought of following in my mother's footsteps, but that time had passed long ago.

I shoved the small volume into my cloak and read the words etched into my mother's tomb. Below her name was a banner which read "Taken in the First Wave." I could still recall that day with crystal clarity.

I had been in my room in the south wing of the Court, my parents sharing a chamber down the hall from mine. It was midday, and the warmth of the sun poured through the narrow window slats, bathing me in strips of light as I lay on my stomach reading through my mother's grimoire – something I had loved to do. My mother had been a trained healer, but she also knew other magic. She had been brought in during the end of the reign of King Aric's father who had passed on to the Goddess in peace with the help of my mother's powerful spells. They say her magic is the reason she passed in the first wave. Her life force was so deeply connected to her magic that when the Blight stole it, she had nothing left to fight back with. It was also the reason I had refused to have anything to do with magic since that day. Relying on magic made you weak. It was true that all fae were born with magical abilities, but you had to train those abilities in order to strengthen them, otherwise they lie dormant. That was exactly where I wanted to leave any abilities my mother might have passed on to me.

The first wave of the Blight began with a great rumbling within the Court walls. It began low and grew to a roar, forcing me to clap my hands over my ears. I raced to the window. Everywhere I looked, fae were lying in the streets, writhing in pain. The grimoire tumbled from my hands to the ground and I grasped my temples as pain shot through my head. The sky flashed brightly several times, blinding my vision. I stumbled back to my bed and called out for my mother as the rumbling died down and was replaced by screams of terror. I could hear people calling out for their loved ones. Everyone must have been temporarily blinded by the brilliant light.

With trembling hands, I felt along the edges of my room and followed the line of the wall down the hallway to my mother's room, calling out her name the entire way. If I could only get to her, she'd know what to do. She never answered, but I could sense she was nearby. My knees scraped against the rough stone floor before I reached the delicate lace edging of my mother's bedspread. I could make out the shape of my mother lying in bed. I clutched her hand in mine, but it was cold. Too cold. She had not died that day, but she never regained consciousness.

There had been a second and third wave of the Blight since that day, and the passage of time dictated that we were due for another soon.

I knelt down over my mother's grave to pray one last time to the Goddess. I had prayed so many times for my mother's return – a prayer that was never answered. Now I prayed that I would be returned to her, whether in body or in spirit, I needed to be returned to Dell'Aria. Maybe it was best that I refuse this mission. My father was right about one thing, none of the Soulstealers the Hunters had brought back had revealed anything that we knew of to the King. We brought them back, they disappeared, and we were sent on another mission. Perhaps if I could convince the King to let me speak to Pryn, I could get him to talk to me. He had saved me for a reason.

"I miss her too."

The sound of the King's voice was unmistakable. I turned and saw him leaning against the frame of the door, one bare foot crossed over the other. His bare chest was visible from beneath the open robe he wore cinched at the waist. The fabric was a darkened purple like the night sky of Dell'Aria. A storm was set deep in his eyes.

He walked into the room and stood in front of me, tracing one finger over the top of my mother's tomb.

"She was a strong woman, much like her daughter. She was like a mother to me. You know her memory will always be held in high regard."

He tilted his head down towards where I lay prostrate on the floor and reached his hand out to help me up.

I stretched my hand towards him. The King was the only man besides my father who had not feared to touch me in kindness, but I had always wanted more from the King's touch. Electric sparks seemed to jump across the expanse between my hand and his.

From behind me I heard a small barking sound followed by the stomping of boots on the stairwell. Pika bounded into the room and twirled around three times before sitting at my feet and giving another yap.

"Looks like he found who he was searching for," said the King.

Pika ran towards my scabbard and scooped it up in his mouth before I could get a grip on it. He ran out of the room, and I quickly jumped to my feet to follow him, only to run smack into the broad chest of Siam. I fell back onto my ass, and Pika bounced over and dropped the scabbard into my lap.

"At least this one knew where you were hiding," said Siam.

"I was just speaking with King Aric." I dusted myself off for the third time in the last day and clipped my scabbard back onto my belt.

"King Aric? Have you been drinking? King Aric is upstairs in his keep, I left two Guards by his door myself. He is preparing to send you off at the docks, and I intend to make sure you are on time." Siam puffed out his chest and straightened his wings as he pointed towards the stairwell. I almost felt bad that I was going to have to prove him wrong.

I turned to look back into my mother's crypt and it was empty.

CHAPTER FOUR

I took the steps two at a time, wiping Pika's orange drool from the sheath of my blade as I ran – pikaki drool was impossible to get rid of. Siam was hot on my heels, but even without wings I was faster than most of the other fae. Shorter wings meant less drag.

Outside, fresh air flooded my lungs and erased the stale scent that lying in the crypt all night had left on me. I heard the staggered breath of Siam as he came up behind me.

"No detours, Valora. This is an important mission."

"More than you know, Siam." I took off before he could question me on my meaning.

I had always wondered how much the Royal Guard was told about our missions. I hadn't yet decided that I was going Earthside. This Soulstealer supposedly brought promise of a cure to the Blight, but I was far from hopeful. In five cycles none of the Soulstealers we brought back had divulged any information about how or why they continued to plague our city with the Blight. My mother was already dead, and no amount of information would bring her back.

I squinted against the light of the morning sky. The docks were a little over a mile on the opposite side of Dell'Aria. As I sped past the spires of the temple, the land dipped down slightly. Over the tops of the huts I could see the great airships being readied for launch. Rays of fuchsia bounced off the wings of the crew of the Peixes as they spread through the sky and checked all sides of the craft to make sure that we would reach our destination.

Despite Siam's admonition, I took a slight detour to the hut I shared with Kali.

Before I reached the door I caught sight of her through the rows of ice fruit trees. I made my way through the fallen branches to the outskirts of the field where a few trees that still bore fruit clung to the outcroppings, the branches dangling dangerously over the edge. Kali had wedged her feet into the crevice between two large trunks that bent out over the edge, her arms dangling over the sides. The wind blew through her hair, causing the beads to click together like a wind chime. Scraps of featherless skin left covering the battered frame of her wings flapped in the breeze.

I stepped up beside her. "You know you need to be careful out here. These trees could give way."

"Isn't it funny how these trees are the only ones still alive? These trees which seem to want to dive off the edge and plummet to their death? They live, and yet they want death. Can't stand to watch their friends dying around them. Something at the core of Dell'Aria is rotten, Valora. Something is rotten, and these trees can sense it."

"That is why we do what we do, Kali. That's why the King appointed Hunters, so we can find out what is happening and fix it."

"Nothing will fix this. Find out how to return all the magic to Dell'Aria, and these trees will still be dead. The ones we have lost to the Blight will still be dead. And I will go back to piloting supply ships."

My voice caught in my throat. I had always thought Kali accepted her fate, that she held the title of hero with pride. I had always tried to live by her example. None of the fae would ever see me like they saw Kali, but maybe one day I would see myself like Kali.

Kali jumped down from her perch. "Let's just forget about this, okay? I need to get you down to the docks. So you know, I'll be helping to escort you through the Riparian forest to the Portal."

"I'm not so sure I like that idea."

"You don't have a choice. They needed someone who was trained to open the Portal. Who else do you think is going to do it? There aren't many of us left that can."

It was true that Kali's ability to open the Portal was an anomaly. The Queen was supposed to be the only one with the knowledge of the ritual needed to open it. But when she disappeared there was a call for those who would admit to knowing the ritual to step forward. It was well known that the fae used to freely travel Earthside before the command to close the Portals after the Fae Wars. Some families continued to pass on the knowledge even though it was forbidden.

I reached out and wrapped my arms around Kali, giving the jagged feathers of her wings a little ruffle. "You are right, as usual. Did you learn anything about Brokk?"

Kali got a little smirk on her face. "Well, it must have already gone around that he is accused because no one gave me anything willingly, but you would be surprised what a few glasses of ice wine will do to loosen the lips." Kali paused and eyed the shadows. "Let's walk and talk, we need to get you to the docks on time."

She took me by the elbow, walking quickly down the dirt path. Fae were busily going about their day. It used to be that the Hunters would be sent out on their missions with fanfare. However, now it had become so commonplace that it was just another day at work. I didn't expect any special send off for this mission just because it might be my last.

Kali leaned in and spoke quietly. "The fae I spoke to knew him well."

Kali raised her eyebrows and gave a slight smirk as she waited for me to take in this information.

"You mean you spoke to someone who consorted with him? Who?"

Kali slapped her hand over my mouth. "Do you want the whole colony to know?"

"Well, it is not like it is a big deal."

"Yes, but he is a Soulstealer. I don't want my name associated with a Soulstealer. You know the way it has become."

No one trusted anyone these days. If your neighbor or friend was accused of being a Soulstealer, then you might be accused of being in league with them.

"Did she tell you anything else about him?"

We were getting closer to the docks, and the gleam of the solid copper underbelly of the craft sparkled in the morning light as we approached.

"Apparently Brokk was some kind of Builder, but she never knew what he was working on. He wouldn't allow her back to his dwelling and never spoke of what he did. When he disappeared she went to his hut, and it was empty."

"I can't imagine he would have packed everything he owned and taken it with him," I said.

"No, Valora, it had been emptied. Whoever did it must have known him or known what he was working on and tried to hide it."

The Soulstealers' manifesto had never been uncovered. Just why they were choosing to suck the magic out of our city and abandon it to ruin had never been clear. We were at war with them, that much we knew.

I jerked to a stop on the path. One more turn and we would be at the docks. "Kali, you must know that I haven't made my final decision yet. This Soulstealer must also be skilled in magic if he has hidden from King Aric amongst humans all these cycles. I might not be the best fae for this mission."

⇦⇧

"I haven't seen this kind of procession since the first mission."

I turned to see what Kali was looking at. Behind us the Royal Guard was in full formation. Their ranks had dwindled over the years, but they were no less majestic in their full white uniforms symbolizing the purity of air. The edges of their sleeves and pants were piped in the brilliant purples and oranges that swept across our sky, and their wings were spread wide to part the path for the carriage that usually transported the Queen. It floated down the road without wheels on the magic that held it aloft. The procession came to a halt as it reached Kali and me.

Siam stepped forward through the crowd and addressed me. "The King would like a private word with you before you begin your mission."

Kali gave me a small wave as she departed. "I'll see you on the ship."

The surrounding crowd stared at me. Some were in awe. Some were in disgust. Many likely felt a mixture of the two. I knew that I was never meant to hold a place in their society, and most of them made sure I knew it on a regular basis. I was the only fae in Dell'Aria, other than those wounded in battle like Kali, who could not fly.

Every other fae born like me, and there were not many, were put to death. The only thing that had saved my life was my mother. She begged my father for my life to be spared. She said it would be the only thing she ever asked of him for her entire life. She could never have known how short a time that would be.

Siam knocked me out of my daydream as he herded me towards the entrance of the carriage.

"No need to rush me, Mister."

I shoved back at Siam before pulling open the door of the carriage. He was as much of a bully as his brother Orris.

I tripped in the curtains and pitched forward, landing on the soft carpeting inside. I pulled my feet up underneath me as the door shut closed. The inside of the carriage had two cushioned benches which faced each other, one of which was occupied by the King. His face was in shadow, and the room was silent. All of the noises from the outside ceased at the door.

"I finally have a chance to speak with you alone. Please sit. We don't have much time."

I pulled myself up to sit on the bench opposite the King. This could be the only chance I had to get him to listen to my plan.

"I am not sure it is the best idea that I go forward with the mission. The last Soulstealer I brought in – Pryn – it seemed like he had some information that he might be willing to share with me. He was the priest that oversaw my mother's training as a healer. If he hasn't told you what we need to know, maybe he would tell me."

"I heard of your tangle with the dragon on Mount Elbrus. Very brave. Kali thinks highly of you, and that means a lot to me. I care about all of the fae of Dell'Aria."

He reached out and hooked his finger around the chain of my amulet, pulling it from its hiding place beneath my leather armor.

"You still carry this?"

"Yes," I stammered, trying to regain my composure. King Aric had handed me the amulet shortly after the death of my mother. He asked that I always wear it, and I always had. It had given me an immediate sense of well-being. There was nothing that could make me remove it, and even when Siam had threatened to take it from me during my training at the academy, I had just shoved it into my shirt and encouraged him to retrieve it himself. Considering how little contact he liked to make with me, it was a challenge he chose to ignore.

"Good. I wanted to make sure that you had it. During your time on Earth, please, do not lose this. It is more than a piece of jewelry. It will keep you safe when you least expect it."

"I wanted to ask you about that. The stone glowed when I entered the dragon's cave. I thought I had been caught in the dragon's spell, but then it released me. Does it counteract magic?" Even though I was loath to have anything to do with magic, I couldn't rule out other causes for the dragon's spell failing.

"As I said, it is more than a piece of jewelry." King Aric still held the amulet in one hand as he parted the curtain and peered outside. "We're here. We have little time."

He pulled quickly on the amulet and closed the distance between us. I wasn't sure if he was trying to free the amulet from my neck or draw me towards him. I quickly learned my answer. I had never been this close to the King, to any man. I closed my eyes and tried to slow down my breathing.

"I like you, Valora. You are different. Like me. Both outsiders because of our birth. A fae who cannot fly and a King without a Queen. Both of us at a disadvantage."

His hand went to the back of my neck and his lips found mine, as he took my first kiss from me. I quickly melted into his embrace, not knowing what to do with my hands. In the same instant it was over, and we were sitting on opposite benches leaving me wondering if my imagination was again playing tricks on me. But the surge of lust that twirled through every ounce of my being told me otherwise.

I opened my eyes to see his face no longer in the shadows, and that's when I saw it -- the ashen tinged skin, the deep lines in his face, the markings of the Blight.

I took a sharp intake of breath and brought my hand to my mouth. No use being subtle. The King put a finger to his lips again as he rested back on the bench.

"You come back to me safe, Valora. I will await your return." He reached forward, and I thought for a moment that I might be able to kiss him once more. Foolishly I leaned forward as he opened the door to the carriage. The noises of the dock flooded inside, and I knew it was time for me to go.

Before I left I turned to the King. "I will return. And I will bring you the cure."

I took the amulet and placed it back under my bodice before exiting the carriage.

❧

I squinted into the sunshine as I exited the dark respite of the carriage. The sun had started to rise in the sky and my sense of time was off balance. I could still feel licks of energy running through my body from the touch of the King. I was thrilled and scared. I cared deeply for the King, but now he was showing signs of sickness and was entrusting me to bring him back the one person who he thought had the cure. *How could the King possibly have this much faith in me? What if I disappointed him?* The responsibility of the task before me weighed even more heavily on my shoulders.

The crew of the Peixes airship were busily making the final preparations. When I was not lead on a mission it was I who would be responsible for tightening the ropes on the sails and making sure all the cogs and wheels that controlled the massive tail were well oiled. Today the Peixes glided through the sky as smooth as a fish through water. The great sails reached high into the heavens. A glint of copper light bounced off the casing of my motorcycle and caught my eye as it was pushed up the bridge from the dock to the ship. The King's Guard unloaded a small black trunk from the back of the King's carriage and handed it to the crew that was loading the rest of the supplies.

I had no choice but to be ready for this mission. I put my hand to my breast, to the amulet hidden within.

Kali shouted down to me from the deck as I walked up the gangplank. "Everything is ready for departure to the surface. They have been having some trouble with the dwarves in the area. Nothing we can't handle though."

"Dwarves? I thought they had been mainly sticking to Mount Elbrus. What are they doing in the Riparian?"

I hopped over the short railing to stand next to Kali.

"Never can tell with the creatures of the Underworld. The sooner we can get this all over with, the better. I hate having to crawl around Underworld. Everything down there is out to get us in one way or another," said Kali.

Before our ancestors had established themselves entirely in Overworld there was a time that they tried to maintain colonies in Underworld. Fae were deployed to man the colonies, and most of them were decimated by the attacks during the Fae Wars. Once the Queen at the time was ousted from power, the next one decided to pull the remaining fae from Underworld back to Dell'Aria.

But it was too late for Kali. The Healers tried to put her wings back together, but the dwarves at the time had purchased some black magic from the ogres, and their weapons dealt serious and lasting injuries to her. From then on Kali was the Captain of the Peixes, just as reliant as I was on the airships for transportation from Dell'Aria to the surface.

It was well known throughout the Realms that the fae were the strongest with magic. It was why our ancestors had retreated to Overworld many life cycles ago. We were no match for the physical strength of most of the creatures of Underworld, and it was the only way we were able to protect our resources without expending too much of them. But it also meant that we were shut off from all races other than our own. We were told it was better that way.

"I think I am ready," I said to Kali.

I turned back towards King Aric's carriage, and it was already gone. In its place stood my father who stared at me from a crowd of about a dozen other fae hanging around to see the Peixes depart, likely family of the other fae aboard. As I lifted my hand to say good-bye, so did he. Father had never come to see me depart before. The kiss from King

Aric had hit my stomach with waves of pleasure and anxiety. The wave from my father set my heart aching. Despite our strained relationship, I still cared for him deeply. I desperately hoped I would be able to return to see them both again.

I reached down to the other side of the bridge and helped Kali slide it back into place under the decking.

"So how long do you think it will take us to reach the Portal?"

Kali squinted. "Depends on how much trouble those dwarves give us. But we should be there by nightfall."

The crew of the Peixes had all but stopped working. Their attention focused on Kali, Captain of the Peixes, and me. The full weight of the mission started to sink in along with the stares of the other fae. I kept repeating to myself that I was doing this for the King, but I also knew I was doing this to prove to myself and every last one of the fae that I was as capable as they were.

The fae of Dell'Aria were weary in this battle against ourselves. There was no real face of the enemy except for our own kin. Trust was running thin in all directions these days.

"All right, everyone, listen up," Kali said. "We are headed for the edge of the Riparian forest. That much you know. Valora here is lead on this mission. I will need several volunteers to act as escort. Scouts have located a pack of dwarves in the area who have set up several traps. I will need some of my best and brightest to make sure Valora gets to the Soulstealer within our window of time. We won't be spending too much time in Underworld if I can help it."

Kali finished her speech. The crew of the Peixes avoided her stare, their eyes coming to rest on anything but her. None of them wanted to be involved in something that required them to put their lives on the line for me.

The ship began to move away from the docks and down on its way to the towering evergreens that rimmed the Riparian forest. The shuffling continued.

"Do we need to draw straws? Are you all that much of a coward?" shouted Kali.

Orris stepped forward, his belly parting the crowd.

"Oh, good, Orris, our first volunteer," said Kali.

Orris held up his hand. "No, I am not volunteering to help this cripple. I am just the only one who is willing to step forward to say so. Why is it she was chosen for this mission? You say this mission is one of the most important, yet you put the fate of our world into the hands of a fae who is only here because no one else would take her? If that Soulstealer hadn't gotten away from me on the last mission, she would be a splat on the plains."

Kali stepped forward, coming within a few inches of Orris, her crooked wings spreading to the sides. Through every rip and tear you could see the pain Kali must have gone through. You could see how she struggled for her life.

"Listen here. You must think I have gone soft, Orris. Is that what you think?" Kali spat out the last few words.

Orris did not flinch. Since his brother Siam was Captain of the Guard, his tongue was allowed to wag a lot more than most. "Either you or the King, Captain."

That was the last straw for me. Orris could speak ill of me all he wanted. I was used to it. But I wasn't going to let him speak ill of the only one who stuck by us through this horrible tragedy. I flew at Orris before I really knew what I was doing. My hands grasped at his throat.

"Don't you ever speak like that about the King, you fat bastard," I screamed.

Orris swung his fist back, but before he could bring it forwards, the fae behind him held him back. Kali pulled me off him.

"Orris!" Kali's voice commanded attention. "You either support this crew and all of the Hunters, or you can fly your ass straight back to Dell'Aria and clean the pigeon shit off the great temple. Are we clear?"

"Fat bastard probably couldn't fly back if he wanted to," I muttered under my breath.

"Don't you question my ability to fly, you cripple. You should have been put to death like every other useless fae ever born in Dell'Aria. You just got lucky you have family in high places."

"Something we have in common." I sneered.

"Don't you ever talk about my family. Family means everything to me."

"Enough, both of you." Kali threw her hands into the air. "We settle this now. Straws it is, I guess."

As the remainder of the crew clustered together in front of Kali to pick their fate, I faded away from the crowd to take in the view from above.

The crew didn't try to muffle their cheers as each drew a straw long enough to get them off the hook. I knew from the loud groan when someone drew the short straw. Kali leaned against the railing next to me as I watched Dell'Aria get further and further away.

"It never ceases to amaze me how thick those guys can be." Kali touched her hand to my back.

I shrugged my shoulders. "I have already forgotten about it. You know what never ceases to amaze me?"

"What?"

"That."

I pointed back to Dell'Aria, a flat island floating among the clouds. It defied gravity because it was infused with all of the magic of many life cycles of fae who had worked and toiled to bring it to life. And now it was crippled.

Large copper pipes snaked down from the craggy underbelly of my home and ended at the Selkie colony in Lake Mavrovo far below. King Aric had forged an alliance with the Selkie Queen, Elemi. The Selkie were descended from the fae and had evolved to living their life in the water. Although we rarely had any relations with any of the other creatures of Underworld, the Selkie Queen had seen our problem as her own. Should the magic holding Dell'Aria fail, it would surely fall straight down into her underwater kingdom and destroy it as well. I would like to think she was reaching out to us and allowing us to siphon their magic out of the goodness of her heart, but really it was just pure logic.

The same reason why King Aric chose me to go Earthside on this mission alone. I would blend in the easiest, no one would question the decision to send me there since I was considered expendable to most, and I would never deny his request for me to do so.

I sighed and leaned over to rest my chin on the back of my hands perched atop the railing. Thinking of King Aric had me thinking about that kiss.

"Don't worry," Kali said. "You will see him again."

I shot up in surprise. "What are you talking about?" *How could Kali know about what happened between me and the King?*

"Your father, of course. I saw him at the docks."

"We are getting closer to Riparian," I said, glad to change the subject. The Peixes descended onto the open plains.

Kali patted me on the shoulder. "I'd better get suited up. You, too, hero. We're going to be entering into some treacherous territory."

I followed Kali along the length of the ship deck. The crew had gone back to their assigned tasks. I jogged down the steps that headed below deck into the area where we kept our supplies and started to suit up into my usual Hunter gear.

"Hey, you won't need that heavy armor, Valora. I have something special."

Kali hobbled over to a black chest on the floor, the same one I had seen unloaded from the King's carriage. Her injuries had also taken a toll on her legs. Kali made it hard for me to feel sorry for myself. Except that her injuries made her a hero in the eyes of the other fae, and I feared I would only ever be considered a cripple no matter how valiantly I fought for Dell'Aria and my King.

Kali opened the chest and pulled out a pair of black leather pants and a coat. Something about them seemed familiar.

"That's not standard issue. Where did this come from?"

Kali swung the coat around and held it up for me to slide my arms into. The inside of the coat was lined with a glittering gold surface, and suddenly I remembered where I had seen it before.

"Remember that dragon you played fetch with last mission? You're wearing him," said Kali.

"The only person who can order the slaying of a dragon is King Aric."

"You certainly have caught his attention. I don't know how, but you have," said Kali. She gave me a quick wink.

45

I pulled on the pants and ran my hands over my legs. The inside of the pants was supple, but the leather itself was incredibly strong.

The dragon was a creature of Overworld and thus under our domain. They were creatures that ruled themselves, but the fae considered them sacred creatures and would not allow others to sacrifice them. The slaying of a dragon could only be ordered by the Fae Queen for certain ceremonies. Dragons held powerful magic.

The longer the leather was wrapped around me, the stronger it made me feel. King Aric had given me another gift. One I would never be able to repay him for, though I was certainly going to try.

Kali took me by the arm. "Do you still have the ring I gave you?"

I showed her my hand. "Are you really that worried that I won't be coming right back?" Not that I wasn't worried about the same thing.

"Right. Keep it handy, just in case." She paused and took a look around before continuing. "I don't like the things I have been hearing the others whisper under their breath. They are wishing you harm, Valora. I think they would just as well close the Portal behind you and leave you Earthside."

"You know they are all talk. Besides, King Aric said it himself; I need to bring this fae back. It is very important."

Kali took my arm and turned me towards her before I could race up the stairs. "He told you this and you alone, Valora. No announcement was ever made. I believe you. But the crew thinks this is just another mission."

"But I am going Earthside. Why is it they think that is just another mission? Why can't we tell them?" I wanted to find this fae to help the King find a cure, especially if he was ill, but I also wanted the other fae to accept me.

"They don't know, Valora. Only I know the Portal is to be opened. I spoke to King Aric while you were visiting your mother last night, and he thought it best that we keep most of the details of this mission a secret."

She had spoken to King Aric? Had she seen what I saw? Did she know he was ill? "You didn't think it was a good idea for me to go before. Do you think it is a good idea now?"

She nodded and dropped her eyes to the floor. "We will have an escort through the traps set by the dwarves, but the rest of the way to the Portal is just you and me."

I hit the wall with my fist. "Dammit. I told you I didn't want you to be put in danger."

"I won't be. Remember, I am the war hero here."

I stared her straight in the eyes. She knew I would never ask her to risk her life for mine, and I knew I would never be able to talk her out of it. Slowly I responded. "In and out."

"Meet me topside in five minutes. Sounds like we are docking, and we need to get moving before it gets too dark." Kali hobbled up the stairs.

CHAPTER FIVE

Four others had been chosen to escort Kali and me to the Riparian forest. They stood in formation, two flanking us on each side of the ship deck. I revved the engine on my motorcycle, and it came to life beneath me. The vibrations rattled through my body. Kali clutched me tighter around the waist.

"I still don't know how you can stand this thing." Her voice shook in my ear.

"I still don't think it is a good idea for you to come along," I said, mimicking her.

"And you don't have any choice. Don't make me pull the 'I am your Captain' card. You know how I hate throwing around my authority." I glanced in my rear view mirror to see the grin on her face that went along with her sarcasm. Kali was like the big sister I never had.

"Okay, but make sure I can breathe, or we are both in trouble."

Kali released her grip only slightly. "You ready, Valora?"

I answered her by gunning the engine. We lurched forward down the ramp from the ship onto the plains that bordered the edge of the forest. My bike easily parted the three foot tall ginger-grasses that tickled at my ankles. I reached out and snatched a handful, tucking it into the inside pocket of my jacket where I had put my mother's grimoire.

The escorts on either side of us extended their wings and shot forward, keeping pace as best as they could. I gave a smirk when I saw that Orris had been chosen to go on this mission. His face reddened as he tried to suck in his sloppy middle. I was all too happy that he was having trouble keeping up with the rest of us. As we approached the dense boundary of the Riparian I slowed to a stop and the other Hunters dropped down beside us.

Kali hopped off the back of my bike and commanded the attention of the Hunters.

"We need to stay along the path. Orris, if you and Cabe will take up the rear then Waaren and Wid can take the lead. Keep all eyes out for the dwarves. They have been trying to extend their domain and have been causing havoc around here."

The beads in Kali's hair clicked as she turned her head from side to side to get one last look at the forest border. "I have my arrows, but you are better at hand to hand combat. Let me walk the bike through," she said.

Kali took the handlebars of my motorcycle as we crossed the boundary between the plains and the Riparian, darkness descending on us. The canopy was so thick that most of the remaining daylight was blocked out anyway. Wind swept through the air and curled around us. The trees knew we did not belong. I only hoped that the elven folk who lived deeper within the woods would not have time to receive the message from the tree sentinels before we reached the Portal.

"Just where is this Soulstealer and what is he doing in

here?" Orris scanned the trees to either side of the path. He might be an asshole, but lucky for me he didn't want to die today any more than I did.

Before I could answer I heard a yelp, and Wid disappeared from the path ahead of us. "Dammit, get down everyone," Kali yelled. Everyone hit the dirt as a volley of slings and arrows skimmed our heads.

Wid yelled from the pit where he had fallen. His brother Waaren crawled on his belly and reached his hands down to help him up out of the trap.

Kali and I crouched behind my bike. The volley of arrows had come from the east side of the path. I grabbed at my temples as a nagging pain shot through me.

"Any idea how close we are to the Portal?" I shouted over the whistle of weapons. No use trying to hide our position now. They knew exactly where we were, and we had fallen into their trap.

Kali traced her finger over a weathered map she pulled from her pouch. "Just around that bend."

Wid came to his feet twenty feet in front of me. Waaren tried to coax his brother towards cover, but he just stood there. A rippling movement pulsed across Wid's face as he brought his sword upwards. Waaren had already turned to take cover and didn't see what his brother was about to do.

"Waaren, look out!"

But it was too late. Wid's blade sliced across Waaren's middle. A mask of shock and horror froze Waaren's features as he clutched at the ruins of his gut before falling to the ground. The ripple effect of pain shot through my head as Waaren died before me.

Kali got up from her hiding spot beside me and quickly shot an arrow through Wid's head, dropping him to the ground beside his brother. Wid's features morphed. His jaw extended revealing the sharpened bottom incisors of an ogre.

I crawled on my belly past the body of the ogre and peered into the pit that Wid had fallen down. In the bottom was his broken body.

Kali yelled across to Orris who had hunkered down with Cabe just behind one of the tree stumps. "There are ogres in these woods. You guys head back. Valora and I only need to go a little further."

"Don't need to tell us twice." Orris ran ahead of Cabe, back the way we came.

Cabe turned and gave Kali and me a quick salute just as a massive troll came through the tree line to his right. I heard a sickening crunch as his hammer came down upon Cabe who didn't even have enough time to cry out. Another sharp pang zipped through my skull.

"Go, go, go," I shouted.

I choked back the tears and pushed my weight against the bike to get it moving down the path. The copper tank on the front of my bike caught a stream of light that pierced through the canopy and also caught the attention of the troll. Orris had disappeared. The troll came down the path towards us.

"Just around the corner," Kali repeated as she pushed at me. The path suddenly came to an abrupt end at a large piece of dead fall.

"Holy crap." I stopped the bike and sheathed my blade, reaching for the mace I had strapped to my belt.

"You can handle this. I need to get us past this hunk of wood. The Portal is on the other side," said Kali.

"How the hell am I supposed to do that?"

The troll lumbered closer to us, each of his footsteps causing the ground to shake beneath my feet.

Kali turned her back to the troll and focused on the tree.

She muttered under her breath.

"I really hope you know what you are doing," I shouted.

I swung the mace above my head, ready to lob it at the troll and hoping that it would do more than just piss him off. The head of the mace was just about as large as one of his hands, so I wasn't sure how much good it was going to do. You really couldn't ever equip yourself for a fight with a troll. Mostly you just had to run, an option which was not currently available to us.

The troll opened his mouth and let forth a loud yell. Spittle shot off his flaccid lips. He was close enough that I could smell the rot of death and decay on his breath. I answered his cry with one of my own, but it was like a mouse yelling at a lion. He was only ten feet away when I swung my mace in his direction.

A whoosh of air came from behind me, and I watched as the tree that had been across the road hurtled over my head and slammed into the troll, pinning him to the ground beneath its weight.

I turned to see a sparkle of light surrounding Kali. The tell-tale sign of magic weaving. My mother had practically glowed wherever she walked.

"He's going to get that off in less than a minute, and I need to get you through that Portal," Kali said, her voice strained.

She motioned for me to follow her down a smaller path that forked off the main one. She seemed to know exactly where she was going. Several twists and turns later we came to a stop in front of some thick shrubbery that appeared to be a dead end.

She parted the brush, and I pushed my motorcycle after her. Branches whipped at my face, and suddenly I was in a small circular clearing. At the center Kali was casting some kind of spell. The Portal crackled to life, becoming a swirling vortex of energy. I had read about the Portal in the many texts contained within the Court, but to see it was another story. It both amazed and frightened me. I looked across to Kali and realized that this trip could be a one way ticket. We were dealing with ancient and fickle magic.

"Just concentrate on the mission," Kali shouted across to me as the rumbling from the Portal grew louder and the wind whipped up to a frenzy. "Remember, you need to find Brokk. The Portal will take you where you need to be. When you have him, then return straight back through. I will be waiting for you."

Kali smiled and nodded. She was trying to encourage me, but through her thin smile it felt to me like she was as uncertain about this as I was.

"I love you, Kali."

I edged my leg over the side of my bike and focused my thoughts forward to Brokk. I tipped my bike forward into the swirling vortex of purple and white light and fell forward. I took one last glance at Kali. Behind her, in the shadows, I thought I saw the face of King Aric. But it couldn't be.

I refocused my thoughts. Brokk. I must bring back Brokk.

A blast of energy hit my center and I grasped tighter onto the handlebars of my bike. The scream I was biting back sprang forth as each molecule in my body released and reformed.

CHAPTER SIX

Moist ground cushioned my fall. Sound and vision began to come back to me. A steady ticking sound came from the wheels slowly turning round and round on my motorcycle which had fallen on its side. Dried leaves crackled under my hands and the chill in the air clutched at the warm breaths I exhaled and formed a foggy mist in the air. The hooting of some airborne brethren of mine sounded far above me. My vision sharpened in the darkness that surrounded me.

It was night here on Earth, and I was in a forest much like the one I had come from. I half wondered if I had been transported at all. I looked behind me to the swirling vortex of the Portal at the base of a massive oak tree. Kali was gone.

I pushed myself up and righted my bike, leaning against it as I regained the last of my balance and my legs became steady again. In and out. I had to find this Soulstealer.

I closed my fingers around the hilt of my sword. It was still there. The mace was long gone, but not needed. I tried to regain my bearings. I had landed deep within a forest. It seemed a likely place for a Soulstealer to hide, but I sensed nothing except for the animals that inhabited this forest, which was not as foreboding as the Riparian. This forest was half asleep and naïve to my presence.

Ahead of me about half a mile a light shone through the trees. I left my bike by the Portal and made my way through the underbrush towards a lone cabin. Warm yellow light flickered in the windows, reminding me of the hut I shared with Kali. The house was quiet. I sensed no one. *But the Portal had brought me here. Brokk should be near.*

As I got close a sharp pang burst through my head, interrupting my concentration. The same as when Wid and Warren had died, and the hammer had come down on Cabe right in front of me. We had lost another fae. *Kali! But how would I feel that through the Portal boundaries? I shouldn't.*

A groan came from the back of the cabin, and I flattened myself against the side wall. Something hit the ground with a thud, and the cry of a bird of prey echoed against the clear night sky. I slowly made my way along the wall. I reached down and silently drew my sword from its scabbard, holding it at my side.

Taking a deep breath, I peered around the corner. The scent of blood reached me before the realization set in. Leaving all sense of caution behind me, I rushed forward, dropping my sword to the ground beside the fae. It must be Brokk. His throat had been slashed only moments ago. I touched his neck to check for any signs of life, but there were none. His eyes were wide in a look of surprise. Blood pooled below his neck and dripped down onto his downy white wings that lay askew beneath him.

This was the fae that was supposed to hold the answer to the King's illness, to the Blight that was threatening Dell'Aria. And now he was dead. *How could I return home with nothing?*

A rustling in the forest told me I was not alone. My Hunter instinct kicked back in, and I grabbed my sword from the ground, gripping it tightly with hands slick with Brokk's blood. I stood stock still and heard no other sound, saw no movement. I looked back the way I came just as sparks sprang forth from the Portal and then went dim.

In that moment I was not sure whether I should be more worried that the fae I was sent to collect was dead at my feet or that the Portal had just closed leaving me trapped Earthside.

I took two steps forward and heard the click of a weapon behind me.

"Don't move."

Defying orders and running on pure adrenaline, I grasped my sword and swung around to face the voice behind me. A human. I stared back at Brokk's body knowing there was no way I could hide the evidence of his wings, of who he really was. Brokk had likely used a glamor spell. I could easily hide my small wings with the jacket I wore, but other fae had a harder time doing so.

"I said, don't move." The man stepped forward, and light from the back window of the house fell across his face. His hair was long and dark, hanging just below his shoulders. The light caught his eyes, and I could see they were moist with tears.

Black markings snaked up his bare arms, defining well-toned muscles, though the hand holding the gun pointed at me shook as he spoke in an equally shaky voice.

"I already called the police. You just stay where you are."

I brought my hands up, still clutching my sword. "I know this looks bad, but I am not responsible. Whoever did this is close by. You need to let me find him."

I stepped backwards, testing the resolve of the man who held me at gunpoint.

He leveled the weapon at me again. "No! Don't move! I am not going to tell you again. Drop that sword." He gestured to me with the end of the gun. "And drop to your knees."

There wasn't much I was going to be able to do against his gun. I complied with his demands, trying to think of how I could turn this situation to my advantage. I knew there was someone in the woods. I could feel them watching. It was likely the same person who had slit Brokk's throat moments ago. If only I could break free, I was sure I could catch up with whoever it was. But I had no choice. I dropped to my knees.

"Put your hands behind your head." The man was becoming more comfortable with the weapon he was holding. The shaking in his hand and voice had begun to subside. I was going to lose ground soon.

He circled around me. The barrel of his gun hovered at the back of my neck.

"Why did you do it? Why? Brokk would never have hurt anyone. He was gentle. Kind. Why?" I could tell the tears were coming again.

This man knew Brokk. If he knew him, maybe he had information I could bring back to the King, something that would help.

He parted my hairline with the gun, and the iron barrel pushed into my neck, searing my flesh with an audible sizzling sound.

"Arghhh."

I flew forward without any control over my reaction. The iron was like poison to the fae. He may as well have shot me with the bullet. The damage was done.

I lay on the ground writhing in pain that radiated from the back of my neck and into my arms. I was hit with a few convulsions before rolling onto my back. I stared up at the stars which dotted the night sky. They were bright and twinkling. I had been told about the night sky here on Earth, but I had never imagined it would be so beautiful. I only hoped the Goddess Varuna would be able to lead my spirit all the way back from Earth to my mother.

The stars came closer into the field of my vision. I knew I was losing consciousness. The man knelt before me. I could see in the light that his eyes were dark velvet brown. He stared at the gun in his hand and back towards me.

"I didn't mean to harm you."

He set the gun down on the ground and closed his eyes, bringing his hands to his chest in prayer. Little did he know that his God wouldn't likely do anything to help me. He then reached his arms, snaked with slashes of black ink, to the sky before placing them on my stomach. He muttered a few words and went into a trance. The pain in my neck receded just as the presence in the woods receded. I had lost my chance. And somehow this man had given me another one. *What kind of power was that?*

The man opened his eyes and studied me. I needed to find a way back to my bike and a way to reach Kali. She would be able to help me. At least I really hoped so. But right now, there was no one who could help me.

The man rocked back on his heels, stretching his hands out in a search for his gun.

I brought my sword forward, the sharpened tip resting under his chin before he could reach his weapon. "I greatly appreciate your assistance. But I really need to be going."

I kept the tip of the blade under his chin as I crawled to my feet and kicked his gun into the brush. He raised his hands into the air.

I glanced back at Brokk's body. His face had gone ashen, like the King's face had been when I last saw him. I noticed the front of his shirt had intricate cording woven in three sections down the front. Not the same as the priest's gown worn by Pryn, but similar enough.

My distraction was my undoing. I gasped as the tip of my sword was thrown to the side. The man regained his nerve and dove for the gun which I had only managed to kick about ten feet away.

"Dammit." I ran towards the man who had gone headlong into the brush and grabbed one of his ankles pulling him out into the open in one quick and sharp movement. The last thing I saw was the glint of gunmetal with the man's finger wrapped around the trigger. The sound of the shot pierced the quiet night sky and my vision again went dark.

CHAPTER SEVEN

The Portal had squeezed me in one end and spit me out the other, but the head rush from that trip was nothing compared to the pounding in my skull as I tried to open my eyes.

The outline of a man with broad shoulders and long hair filled the edges of my fuzzy vision. His back was to me, and he was shuffling about the room. The strong smell of a familiar herbal tincture hung in the air. A few white pillar candles, bubbling over with thick rivulets of wax, sat atop a wooden table casting their dim light on a blackened cast iron stove in the corner. Steam boiled out of a deep pot with flames licking up the sides. Somehow they had found me. I had been returned back to Dell'Aria.

"Aric?"

The man turned, but the darkness of the room still shrouded his face.

He took a step towards me. "Shhhh, you need to rest. Help is on the way."

"I don't need any help. I think I just lost my footing and hit my head somehow. I've got an awful headache." I squinted and tried to focus in the low lighting. "He was already dead. Brokk. When I got there someone had killed him. I am sure you are disappointed in me."

He took two long strides, closing the distance between us. All of a sudden I could see his face in the candlelight. The man. The one who had shot me. His features twisted with grief and anger. My memory quickly returned.

He shoved his finger into my chest. "Still sticking to that story? I don't buy it. His blood is still all over your hands. There was no one else around." Our eyes met, and he backed off me and began pacing back and forth across the small space of the one room home. Suddenly he stopped and stared at me. "It doesn't matter what you say. The sheriff is on his way with a medic. They'll check that arm of yours and then bring you in. You can tell them you are innocent all you want. I doubt they will believe you, either."

I tried to pull myself up to a seated position and realized I was tied down, my hands and ankles attached to the legs of a cot that sat low to the ground. I tugged slightly and realized the rope was some kind of synthetic cord. It would be difficult for me to break free of it in the state I was in right now. My only hope of getting out of here alive was to get this man talking to me.

"So you knew Brokk?"

"Of course I did." He paused, took a seat on a stool near the stove and began to absentmindedly stir the pot with a wooden spoon. The markings on his arms were black symbols that I didn't recognize. "He was all I had out here."

"I know you don't believe me. But I need you to listen. You are right, I am here for Brokk. But I was not here to kill him. I was sent to bring him back home. You see his...family just learned about where he was and wanted someone to come out and make contact with him. Did Brokk ever talk about his family with you?"

The man had to have seen the wings lying askew under Brokk's body. My mind raced. I had no idea how much the Soulstealer had shared with this human.

He stopped his stirring. "No, he didn't."

I heard the sound of an engine, not unlike my motorcycle, pulling up outside the house. I hoped I had hidden my bike well enough so that no one would find it.

"That would be the sheriff." He rose to his feet and went to the door.

"No, please, you can't let him take me." I tried to hide the torrent of fear that ran through my voice. I knew that humans clasped their prisoners in irons and encased them in a room with iron bars. It was one of the reasons we were forbidden from coming Earthside. If we were caught, then our true nature would certainly be revealed. It was a warning we had been taught since birth. Hide your true nature from anyone outside the Realms. Even Underworlders would kill us and tan our hides for use as magical armor. Armor, like the dragon hide leather that covered my legs. I suppose I was getting what I deserved.

"If you are innocent, you have nothing to worry about, right?" He opened the door to a portly man whose thumbs hung by his belt loops. His tan polyester uniform stretched thin over his belly.

"Hey there, Dooley. What's this about a dead person in your woods?" The man seemed older than Dooley, but then again, it was difficult for me to tell a human's age. Streaks of gray played at his temples where most of his hair resided, the top having thinned out considerably. Dooley stood on his toes to see past the sheriff's shoulder.

"Didn't you bring anyone else? Like a team?"

The sheriff looked behind him at his cruiser and jabbed a thumb over his shoulder. "That is my team."

"Ralph. It's Brokk."

"Brokk? Why the hell didn't you say so on the phone? Where is he?" Ralph tried to push past Dooley, but he held his hand up.

"He's around back. I didn't say anything on the phone because, well..." Dooley pointed in my direction.

If Ralph was surprised when Dooley had mentioned Brokk, he was even more surprised to see a woman clad in tight leather pants, bustier and jacket strapped spread eagle across a cot at his feet.

"Hi there, it's nice to meet you. I would wave, but as you can see I am a little tied up at the moment."

Ralph lowered his voice and whispered to Dooley. "Man, if this was what was distracting you I totally understand. But where's the perp?"

"You're looking at her."

Ralph ran his hand over his face and clutched at his chin in disbelief. "Well, and they said being sheriff in the sleepy suburbs of Seattle wouldn't be interesting. She seems well tethered for now. Show me where you got Brokk, and tell me what the hell happened."

The two of them went out the front door, leaving me alone. I weighed my options. I had recovered much of my strength and felt sure I could now break the ropes easily. But I wasn't certain I could get past those two men with their guns.

If I found out who killed Brokk, I would have something to bring back to the King. But the first thing I needed to do was to get myself out of this situation.

I strained against the cording that held my right hand bound and smiled as I heard the satisfying snap of it breaking free. In a manner of seconds I had the remainder of the binds untied. I rubbed at my arm feeling the wound where the bullet from Brokk's gun had grazed it. I couldn't be sure if Dooley had missed on purpose or if I had his bad aim to thank.

Through the window I could see Dooley and Ralph hovering over Brokk's body. The sheriff was speaking into a device on his shoulder, and Dooley had gone back to pacing. Neither of them examined Brokk's wings or made any fuss about it. Either they were somehow still under the influence of Brokk's glamor spell, or they already knew about him.

The room clearly held evidence that the Soulstealer had made his home here with this human. But it didn't make sense to me why he would do that. Pryn had bedded down with a dragon, and Brokk chose this human. Which was more dangerous? Whether he knew it or not, Dooley had to hold another piece to this puzzle.

❧❦

I snuck out the front door and gave the rear of the house a wide berth. It was still dark, so I couldn't have been passed out for long. If I could contact Kali, maybe she was still nearby and could open the Portal.

When I reached my bike the sick feeling in my stomach got worse. Where there was once a swirling vortex of light was now just a knot in the base of the tree trunk.

I ran my finger over the smooth black stone on the ring Kali gave me and pressed it to the small rear view mirror on the handlebar of my bike. A shimmer passed over the surface of the mirror and revealed the inside of the hut I shared with Kali. Or what used to be our hut.

It had been ransacked. Everything was hanging out of the drawers, and our few belongings were scattered about like someone was searching for something. My vision was partly obscured by our stash of weaponry. Obviously whoever had torn through our hut had done so in a hurry and had not bothered to peel back all the layers of weapons we kept in the corner to find the mirror.

I could only hope that Kali was okay. All I knew for sure was that I was stuck Earthside with no way of getting back. This Portal could only be opened from the Realms, and I had no idea why it had been closed.

A stick snapped behind me. I whirled around in time to see the small form of a dwarf peering at me through the brush. I could tell it was dwarf not only from the size but also from the smell. This dwarf had brought with it the ashen smoke from the fires that burned deep within the rock of Mount Elbrus.

I reached for my sword and realized that Dooley must have taken it from me. My scabbard dangled empty, and I had nothing to defend myself with.

The dwarf spoke through the brush. "Looks as though you are in a predicament, fae."

"One you have personal knowledge of, no doubt, dwarf."

"You think I would bother to kill a fae? Nonsense. I am only here as a Collector. A Collector of things that are useful."

"As I hear it, dead fae are of particular use to your kind. So it was you in the brush watching that entire time? If you are so harmless, why don't you show yourself then?" I tried to see the dwarf through the undergrowth but I wasn't able to see much.

"I suppose I can since you have nothing to swipe at me with." A short and stocky female dwarf jumped out of the bushes and landed about ten feet from me. She had her

65

yellow hair tied back, and she was clad in black iron plate mail, a small war hammer and brown satchel hanging at her side. The same dwarf who had spoken for me in the dragon's lair, though I thought she had done so more to save her own skin then mine.

"The name is Franca. And I was not the only one here in the woods. If you think I alone am capable of slaying a full grown fae, than you are sadly mistaken."

The dwarf was half my size. She had her fists on her hips and stood her ground. No fear or hesitation.

"Well, not without the traps your people are always setting as you lie in wait for us."

"Are you crazy? We don't have any intention of trapping you. If the fae run into our traps it is because you are not watching where you are going. It's those horrible trolls and ogres we are trying to get rid of. That and the fae that seem to be hiding out in our mountain."

So she recognized me, too. "If you were not the only one out here then who else was?"

"Another fae. Like you. He disappeared through your Portal, and it shut behind him."

So that's what had happened to the Portal. "Him?"

Franca sat down on a nearby fallen log. "Really, he moved too fast for me to get a good sketch of him. But he was no dwarf."

Franca, however, *was* a dwarf, and I had been raised to trust them about as much as humans, which is to say, not at all. But if I was going to pick between the humans who thought I had killed Brokk and wanted to put me in irons and a dwarf who knew I was innocent, I decided to pick the dwarf. I sat on the log next to her and extended my hand in greeting.

"My name is Valora of Dell'Aria. I was sent here to bring this fae back to Dell'Aria, and I suppose you know the rest of the story."

She nodded. "These woods are a great source of the elderberry. They have great medicinal properties. The fae must have cultivated a field of them here since he took up residence."

"Elderberries? But I didn't know that they could grow outside of Overworld."

"They can't. Not unless they are tended by the fae. We caught wind of his field, and I was sent to collect some of them. It took me days to travel here from our Portal. Without Brokk they will all wither and die. Might as well not let them go to waste." She got up and turned to go back into the forest.

I caught her by the shoulder. "Wait, Franca. Did you say you have another Portal?"

"Yes, of course. But we are not as great magic users as the fae. The Portal has a bit of a mind of its own. I am just glad it got me within a few days travel. The way back is straight to Mount Elbrus."

I took another deep breath and inhaled her smoky scent. I had already begun to get homesick, and she was the closest thing I had at the moment to home. "Please, take me with you. I need to get back to Dell'Aria. Something is terribly wrong there."

Franca shrugged. "Don't suppose I care if you tag along. But are you certain that the answer to your problems is back through another portal?"

"What do you mean by that?"

She shrugged again. "Dwarves may not have the magic the fae do. But we do have a little thing called intuition. Come quick, daylight is approaching." She popped through the brush, and I quickly raced to follow her.

CHAPTER EIGHT

"Franca, wait." I stopped short and listened for a sign of where she had raced off to. Her speed surprised and impressed me.

I heard the familiar click of a gun behind me. Franca had led me straight back to where I had come from, and I was in such a hurry to follow her that I had not been paying attention.

"Turn around slowly, Miss. It's not my intention to bag up two bodies this evening." I turned to see the sheriff about fifteen feet to my rear. He had obviously been searching the woods around the house for me, and I had made his job easy. Unlike Dooley, Ralph held his gun firm and straight. Dooley had missed me when he took a shot. Ralph would not.

"Go ahead and get those hands up in the air and walk towards me."

I remained silent, lifted my hands and walked towards him.

"I am going to have to bring you in for questioning. Seems you may have been in the wrong place at the wrong time. You aren't under arrest, but I need you to answer some questions for me. Turn around and place your hands behind your back."

My breath caught in my throat. "You don't need to put me in shackles. I will go willingly with you to answer questions."

"That's mighty kind of you, but, you see, these are for your protection as much as mine." He held up some white plastic zip-ties in his hand. "And we stopped using the shackles a long time ago. Budget constraints."

I turned around and placed my hands behind my back. At this point I needed to get out of the area and into some shelter.

"Sorry, but I have to pat you down for weapons. Dooley said he took a sword off you. You have anything else I should know about?"

I returned his question with silence. I certainly had something I didn't want him to know about. After he finished running his hands up and down my legs and checking my pockets he ran a flat hand down the back of my jacket, which was anything but flat. His eyes widened as he slowly removed his hand. My father's words about learning at least a basic glamor spell echoed in my ears.

"What's your name?"

"Valora Delos."

"Where are you from, Ms. Delos?"

"Somewhere a long way from here."

৵৹৵

For whatever reason, Ralph choose to ignore what he had felt. He led me over to his car and opened the rear door motioning for me to sit inside.

"I've got her, Dooley. Don't worry. The coroner will be over in a few hours. He was fishing on the Snoqualmie River and has to make the trip down." Ralph shut the door, and I was no longer able to hear the words between the two men.

Ralph went over to Dooley and placed his hand on his shoulder. Dooley's head hung low as he said something to Ralph. Ralph responded by drawing Dooley into a hug, giving him a quick squeeze and patting him on the back. He pointed towards me. Dooley looked at me and then back at Ralph and nodded before turning heel and walking back into his house.

Ralph opened the driver's side door and fell into the seat with a jolt as he pulled the door closed. Without turning around he said, "Well, Miss, I certainly hope you didn't have anything to do with Brokk's death. You see, he meant a lot to Dooley and to me, too." Ralph pulled his sun visor forward to reveal the picture of a young girl on the other side. He placed a kiss on his finger and onto the picture. "Don't worry, honey. Daddy will think of another way."

Ralph pulled his car backwards over the rocky and unpaved road that led up to Dooley's cabin. Through the window I saw the flash of yellow hair in the brush. *Damn that dwarf.* The car reached the paved road and started a downhill descent. The path down was winding, and dawn was approaching. I had never expected to be here this long, and I was not prepared for what was to come.

I took a deep breath and tried to find my center. Tried to call on the Goddess Varuna for guidance. But as the car travelled further down the mountain, away from the Portal and away from the sky I was used to calling my home, I could feel my connection to her and the rest of the Realms slipping away. I had never heard of any other fae who willingly came to Earth and stayed. Brokk had obviously been one of them. But we had always been taught that those that left the Realms for Earth did so because they were trying to hide from a fate worse than death, and surviving Earthside was preferable, which didn't say much for Earth.

I squinted as the sunlight got brighter. My hands were tethered behind my back, and I was unable to shield my face. I had not lost all of my fight yet, but I was close to it. The adrenaline from the trip through the Portal and having Brokk's blood on my hands was wearing off. I shut my eyes against the light of the sunrise and lay my head back on the seat behind me. The rocking motion of the car slowly lulled me to sleep.

At the beginning of today I had found myself in the arms of King Aric. And now I feared I would never see him or Dell'Aria again. The cold vinyl of the seat was a poor substitute for the warmth of the King, but as I slipped into sleep my mind created for me visions better than the reality I was in now.

CHAPTER NINE

I was woken by a gentle shaking on my shoulder. "Ms. Delos, we are almost to the station, but I need to stop in the house right quick and make sure my daughter gets up in time for school. You understand?"

"Sure." I peered over Ralph's shoulder and saw a structure which contained several dwellings. The area was densely populated, and traffic was picking up. Trees, barren of leaves, lined the streets. People walked down the sidewalk to my left and through the area where Ralph had parked his car. I was suddenly claustrophobic, trapped without a weapon amongst all these humans. With my hands pinned behind me, my mother's grimoire pressed awkwardly into my side, reminding me that it was a weapon I chose to ignore.

Ralph stood up as he was about to shut the passenger door.

"Wait, I need to ask you a favor," I said.

"What is it?" He ducked his head back in.

"I need to go inside with you and use your restroom." I tested the plastic tethers holding my wrists together and was confident that I could snap them free.

Ralph nodded and stood to hold the door open for me. "Now I am going to cut these ties so that my daughter isn't afraid. But don't think I won't keep you still in another way if I need to." He patted the end of the gun hanging from his belt, his crooked smile more menacing than friendly.

"Understood." He cut the plastic ties binding my wrists, and I followed him up the stairs and into his small apartment.

A young girl bounded up to him and kissed him on the cheek. She was all too thin, but energy burst forth from her small frame. Above the doorway was a skylight that lit up the clear blue pools that were her eyes. I was immediately drawn into her gaze. The girl hesitated when she saw me and then extended her hand in greeting.

"I'm Kit. Who are you?"

I took the girl's hand in mine and felt a familiar spark that sent a shock through me. She was not human. I quickly masked my surprise. "I am Valora, a friend of your father's."

She tilted her head to study me. "A friend?"

"Don't worry. I am only here to use your bathroom and answer some questions your dad has for me. Then I will be on my way."

The girl nodded and skipped through the door. "Going to school, Dad, see you later."

I shut the door behind me. Ralph was still standing in the entryway. "Ralph?" I touched him on the shoulder.

Ralph blinked and turned his head towards me. "She is a lovely girl, isn't she?" He returned his gaze down the hall and out the sliding glass window at the back of the house that led to an outdoor patio.

"Yes, she is. Her name is Kit?"

He nodded.

I realized where I remembered those eyes. She had the eyes of a Selkie. Of course, Selkies did not exist here on Earth. The largest colony I knew of lived in Lake Mavrovo in the Underworld below Dell'Aria. Water Fae.

"You're like him, aren't you? Like Brokk? Besides the wings you're obviously hiding under that jacket, you even talk like he did."

Ralph turned to me and unsnapped the clip holding his gun to his belt. His hands clenched around the leather grip. "You might think I am not all too smart, bringing an accused murderer to my house instead of the county lock-up. But we both know that wouldn't be the best thing for either of us. Right?"

Ralph perched on a nearby stool, keeping his manner casual, but the white of his knuckles as his finger froze over the trigger of the gun told me this was anything but a friendly conversation.

"I am not sure what you want from me or what you think I can give you, but Brokk and I are nothing alike."

The Soulstealer had likely been heavily involved in whatever was happening in Dell'Aria. Why else would he have fled Earthside? His death wasn't going to keep me up at night. But who killed him and why, that was another story. Dooley was the only clue I had. He was also the only thing I would be able to bring back to Aric.

❧

"Mind if I go ahead and use the bathroom?" It was the only way I could think to get out of his line of fire for the moment, and I needed to talk to someone back in Dell'Aria.

"Oh sure, it's right through there." Ralph gestured with the gun to a door off the hallway.

I leaned against the closed door and noticed that there were no windows. I needed to get out of here. I wasn't sure what Brokk had gotten himself mixed up in, but the girl was a different story. She was definitely not human. All my sensors had registered that. *But how could a Selkie child survive in this world?* It was one thing for fae like me to walk outside the Realms, but the Selkie required regular rejuvenation in the pools of life that they made their homes. Everything I knew told me that an Earthbound Selkie couldn't survive.

If I could only get through to Kali then maybe I could find a way home, and then I could figure out the answers to all these questions that were pressing against me like the small confines of the room. I placed my ring stone to the mirror, and it shimmered to life. This time the corresponding mirror in our hut had been brought out into full view. Through it I saw Kali curled up in a ball on her bed. It was night time in Dell'Aria.

"Kali, wake up, Kali."

Kali shot up out of bed and rushed to the mirror. We simultaneously said, "What happened?"

"You first." I told Kali everything that had happened on my side, and when I was done she took a seat at the table the mirror was resting on.

"Valora, another wave hit Dell'Aria just before the Hunters returned from their mission. So many dead and wounded. A section of the outer isle has fallen. Others are saying the Selkie Queen is up in arms and threatening to dismantle the copper piping that she says is draining the pools of life from the energy needed to sustain her people. The King has not appeared, and many fear he may have fallen ill."

Kali took a deep breath and although I could tell she wanted to tell me more I interrupted with my own question, one I had to know. "Is my father okay?"

"Yes, he has made a few announcements in place of the King, but he will not say where he is. Valora, I know it isn't true, but there are whisperings about you, too."

"What are you talking about? I have been here less than a day. The fae was dead when I got here. The King himself assigned me to this mission, or is that still a secret?" *One that was doing me absolutely no good.*

"I think Orris started the rumor. He has been saying that you have likely been making trips back and forth through the Portal for many cycles. That you often go off alone. That you are in league with the Soulstealers. Valora, it does not help at all that the wave hit just after you disappeared through the Portal. I think others are beginning to believe the rumor is true."

"Of course they are. What happened to the Portal? Why did it close?"

"I don't know for sure. I was standing there waiting for you to return, and there was a sudden flash of light. I was knocked to the ground, and when I woke up the Portal was closed. I rushed back to the Peixes thinking you must have gotten through somehow. Everyone was there but you. That was when we saw the wave flash over the colony. I am so sorry I abandoned you, Valora. I had no idea where you were."

"You take care of what you need to there, Kali. I need to figure out what is happening here. I have seen more of our world here than I ever expected to. I came here for answers, and I will find them. When I found Brokk there was someone watching me from the woods. They ran off, and I saw the Portal close. Did you see anyone come through on your end?"

Kali brought her hand to her mouth. "I did not see anyone come through on my end. I will work to find a way to get the Portal open again, Valora. Stay in contact with me. Can you reach me tomorrow at this same time?" Kali placed her hand against the reflection of mine in the mirror.

"I will do my best." I took one last look around the hut I shared with Kali and blew her a kiss before taking my hand from the mirror. It shimmered to the present, and I stared back at my reflection. My face was smeared in dust and grime. My short black hair was stringy with dirt and sweat. The dragon leather covering my shoulders felt hot and heavy. Time was not on my side. I needed to figure out what had happened to Brokk and what he was doing here. And I needed to find out quickly.

I opened the door of the bathroom and found Ralph seated on a couch in the adjacent room. In his hands was an amulet which contained an ocean blue stone. He held it up to the sunlight pouring through the window. The stone had a depth to it like looking through a clear ocean floor, seemingly infinite, the amulet of the Selkie Queen.

"Ralph, we have a few things to talk about."

CHAPTER TEN

Ralph's stomach pooched slightly over his pants as he sat staring at the amulet.

"Ralph, where did you get that?"

"I suppose I could tell you. The only other person I ever told was Brokk. I'm not sure what else to do now. My life is over if I lose my daughter. She means everything to me."

"I understand, Ralph, but I don't want to get your hopes up. Whoever you think I am, whoever you think Brokk was, we don't possess the same skills. I can barely help myself." The words of my mother came back to me as clearly as if she were beside me speaking them. "But I was once told that I could do anything that I set my mind to, and I promise you that I will do everything I can to try to help your daughter." My words seemed to calm him somewhat, and he went on to tell the story of how he met the Selkie Queen.

"I really enjoy fishing. I stay pretty busy as the sheriff around here, always having to deal with the scum of this town. But I never was able to find me a wife in my younger days. Couldn't get any gal to believe that being sheriff of this tiny town was worth anything."

I could see in his eyes all the rejection he had been served and all the memories flooding through his mind as he recalled the years spent in solitary, a look I had seen in the mirror many times. I tried to bring him back to focus.

"The fish?"

"Oh, yeah, sorry. So one day about eight or so years ago I was in my skiff out on Yellow Lake. It was the break of dawn, and the waters were still. No one else but me on the lake. I had my line in the water for about an hour or so. I was actually just about to pull my line and head in. Fish weren't biting and I needed to get myself ready for work. Then I saw this flash not ten yards from the end of my boat. A blast that big I thought would have rolled me and the skiff over, but the waters remained calm. Barely a ripple. The light died down, and then I saw a head poke up out of the water and realized it was a lady. I yelled to her to ask if she was alright. She didn't answer me, but she did swim to the side of my boat. Bluest eyes I had ever seen." He looked again at the amulet, and his cheeks flushed. "I don't suppose I have to tell you what happened next."

"Oh, no, I can guess." I leaned back into the couch. So the Selkie Queen had a portal, and she was using it to travel Earthside to have dalliances with humans. That was not unusual. *But what would make her leave a child she knew would not survive here on Earth with Ralph?*

"What did she say to you when she brought you Kit?"

"I didn't see her again after that day. I went to the lake every morning for six months, hoping she'd come back." He grinned wryly. "Hoping I wouldn't have to turn myself in for a psych eval. I was beginning to think maybe the job was getting to me. But then one morning I saw the same flash of light. I raced over, and there she was. Floating on a large lily pad with the same blue eyes as her mother. She had this amulet and a small blanket with her, and that was it. I never saw her mother again, but I loved Kit from the minute I laid eyes on her. She's my life."

"Can I see it?"

Ralph handed me the amulet. I turned it over and over. It was definitely the amulet of the Queen. The markings proved as much. But I was still confused as to what purpose it served. I brought my hand to my throat and fingered the chain of the amulet I wore around my own neck. The one given to me by King Aric. "This will save you when you least expect it," he had said to me. I didn't know the purpose of it, either.

"So you never found out what this was for?"

Ralph shook his head. "No. Brokk didn't know, either. He came to me in the hospital when Kit started to get sick. Said he could help us. You can't say anything to Dooley. He doesn't know anything about this, and I'd just as soon keep it that way. Brokk wanted to keep his secrets, and I wanted to keep mine. We had a mutual understanding, one I hope you will honor."

I nodded. Ralph believed Dooley had no idea who Brokk was. The safest place for Brokk to hide out would be a place where no one knew or suspected him. The phone rang before I could pry any further.

☙❧

I set the amulet on the coffee table, and Ralph got up to answer the phone. I could hear excited chatter coming from the other end of the phone before Ralph even had a chance to say hello.

"What the hell? Yes, I am coming right back. And I don't want you to be surprised, but I got the gal with me that I took from your place last night." Ralph rolled his eyes.

"Now don't give me that, you know my judgment is a little better and more controlled than that."

I smirked at the thought of what Dooley had apparently implied. Ralph was nice, just not my type.

He hung up the phone.

"Seems we need to get back to Dooley's house," he said.

"Why, what happened?"

I definitely needed to get back out there eventually, but I was in no hurry to come face to face with the guy who nearly put a hole through my head, and Ralph seemed to know more about Brokk than Dooley did.

"Dooley says there are some critters in the woods out back of his house that showed up after the coroner took Brokk's body away."

"The coroner? Dammit, I totally forgot about Brokk's body. We have to get it back from the coroner. This is really important."

"That will be mighty difficult to do seeing that this is an unsolved murder case. Just what do you plan to do with it?"

"Would 'hide it' be a good answer?"

"Right. Secrets." He rubbed his hand under his chin. "I think I can have them hold off on the autopsy for about 24 hours. I played cards with the coroner once, and he owes me a favor. But I don't think they can wait longer than that."

"Okay. I guess that will have to work for now."

As we started out the door, my mind returned to the rest of Dooley's complaint, the reason we were going back out there. The "critters" in Dooley's woods might know who had killed Brokk. That gave me another possible lead.

I followed Ralph out to his car. Propped up against the side of it was the dwarf, Franca.

"Just where did you disappear to last night?" I demanded.

"Nice to see you again, too, Val. She ordering you around, too?" Franca jabbed a thumb in my direction while giving Ralph a wide smile. She had found a loose brown knit sweater to hide her body armor and looked a lot more normal here than I did in my black leather outfit.

"Ralph, this is my friend Franca." I gestured to the dwarf who pushed herself off the side of Ralph's car and extended her hand in greeting.

Ralph quickly shook her hand. "Sorry, miss, but we're on official business and need to get going."

"She is coming with us," I said. There was no way I was going to let the only one who could get me home out of my sight.

Franca sighed. "Well, I wasn't hanging around just letting this car keep me upright. Of course I am going with you."

Ralph looked from her to me and back again, then just shook his head and got in the car.

Franca and I slid into the back seat while Ralph put the car into gear.

"Didn't mean to ditch you. I thought you fae were faster than that."

"Fae? Is that what you call yourselves? I always just thought you were big fairies," said Ralph from the front seat.

Franca looked at me sideways. "Someone has been talkative."

"Ralph is good at keeping secrets." Ralph gave me a short salute. I lowered my voice as I spoke to Franca. "You said you would lead me back to the Realms through your Portal. Does your offer still stand?"

"I suppose. Though I was wondering what I am going to get in return."

"What do you want?"

"Can we just say that you will owe me a favor? I haven't really decided yet."

"Oh, no. I know not to owe any favors to a dwarf."

"Dwarf?" Ralph sputtered.

"Oh, now who is giving away the farm?" asked Franca. "You think you know a lot of things, but you are in this situation now because, and I am just guessing here, you don't know quite as much as you thought."

I really had no other choice than to accept her help. Kali was in no position to help me. At this point I likely had a bounty on my head. I only hoped it wasn't Kali that they sent after me.

"Fine, it's a deal." I shook the dwarf's hand, hoping that I had not sealed my fate in some unknown way.

The car came to a stop, and I saw that we were back in Dooley's driveway. I opened the car door and immediately noticed something strange.

"What is going on here?" asked Franca as she exited the other side.

The wind had died. The trees were still. We heard no animals rustling through the brush. No flies buzzing through the air. The only thing that we could sense was the smell, a sharp tang that bit into your tongue. Fear, acrid and pungent, was rolling off the ground in waves.

The door to Dooley's house flew open, and he stepped onto the porch. It was the first time I had seen him in the light, and my breath caught in my lungs. His long hair was a deep rich brown. His feet were bare and he wore pants that were cuffed at the bottom. His skin was tanner that any of the fae who had spent a dozen cycles parked under the noon sky of Dell'Aria. And other than the shotgun he had propped on his hip and the rips that tore through his shirt, which was peppered with the residue of something or someone, there was one other thing that I noticed.

Dooley wasn't altogether human, either. Part of him was fae.

CHAPTER ELEVEN

"What the hell, Ralph? I told you I didn't want you to bring her back here. Why isn't she locked up in a cell? Did you even fingerprint her yet?" Dooley said all this with tight lips, his words coming out in a growl.

Ralph stood with the car door in front of him. "Now, now, Dooley. I don't tell you how to do your job, you just leave me to mine. Now tell me what it is you got out here."

Dooley stared at me as he spoke to Ralph. "Part of one of them is out back. The rest ran off when I started shooting. But I warn you, Ralph, it's not human. I have never seen anything like it."

I broke away from the group and crept toward the back of the house. If there was a creature from the Realms, I wanted to see it. Before I had taken three steps, Dooley hopped over the stair railing and landed right in front of me.

"Going somewhere?" he demanded.

Dooley had never been this close to me before and I couldn't help but be drawn into his gaze. His eyes, so close to mine, were like melted chocolate, a treat I could not afford the time to indulge in. I took a sharp intake of breath, inhaling Dooley's scent which was all too like my kin of Dell'Aria. I suddenly felt homesick again. The Hunter in me yelled out for me to keep focused.

"I think I can help you with whatever you have in your woods."

"Really? So what is it you do, Miss...?"

"Valora. Valora Delos. I am a Hunter."

"Valora. Well, I would extend my hand in greeting but it is quite full at the moment." He nodded his head toward the rifle in his hand. He had full control of his emotions and his muscles today. There was no quiver as he gripped the barrel. "My name is Dooley Fays. This is my land, and don't think you can just run off after last night. What do you mean you're a hunter?"

His manner was becoming exasperating. "Do you think I would have come back if I had any intention of running off?"

"You are under the control of the Sheriff. You had no choice."

"Is that what you think?" I stared into his eyes.

"She's right, Dooley. I haven't put her under arrest. I have nothing to hold her on. You didn't see anything. She says she was hunting in the woods when she came on Brokk's body. Isn't that right, miss?" Ralph gave me a wink.

I wasn't sure I wanted his help, but no one else was offering anything without strings attached. "Ye...Yes." Franca cleared her throat. "Oh, and this is Franca, my friend. She was out hunting with me last night."

"Yes, I can vouch for her," Franca said. "She is a bit twitchy, but not the murdering type."

"So you hunt with this?" I realized then that Dooley held my scabbard and sword in his other hand. I had been so enthralled with him that I hadn't even noticed.

"Makes it more challenging. Can I have it back?" I reached out, and Dooley pulled away before he slowly handed it to me.

I turned to Franca and Ralph. "Why don't the two of you stay here, and Dooley and I will check in back. Keep watch until we figure out what we have back there."

I let Dooley take lead and followed him towards the back of his house. He pointed, but I needed no direction. On the ground lay the remains of a goblin. Not too far from where Brokk had lain only hours before. The goblin had a hole shot through his chest which explained the flecks of orange on Dooley's shirt.

"You know that black is not the usual color hunters wear when they're out in the woods?" Dooley walked up beside where I was standing over the goblin. "If you wear black you run the risk of getting shot. Hunters usually wear orange, and they don't usually go hunting in the middle of the night behind someone's house."

I knelt down to get a closer look at the body of the goblin. "I am a Bounty Hunter. Hunter for short. Like I said before, I had been sent to bring Brokk back home."

I reached into the pocket of the weapons sash that crossed the tattered muck that was left of the goblin's chest.

"Brokk's home was here. He was my Reiki Master. He taught me everything he knew."

I opened the folded piece of paper I had pulled out of the goblin's sash. "Did he ever tell you where he came from?"

"No. We didn't talk about the past. We only focused on the present."

I handed him the paper. "Presently I would guess that there are more of these things, and I think it is about time you start thinking about the future."

"This is a sketch of Brokk and me." His finger traced the lines of the last picture on the paper. "And you."

"You see, we are both on the same side."

‌❧

Ralph got up from the rocking chair on the porch and headed back to his cruiser. We had convinced him that he needed to go back into town and take care of his daughter. I renewed my promise to help him the best I could, but the first thing we needed to do before dark was come up with a plan.

"The thing you killed. It likely was a scout. A whole team of them will follow." Franca and I had done our best to ease Dooley into the idea that monsters really did exist, but it was proving difficult without using the actual "g" word and admitting that there was an entire world he was unaware of.

"Are you saying that there are armed assassins out there, wanting to kill us, and we can't ask the police for help?"

"I think it is time you shed your coat," said Franca.

"Franca, no!" Franca knew I was a fae. She also knew that I was likely hiding my true nature. What she did not know was that I did not need a glamor to hide long glorious wings from view. All I needed was this coat which had become my security. I never "showed" my wings to anyone. It was not that my true nature was embarrassing; it was that I didn't live up to the vision of my true nature. If I told this guy I was a fae and then showed him my impish wings, he would think I was a bloated pixie.

As if she had plucked the thoughts from my mind Franca said, "No one will judge you here."

Dooley had frozen in place at Franca's words, a wave of confusion crossing his face.

I threw my hands up in the air. "What else have I got to lose? Might as well give away my dignity, too." I tore off my coat like you would rip away a bandage, hoping the abruptness would lessen the pain.

The small black wings that had been pressed down across the tops of my shoulders for the last day sprang to life. I gave them a quick shake to rid myself of the aching that had formed from having them restrained for so long.

CHAPTER TWELVE

We retreated into Dooley's cabin. It took a few tries for Franca and me to explain to Dooley where we were from. He also had to take a few tries tugging at my wings before he believed that they weren't sad leftovers from some Halloween sale. Apparently it was a holiday that had recently passed, and people liked to dress up with wings just like mine. Brilliant.

Brokk had made Ralph swear to keep his secret. I only swore to keep Ralph's secret.

"But Brokk didn't have wings like that."

"No, he didn't. His were much longer and functional. You won't meet another full blooded fae that has wings like mine. They don't usually let those born with defects live. No, Brokk had wings, he was just able to hide them from you. Think about it. Did you ever see him without a cloak or cape or something draped over his shoulders? Most fae also use magic, called a glamor, to hide their true nature." *Most fae, but not me.*

Dooley sat down, his eyes darting from one corner of the room to the other. I figured he was replaying in his mind all the times he had seen Brokk over the last two years. "I can't believe he could hide something from me for so long. And why?"

"People don't tend to see what doesn't fit into their version of reality." Franca flopped onto the bench next to Dooley and gave him a pat on the back. "And I am sure he only hid it from you to protect you. Valora can likely tell you more, but the fae don't normally hang out with humans. There had to be a reason."

"I was the one who sought him out. I heard he was a brilliant Reiki Master. I wanted to stop drifting through life and make a positive difference. I was drawn to the Reiki practice and saw it as a way I could make a deeper connection with the people around me. I've always found it difficult to bond with others. That is, until I started Reiki. Brokk taught me to hone my energies. To focus them so that I could find the source of what's ailing someone. He made me realize that my life had purpose."

"Reiki? So what...was he running an ad in the paper or something?"

"No. Oh, I thought he would have told you. Ralph introduced us. Ralph and I go way back." I sensed there was something he wasn't telling me about why he had known the sheriff for so long, but his distant past wasn't important to me.

"He did say something about knowing Brokk himself, that Brokk had been helping his daughter. Do you know what he was doing for Ralph?" I asked, wondering if Ralph was telling me the whole truth.

"No. Seems there was a lot I didn't know about him." Dooley rose to his feet and went to the other side of the room to where another cot was shoved up against the wall. He dug around underneath it and pulled out a moderate sized wooden chest. It had a substantial lock holding it closed and many copper straps across its top and sides.

"This was all he owned. But I don't have the key." He set it atop the table. The chest looked almost identical to the one Kali had pulled the seal breaker from only yesterday. I needed to see what was inside. As I ran my hand over it I felt the familiar tingle of magic. There was definitely no way I was going to be able to break whatever magical lock it had. I straightened my back as my mother's grimoire decided to dig into my side again, reminding me of what my real disability was.

Although the oil lamps burned bright inside the small cabin, the light outside had faded fast. We had spent a long time trying to explain to Dooley that there was much more to life than the world he knew.

❧

"I need to take a quick shower. Splash some water on my face. Are you two going to be okay for a minute?" Dooley got up from the table. He had dark crescents under his eyes, and I could tell his mind and body were exhausted.

As he walked towards the bathroom door he stripped off his shirt which had been torn in his battle with the goblin and threw it in a small garbage can that sat outside the door. His tan skin was toned from the rise at the top of his buttocks to the back of his neck and shoulders. The black markings were also drawn across his shoulder blades and down his back. A shiver went down my spine.

I was not used to seeing a male without wings, and sensing his fae energy at the same time confused the signals in my brain. I had decided not to say anything about that yet as it was obvious that Dooley had no idea he was part fae. I was running into more people from the Realms than I was humans so far, and I was beginning to think that all I had been told about Earth might not be correct.

"You don't mind me leaving you alone for a while, either, do you?" asked Franca.

"You're not ditching me again, are you?"

"Now why would I do that? You promised me a favor." Franca gave me a wink. "No, it's just that I checked Dooley's fridge, and he has nothing I can eat, and I am starved. I'm going to go foraging for something. The cold season has taken most everything, but there has to be some edible green matter out there."

"Oh, okay." I had forgotten that dwarves mostly foraged for their food. That's probably why the scouts had seen them in the woods. We had a fairly dry cycle, and it was easy to see from Overworld that the foliage that surrounded Mount Elbrus had suffered greatly. We saw a lot from Overworld. We saw a lot and did nothing.

As Franca shut the door behind her, a rumble in my stomach reminded me that the last thing I had to eat was the ice fruit and butter breads back in Dell'Aria. This was never supposed to be a long mission. I actually had no idea what I could eat here on Earth. But Brokk had lived with Dooley, so I was certain there must be something here that would work for me.

I walked to the area where I had seen Dooley cooking the night before. I gave the iron stove a wide berth. On the wall next to the stove was a set of cupboards. Below the cupboards were a small counter and another door below that.

I opened the door below the cupboard and saw that it was a small icebox. To my surprise I saw a bowl of ice fruits sitting inside. Dell'Aria was the only colony in Overworld that grew ice fruits. Kali was the only one in Dell'Aria with a field that still bore fruit. Hunger momentarily overrode my curiosity, and I picked one up. The icy chill of the fruit immediately made my mouth water.

"If you were hungry, you should have just said so."

I had been so absorbed in thought that I had not even noticed when Dooley had come out of the bathroom. I whirled around and saw that he had a towel wrapped around his waist. That was about it. The ice fruit dropped from my hand, and Dooley dropped his towel as he rushed forward to catch it. He quickly caught the fruit and retrieved his towel from the floor, but not before I had caught a glimpse of him. I was surprised that Dooley said he had such a difficult time connecting with people.

Dooley propped the small fruit between his lips while he used his hands to secure the towel back around his waist. He took the fruit from his mouth. "Sorry. I don't suppose you want this anymore, do you? There are others in the fridge."

I tried to put clothes back onto the mental picture of Dooley in my mind so that my voice would work again. "Yes, there are. Where did you get them?"

"Brokk picked them up from the store. Every time he went shopping, he would pick them up."

I shook my head.

"He didn't get them from the store?" Dooley gave me a quizzical look.

"No, he got those from Dell'Aria. There is no other place in the Realms that grows them. Unless you want to tell me that they grow them here, too."

"No. In fact I was always bugging him about where he got them because every time I went to the store they were out. He could never remember the name of them, either, and so I could never ask the clerk about them."

The wheels turned in my mind. I was sent to bring Brokk back to Dell'Aria, but he was either making visits there himself or he had someone there who was still in contact with him. The picture of Brokk's robes and Pryn's robes flashed side by side in my mind. The kindly priest turned Soulstealer who had saved my life and left me with a cryptic message about how I would save all of the fae of Dell'Aria, or so I thought. Kali had told me that a fae told her Brokk was a builder, but he must have been associated with the priesthood somehow.

The Hunters always suspected that a contingent of the Soulstealers were still in Dell'Aria. That is, ones that were not already locked away in the Court. The thought made it hard to trust one another. A city which was once flush with generosity and openness now locked its doors. Neighbors no longer sat around the community fire telling stories of many cycles ago. In a lot of ways I was glad that my mother was not around to see what Dell'Aria had become. It would have broken her.

Then again, I was certain that if she was still here she would know what to do to stop it.

Dell'Aria. Kali. I needed to talk to her again. "Dooley, please excuse me. I need to use the bathroom."

He nodded, taking a bite of the ice fruit in his hand.

I walked into the room and shut the door. The steam from Dooley's shower immediately attached itself to me along with the smell of sweet peppermint soap and his own personal scent. I brushed my hand across the surface of the mirror to clear away some of the moisture and placed my ring to it.

The surface shimmered to life, but the scene was very different than I expected. I had a view of someone's sleeping quarters. The walls of the room were made from rough-hewn stone. There were only two places in all of Dell'Aria made of this material, the Court and the Temple. I had never seen such a room in either. There were no windows. I heard the clink of metal against metal as the door to the room creaked open. Something inside me said I should disconnect from the mirror. This was obviously not Kali's doing. But I could not pull my gaze from the wooden door which slowly creaked open.

Along the walls were sconces where the small flames of candles danced with the breeze as the door closed, and there, standing before me, was King Aric.

His eyes were full with lust and power. I could practically feel it through the mirror, rolling off of him in waves. Across the left side of his face was a fresh wound. Small droplets of blood had barely begun to slide down his cheek from the thin slice.

"Sire! Your face. Are you okay?"

He touched his hand to his face and rubbed the blood between his fingers. "Funny you should be worried about how I am doing."

I took in a deep breath and tried to hold back the tears that were welling up and threatening to break over the rim. But it was of no use. There was my King, blood cascading down his cheek, and I couldn't stop the tears from flowing. "I have failed you. You have every right to be disappointed in me. But you must believe it was not I who did this. Brokk was killed just as I got here. Someone got here before me."

Aric took two steps towards the mirror. "Who? Who got there before you?"

"That's just it. I don't know. I am trying to figure it out, but I was also trying to get home. Though I don't know if I will still be welcome."

Aric bowed his head. "You cannot come back, Valora."

"What?" I pressed both hands against the surface of the mirror wishing I could fly right through it and into his arms. "You can't believe I mean the people of Dell'Aria any harm. Please."

He looked up again and walked closer to the mirror. "Valora. The reason you cannot return is because it's no longer safe for you here. It is not that I don't believe you. And please, when we are alone, call me Aric." A small smile crossed his face, and he ran his finger across the surface of the mirror. "My flower." He broke his gaze and turned his attention to my surroundings. "Where are you? And your coat? Your wings are out in the open."

"Don't worry. I am safe for now. But what about you, what happened?"

"Just a reminder from the Royal Guard of who is really in charge here. My punishment for having the dragon slain for you, the one that tried to take your life. Be careful. Those that would befriend the Soulstealers are not to be trusted. You might think them worthy, but you must be cautious. Promise me you will not say anything of our conversations. I fear what they might do to you if they knew you had a way to contact me directly."

"Of course I won't say anything." I swallowed hard wondering if I could push out what I wanted to say to him most in that moment. "Will I ever see you again?"

"Yes." He smiled then, wide. "You do still have friends here in this city, Valora. Kali was kind enough to bring this mirror to me. I will find a way to restore order here. But until I do, please know that you are safer hiding Earthside." Aric turned his head as a noise sounded outside his door. "The Queen's Guard are vigilant. Valora, contact me again tomorrow. The same time."

He leaned into the mirror and spoke in a whisper. "I love you." The mirror shimmered again, and I was looking back at myself, my mouth gaping wide open, unable to close.

I slowly stripped away the confines of my bodice and the leather pants leaving only the King's amulet to rest between my breasts. I leaned into the shower to turn it on. I stepped in and let the clear cool water cascade over my body, remembering how Aric's long white blond tresses flowed over my bare knees in his throne room only a few days before.

I trailed my fingers lightly down my stomach to rest in the crease between my legs and slid them back and forth as I let the cool water wash over my wings. Waves of pleasure built as I pulled the teeming lust from inside of me, drawing it further and further to the surface with quick sharp strokes until it burst forth. I clasped the amulet as the shaking died down and I was brought back to reality.

I pulled one of the soft white towels from the rack and wrapped it around myself. "My King."

CHAPTER THIRTEEN

I refastened the clasps that held my bodice to me. As I pulled my pants back over my legs I remembered that on my bike was a compartment with a change of clothes and a few other supplies I kept for when I went out on my lone rides through Underworld. You never knew when you might need to camp out for a day somewhere in the Realms.

Holding to Aric's wishes I slid my arms back into my coat and over my shoulders. My wings gave a reluctant twitch. "You'll just have to deal with it," I told them.

When I opened the door I saw Dooley perched on a small stool by the window. He had a rifle in one hand and one edge of the faded corner of the orange curtains in the other. "Maybe I took that shower too soon."

"What do you see?"

Dooley's look of concern melted away to mild amusement. "You seem refreshed."

My cheeks were suddenly warm. He probably thought I got hot and heavy over seeing the towel pool around his ankles. "Yes, I released a bit of that muscle tension under the water. Have you seen any sign of Franca?" I said, hoping to change the subject and the direction my baser instincts were pressing me towards.

"No, not yet." His eyes hovered on me a moment longer than necessary before he looked back through the window. "But I have seen something rustling through the woods, and I don't think it's a deer."

"Just one something?" I leaned over Dooley's shoulder and peered out the window into the woods behind his home. A solitary light shone from his back porch, and the dense evergreens blocked most of it from reaching beyond the lighter scrub brush that played around its edges.

"I can't be sure." His warm breath danced across my neck, and I was suddenly aware of how close we were. I slowly pulled away from the window and looked into his chocolate brown eyes. I was once told that humans were naturally attracted to the fae. Something about our energy, our life force, made it easy to coerce them even without a glamor spell.

He reached out and touched my shoulder. "Would you let me help you?"

I stood up straight, releasing his hand from me. "How could you possibly help me?"

"You probably think it's silly, what I do. But all I know I learned from Brokk, and you say he was a fae. Like you. Maybe I can help you figure out why this is all happening."

"What do you mean?" I drew my coat tighter around my shoulders. "This is all happening because your friend Brokk was a Soulstealer. I don't know why he was killed, and now I am trapped here. I was sent through the Portal for him, and it was all a waste of time." My eyes darted through the room. I located my scabbard, retrieved it and clipped it to my belt. "I need to get out of here. I feel like the walls are closing in."

"Wait." Dooley stepped between me and the door. "They're out there waiting for us to come out. You're playing right into their trap."

"What about Franca? She is likely out there battling them all alone," I stuttered, trying to convince myself of my reasons for going outside. Reasons other than putting distance between Dooley and me.

I tried to push past him and he took my wrist in his hand, holding me in his gaze.

"I lost something, too."

I pushed the rest of the way past him, ignoring his attempts to connect with me. "You don't know anything about loss."

I paused at the bottom of the stairs, scanning as best I could for anything out of the ordinary. The sounds of the forest had returned, and all I was able to catch was the scent of some animal prowling for his supper. A low guttural sound that throbbed through its throat told me he was about ready to pounce. But this sound was brought to me on the breeze and was nowhere nearby.

I pulled the sword from my scabbard as I crept towards the opening between the trees that led to where I had left my bike and the closed Portal. Dooley bounded up behind me.

"If you are coming with me, you can at least pretend that you are a little stealthy," I admonished him.

Dooley cocked his eyebrow at me. "Yes, ma'am."

"Incoming!" I heard Franca's loud cry as she came crashing through the brush to our right and tumbled head over heels before righting herself. She pulled her war hammer from its trappings and swung it to face front just as three goblins, much larger than the first I had encountered, flew through the brush after her into the clearing.

They all brandished the curved blades of their scimitars as they let loose shrieking battle cries. Franca brought up her hammer as two of the three goblins brought down their swords. Sparks flew as the weapons collided and Franca stumbled backwards. I rushed forward into the fray and sliced through the back of the third goblin who went down with a spray of orange blood.

I heard Dooley cocking his weapon as I drew one of the goblins off Franca and engaged him in a little sword play. "Don't shoot, you'll end up hitting one of us," I yelled at him.

The goblin pulled back his lips in a vicious sneer as he took another swipe, almost catching my shin. As he brought up his weapon the light from the porch caught the blade, and I saw a green tinge to its curved edge.

"Be careful. Their blades are coated in poison!" I shouted to the others. The goblin I was fighting brought his sword above his head and before he could bring down his arms I grasped them and shoved my blade deep into his gut.

Franca cried out and clutched at her side where the goblin's blade had found the spot between her segmented armor. She held her hammer before her like a shield as the goblin swept his scimitar downwards in a final blow.

I pulled my sword from the body of the goblin and leaped over his body as I raced over to assist, but I knew I wouldn't make it in time.

A sharp blast rang out from my right, and the goblin's body and sword dropped to the ground. Small wisps of smoke curled forth from the end of Dooley's rifle. He looked at me and smiled. "I forgot to tell you I was a good shot."

Franca lay on the ground, and I raced to her side. "Let me see where you are hurt. How bad is it?"

"Don't worry, fae. You aren't going to get out of the favor you owe me that easily." Franca sat up, gave a groan and lay back down again. "But I might need a short nap."

"Oh, no. You can't fall asleep. Dooley, can you help me bring her into the house?"

"Already on it." Dooley scooped up Franca's small frame with ease and carried her up the stairs.

Bodies of four goblins lay scattered about the yard, blood pooling around them. I thought about how to hide them, but then thought better. Hopefully this would serve as a warning to any others.

❧

Dooley had set Franca on one of the two cots that were propped up against the wall. "The two of you lived rather simply out here," I said.

"Brokk taught me a simple life. It wasn't easy for me to get there, but I have embraced it." Dooley put his hand to Franca's head. "She's heating up."

"Really, you two, I am fine. I just need to sleep it off."

"If you sleep before we heal you then you will fall into sleep forever. You know this, shake it off, Franca." I knelt at the side of the cot and gently pressed the pieces of armor apart. The gash was ragged and bloody, worse than I thought. The green tinge of the poison sat atop the wound, slowly seeping into her bloodstream.

"I am not a Healer. I don't know what she needs," I said.

Dooley put a hand on my shoulder. "I'll help as best I can." He went to his stove and took the pot that he was cooking with the night before. Inside was a substance black as tar that had a faintly medicinal smell. Parts of it smelled familiar to me. If Brokk had ice fruit he was likely able to procure herbs from Dell'Aria as well.

Dooley placed a finger into the mixture and with the other hand gently pushed the hair from Franca's forehead. He began to paint a swirling pattern on her forehead with the black paint. Through the middle was the shape of a cane.

"What is that?"

"It is the Reiki power symbol." Dooley raised his hands and began to move them through the air above Franca's body. His hands moved over the wound, pausing as if moving through molasses, like the wound was emitting some dark energy that he had to forcibly dispel. Gradually his movements quickened, and Franca let out a deep sigh.

She rolled her head to the side and looked up at Dooley, her eyes moist with tears. She reached up and closed her hand over his forearm. "Thank you, Dooley. You truly have the gift."

"Wait. What are you two talking about?" I went to Franca's side again and inspected the wound. It was still angry, but the green tinge of the poison was gone.

"How did you do that?" I asked.

Dooley sat back on his heels looking exhausted. "Brokk was my Reiki Master. He taught me to heal people by manipulating the non-physical energy that animates all living things. I have never had to do anything like that before, though. I think she might need some of the medicine from the clinic." He grimaced as he mentioned the clinic as if it were something he wasn't pleased about.

"I'll be fine for tonight. I really need to rest," Franca said sleepily.

I put my hand to Franca's head. Her skin felt normal, no longer burning with fever. "Are you sure? You were poisoned."

"Don't worry. I can feel some of my strength has returned. He is right. Not everything is out of my system. But I should survive a night's sleep."

I nodded and covered her with a thin blanket. Franca rolled over and was asleep in a matter of minutes. I stayed at her side until I saw the gentle rise and fall of her chest.

I turned, and Dooley was sitting at the table staring at me. Beside him on the table was a small bowl of the tar he had used to paint the symbol on Franca.

"I think now it is your turn." He gestured to the chair opposite him.

"I wasn't hurt."

"No?" I found myself caught in his gaze. If I didn't know any better I would have thought that he had glamored me. There was something intriguing about Dooley Fays, that much was certain. Aric's words came back to me. I should not trust those that were associated with Soulstealers.

"What was it you were saying about the clinic? You think there is a place here that has medicine that can help those from the Realms?"

Dooley smiled and shook his head. "You don't quit, do you? I promise we will talk about it. But first, you need to trust me." He reached out his hand again and gestured to the stool.

I wasn't sure what to expect, but if all he did was a painting on my forehead and make me have a good night's sleep, then I supposed there was no harm in playing along.

I reluctantly plopped into the stool opposite him. "Okay, let's get this over with." I pulled back the hair on my forehead and leaned into him. "Go ahead."

"No. You need to take off your coat." I must have given him a look I was not aware of because the next thing out of his mouth was again, "Trust me."

I shucked off the coat and set it beside me on the table. He had already seen my wings, there was no hiding that from him.

Dooley stood and brought his stool behind me. "This should be a little warm but not hot." He pressed his finger against my left shoulder blade, tracing a zig zag underneath my wing. He reached forward and dipped his finger again into the small pot of tar and placed his finger on the curve of my upper back. He traced an arc down my right side and finished with two small circles on my right shoulder blade.

When he lifted his finger from my back I let out a breath I had not realized I was holding. "What is that the symbol for?"

"It is the symbol for emotional health."

"What? You think I have something wrong with my head?"

"Not hardly." His answer came quick. "I need you to relax as much as possible. I am going to try to access your memory chakra."

"What will that do?"

"If everything works as planned it will bring you to a place in your past, a place where you failed to see everything that was happening around you, a time that you need to relive in order to fully understand where you are today."

"I know where I am, I'm stuck here on Earth."

"Well, technically, you are on the Issaquah Plateau in the mountainous region above Seattle proper."

I could tell he was mocking me. "So you are in league with the dwarf?"

He ran his hands over my back in the space between us. It only took seconds for me to feel his energy pulsing within me. I closed my eyes, and the tension melted from my shoulders. Gradually I slipped into a dream state.

A gentle shaking brought me awake within the dream. I looked up to see the eyes of my father some fifteen cycles ago. The ground beneath me was hard, and I looked up to see my mother's crypt, a place I often fell asleep after the Blight took her from me.

"The King asked me to bring this to you." My father handed me a sheaf of paperwork.

I thumbed through the papers which indicated I had been given a place in the military training academy that trained the guard of the royal court. At the bottom was the signature and seal of King Aric. My training was to begin in two weeks time.

My father silently crept back out of the crypt as I curled up into a fetal position, the orders from the King clutched to my middle. King Aric had saved me again, and I was not going to disappoint him.

I awoke that morning with a renewed sense of purpose. I could barely contain my excitement as I skipped up the curved stairwell to the aviary to say my final farewell to the messenger birds used to communicate with the other colonies in Overworld.

I spent the next ten cycles in training. My days were filled with runs around the battlements of the Court. The Captain of the Guard, Siam, constantly doubted that I could be of any use without a proper set of wings, and I set out to prove him wrong. Mostly he stationed me in the outwork for the outside walls of the Court knowing that an aerial attack against Dell'Aria had not happened in over two hundred years and wasn't likely to happen anytime soon. In the evenings I studied the histories of the Seelie Court and the Royal Guard to prepare for my exit exam. When that day came I was thrilled. I exceeded all of my own expectations that day.

As I danced atop the battlements I spied my father watching me from the window of the keep. My heart swelled with pride. Mother had always done her best to convince me that I was no different than the other fae, and I knew she was watching over me the same as my father was.

I had just rounded the last turret when Siam stepped into the courtyard. He held in his hands the scrolls which would assign us to our posts. The others gathered around him, and I quickly found my way to the ground. There were shouts of glee and groans as those that were given less than desirable duties compared assignments and talked about the celebration to come. I could almost taste the sweet ice wine on my tongue.

The smug look on Siam's face hit me like a ton of bricks. I looked down at the short note he handed me.

"You have been discharged, Valora. The Royal Guard has decided that you would be a danger to your post since you cannot perform a basic duty of the Guard. You cannot fly."

My eyes flashed open, and I realized I was looking at the ceiling. I was lying in Dooley's lap, and he was drawing his fingers through my dampened locks. My cheeks were drenched in tears that continued to fall. Weakness and exhaustion hit me at the same time.

Dooley's face was calm and radiated a sense of peace that amazingly flooded from him through me. "You don't need to tell me what you saw. I was there with you."

CHAPTER FOURTEEN

When I awoke again I was lying on the cot opposite Franca. I could still see the gentle rise and fall of her chest, and that made me feel better. But I knew she needed something else if she was going to completely recover.

Dooley stood in front of the stove in a tight white t-shirt and jeans with frayed edges. He reached back and quickly slipped a tie around his long curly hair to keep it from falling forward. His brown toes peeked out of the bottom of his jeans as he shuffled around in front of the pan. He flipped a small cake in the air, and it landed back in the pan.

"Good morning. I see you're awake." He smiled and turned back to the pan. "Brokk used to like my cooking. I hope you're able to eat it, too."

"What about Franca?"

"She's still sleeping." The scent of cooked meat hung in the air, and my stomach grumbled.

"Don't worry, it'll be done soon," said Dooley.

I propped myself on the stool next to the stove so I was staring at his profile. "You learned a lot about me last night. I don't really tend to share my feelings with others too often."

"I get that. We don't need to talk about it if you don't want to. It was your memory to relive, not mine."

"Perhaps I would feel better if I knew a little more about you."

Dooley cocked an eyebrow in my direction and gave me a delicious smirk. "I'm making you breakfast. When you get some food in your growling stomach, that will make you feel better."

And I thought I was tight lipped. "At least tell me how you know Ralph." I couldn't go straight to asking about Brokk. If he was going to shut me down, I had to start somewhere that didn't really matter, something small.

"Telling you how I know Ralph would require me to tell you my entire childhood, and it wasn't pretty."

Dang, so much for starting small. "You know, if I could read your mind like you can read mine then you wouldn't have to tell me anything. Want to teach me that trick?" The memory of last night flooded back, and I was suddenly self-conscious. It was very rare that the fae could read the thoughts of one another.

"Let's just say that I grew up in foster homes, and I wronged a lot of people when I was young. Ralph tried to help me out. All I can do now is try to make up for some of my mistakes." He placed the cakes onto two plates, scooping some of the fried meat from the pan and placing it on the side.

He motioned to Franca who was still softly snoring on her cot. "I think it's best she stay that way until we can get to the clinic. I called Ralph this morning. He's going to come by after he drops Kit off at school," said Dooley.

"What is this clinic?" I pushed myself up off the stool and went to sit back at the table. The paint that Dooley had used on my back the night before had started to itch.

Dooley turned with a spatula in his hand. "It's a place Ralph was taking Kit to get help before he couldn't afford it anymore, and then he came to Brokk. I've never been too sure about it, but I don't think I can heal her all on my own." Dooley noticed the contortions I was putting myself in as I tried to scratch my itch. He set down the spatula and picked up a wet rag from the edge of the sink.

"Here, let me help you get that off." He came over and rubbed the cloth back and forth over the marking on my back. "I think I got it all." A gentle breeze blew across my back making goose bumps rise all over my skin…Dooley's breath. "All dry."

He brought our plates to the table and pushed a bottle of thick brown syrup towards me. "Try some of that on those pancakes. You'll like them. And that's bacon."

The smell was intoxicating. It had been a long time since I had anything to eat. I slathered the pancakes with the syrup and took large mouthfuls.

"I guess you were hungry. Sorry I haven't cooked for you before now." Dooley popped a piece of pancake in his mouth. "Like I said, Ralph will be over here any time, and then we can go. I don't know what it is they can do, but Brokk's not here and that was where he would go, too."

I took a hard swallow and noticed my plate was empty.

"Oh, did you want more? I can make more," he said.

Dooley rose from the table, and I waved him off. "No, no. I'm good. Thank you though, that was delicious." I hesitated, not knowing if I wanted the answer to what I was about to ask. "Dooley, about what you did last night. You did say you were there with me, right? In my memory? Is that something you do all the time?"

Dooley chuckled and leaned back against the wall

behind him folding his arms in front of him. "Are you asking me if I can read your mind all the time?" A twinkle set to light in his eyes.

"Well, yes. Because it is a very rare ability amongst...my people."

Dooley tipped back towards the table and rested against one elbow. "Actually it is the first time that has ever happened to me. I thought maybe it was because you are fae. Brokk taught me how to perform that ceremony, but he never had me practice it on him. And no, I cannot read your thoughts all the time. It was only during the ceremony. It was as if I could see the pictures in your mind like I was watching a movie, but I didn't know what you were feeling as they went through your mind. I could only assume it was a very painful memory from your reaction to it."

"That's what I don't understand. I thought you were supposed to be helping me figure stuff out. I just relived a very painful day in my life."

"Are you sure? There was one particular face I kept seeing again and again in those visions of yours. White blond hair, blue eyes. Ring a bell?"

"That was King Aric." Dooley's comment surprised me. It meant he had seen things other than what I saw. King Aric wasn't in the memory I had relived at all. "He is the one who sent me on this mission. I was raised in the Court alongside him. He is a part of a lot of my memories."

A knock sounded at the door, and I was glad I wasn't going to have to talk about it anymore with Dooley. I was glad he could not feel my emotions. I had to hide my feelings for Aric. He told me as much during the last time I spoke to him. One thing I did realize during that memory was that there were many times in my life that I had needed Aric, and he had been there for me. He was always there to provide me with a direction when I had none. It was shortly after I was discharged from the Guard that he gave the speech to the people of Dell'Aria about joining the Hunters. I remember after I heard the speech I took the paper Siam had handed to me, turned it over, and penned my application to be a Hunter.

But even though I had found a place to belong I didn't feel like I did belong. The one good thing was that I had found Kali. *Kali.* I wondered where she had gotten to. At least she had known to bring the mirror to Aric. Though how she could have gotten it past Siam and his men I wasn't sure.

Ralph entered the room looking like he had not slept since the last time I had seen him. "Are you okay, Ralph? What is wrong?"

"Let me tell you on the way. We need to get going." Ralph opened the back door of his car for us, and Dooley and I slid in behind him.

I pushed back into the seat, feeling repelled from the cage that separated the front and back seats. "Is that an iron cage?" Something was wrong, bad wrong.

Ralph gunned the engine and squealed out of Dooley's driveway. The car bounced as he sped over a pothole. I reached out to brace myself on the door handle and felt a burning sensation. The handle had been painted with some metallic glaze that was obviously made of one hundred percent iron if my hand had anything to say about it.

"What's going on, Ralph?" asked Dooley. He turned my hand over to inspect the angry red wounds.

"Sorry you had to get mixed up in this, but this fae is going to help me whether she likes it or not."

CHAPTER FIFTEEN

Dooley banged on the cage that separated us from the front seat. "Dammit, Ralph, get a grip. Just because Valora is a fae doesn't mean that she knows what Brokk knew."

"Why do you care?" The car continued to bounce down the road. "Only yesterday you thought she killed your best friend. Maybe she did. She's not from here. You think these things come in peace? You think they mean no harm?"

I clutched at the chain of the amulet around my neck and held on tight, silently praying to the Goddess that somehow she would get me out of this.

"What are you saying, Ralph? Only yesterday you were trying to convince me that she was innocent."

I looked up in time to see a rippling movement pulse across Ralph's face in the reflection of the rear view mirror. I leaned my head into Dooley's neck and whispered into his ear. "I don't think this is Ralph."

Dooley gave a slight nod of his head. He stroked my hair and bent down to whisper in my ear. "What do we do?"

It didn't seem like there was anything we could do. At least nothing I could do. The ogre had been careful to make sure all the surfaces I would have to touch to bust out of this car were coated in iron. As the wheels in my head turned, a cooling sensation spread through my hand. The red stone in the amulet pulsed with light. The burn on my hand was gone.

"You have the amulet!" roared Ralph.

I looked up to see the ogre's eyes in the rear view mirror. The car fishtailed as he slammed on the brakes. He quickly leapt out of the car and opened the back door. Dooley and I fell to the ground in a heap. The ogre grasped the chain of the necklace and picked me up. I grabbed at the amulet, but the taut chain constricted my airway.

Dooley beat down on the ogre's arm trying to free me, but it was like he was made of rock. I kicked at Dooley trying to get his attention.

"Sword," I managed to sputter as the ogre's grasp on the chain continued to choke me.

Dooley pulled my sword from the scabbard, and the ogre suddenly dropped me to the ground and backed away. I rubbed at my throat and took a few deep breaths of sweet air as Dooley danced around the ogre with the sword, obviously not his weapon of choice.

"Throw me the sword!" I yelled, getting to my feet.

"Are you sure this isn't Ralph? Maybe something has just gotten into him or something. I don't want to hurt him."

Just then the ogre's form started to shift. There was a bubbling along the surface of his skin. He didn't remove his focus from Dooley. Slowly Ralph's form morphed back into the ogre's real shape.

"Holy hell!" shouted Dooley.

"Dooley, throw me my sword!"

Dooley tossed my sword over the ogre's head, and I caught it. The creature turned around, and I got a full view of the last of Ralph's face melting away to the reveal the greenish skin of the ogre who stood about three heads higher than me.

"We need to get it off the road," I yelled to Dooley.

The ogre had pulled the car over to the side of the roadway, but we had managed to end up in the middle of the street. I took off my amulet and held it aloft.

"Is this what you want? Come get it, freak."

The ogre lumbered towards me. The road didn't seem well travelled, but it was midday and you never knew who might happen by. Just as I said that, I heard a familiar rumble from around the bend.

The ogre was taking slow swipes at Dooley and me. We both managed to miss the lobs from the lumbering giant, but we were no closer to getting rid of it. I stabbed forward a few times, but my blade just made small incisions in its hide, only making it angrier. My sword was not meant to hunt ogres.

The rumbling got closer, and Franca rounded the corner at the helm of my motorcycle. She let loose a battle cry and swung her war hammer over her head as she neared us. The ogre turned as she passed by, and Franca's hammer beheaded the ogre. Dooley and I jumped out of the way as its body pitched forward and landed with a thud on the ground.

Franca circled my motorcycle around and came back to where we were.

"Looked like you guys needed some help." She attached the hammer back at her side.

"How did you get my bike here?" I ran up to it and noticed that there were a few things out of place.

"I believe Earthside they call it 'hot-wiring'."

Dooley rushed to Franca's side. "You aren't well enough

yet to be walking around."

"How did you know, sport?" As if suddenly deflated, Franca slumped against Dooley's shoulder, her oversized sweater bunching to reveal her armor underneath. Its weight suddenly became apparent to her and to Dooley.

As I got closer I could see that under her eyes were dark circles, and she had an unhealthy pallor to her skin.

"I had no choice," she said. "You two went out the door so quick I wasn't able to tell you that friend of yours was no friend. I could smell that ogre a mile away. Do you know where it was going to take you?"

"No." Dooley carefully set Franca to rest against a boulder on the side of the road. "We were lucky it stopped. It got a glance at Valora's amulet and pulled the car over."

"What is that amulet of yours? Why would he want it?" asked Franca.

My gaze focused on the amulet. I answered without looking at her. "It was a gift from someone special to me. He said it would save me in a time I least expected it to."

"And that it did," said Franca, sweat breaking out on her brow.

"I want to find out what has happened to Ralph, but we need to take her to the clinic first and fast," said Dooley.

"Let me help you get her into the back of the cruiser. I'll follow you on my bike." Dooley and I picked up Franca. Despite her strength she was surprisingly small framed and light. Most of her weight came from the segmented plating she wore under the Earthside clothes she had procured so she wouldn't stand out.

As I turned to go to my bike Dooley caught me by the arm. "I'm going to turn on the siren to get us there faster. Don't fall behind. And be safe." He gave me a quick peck on the cheek. His eyes searched mine briefly before he turned back to the car.

I slung my leg over my bike and pressed my hand to the instrument panel, hoping that whatever Franca had done to get it here hadn't fried the magic holding it together. The bike responded with an illustrious roar between my legs, humming with a high pitched squeal before falling back to steady lull. Dooley turned on the lights and siren of the cruiser, and I raced to keep his pace.

Dooley entered a large road with fast moving cars. A light rain fell from the sky, coating my skin with a chilling mist. I settled into the rhythm of the ride and let my mind drift as I followed closely behind him.

At some point I was going to have to sit down with Dooley and let him know what it was that I saw in him. Of course, there was no way I could tell for sure, but everything inside me told me that Dooley was at least part fae. I know he thought his power came from the Reiki rituals that Brokk had taught him, but I knew nothing but fae magic could have hooked into my subconscious like he did.

I watched the sun on the horizon and thought of Aric. I would need to find a way to reach him again. I hoped that Siam had not confiscated the mirror. Without Aric's guidance I was just struggling along in this world without direction. I wasn't sure what it was I was supposed to do. He said I should hide out here. But hiding was the least of my worries at the moment.

As if I didn't have enough to worry about, a story my mother told me when I was small pushed its way into my thoughts, the memory as vivid as if it had happened yesterday. I had asked my mother how she knew my father was the one fae she should devote her soul to. The fae often took multiple lovers, but they pledged their soul to only one fae, the one they would make a home with and raise their children with. I remembered her answer to me.

"Your father spoke to me."

"What do you mean, Mama?" I had said to her. "Many of the fae speak to you."

"Not in here." My mother tapped her finger against her temple.

That was the first story she had told me. After I had reached maturity she told me another story, and I blushed at the thought. *Valora Delos, you are not going to be testing that theory.*

CHAPTER SIXTEEN

Dooley turned off the lights and siren as we entered thicker traffic. I could see that he was leading us directly into a major city. Cars zipped in and out of traffic with frightening speed.

Hanging onto my bike, I followed Dooley off an exit to the left. We wound around a narrow road and up to an open parking lot where we came to a stop.

People were exiting through an archway marked "Japanese Botanical Gardens," and it appeared as though things were closing up for the night.

I left the bike and went over to Dooley's car. "Is this where the clinic is?"

"No. She's getting worse. I think I can get what I need to help her here. We'll have to continue on to the clinic after I get her stabilized."

Franca rocked herself back and forth in the rear of the car, in obvious pain. Dooley popped the truck of the car and grabbed a small backpack which he slung over his shoulder.

"Wait, I want to help." I went to my bike and grabbed my satchel then followed him as he went to the booth by the archway.

"We close now. No more admittance," said the man behind the glass.

Dooley pulled out a small card, and the man waved him through. "Be quick. I need to close up."

"Thank you." Dooley motioned for me to follow him.

"What was it you showed him?"

The small stones on the pathway crunched under Dooley's footfalls as he hurried towards a corner of the garden. "The owners have a great respect for the practice of Reiki. They give me access to collect samples of some of the plants they grow here which are essential to the rituals I perform. There are dried versions, but they're not as potent."

Despite the cold weather the garden teemed with life. Brilliant pink blossoms dotted the crooked branches of the trees. A burbling brook raced underneath a wooden footbridge towards a lake filled with bright orange and white fish that swam lazily through the cool waters. Small statues, like tiny temples, sat atop every rise watching everything. It was a world onto its own and one I felt very at home in.

Over the bridge and down the path a ways we came upon a small rise, and atop it rested a tough old thorn tree. Its trunk sprang from one spot and quickly forked into two large branches that grew away from each other. Branches in competition for space dueled one another with sharp thorns. At the top sat a cluster of leaves which were adorned with small white flowers.

"It's the Hawthorn tree. I need to collect some of the leaves and flowers. It should strengthen her heart and give her more time." Dooley reached out and gingerly grabbed onto the thorny branch of the tree. He would have to climb up several feet in order to reach any of the leaves and flowers which were perched atop the tree, just out of reach, the lower leaves having already shed in the cold crisp autumn air.

"Dammit." Dooley shoved his finger into his mouth and shook off the sting of the thorn he had just grabbed.

"Wait, get down from there. This is something I think I can help with." I made sure we were alone and shrugged off my coat, dropping it to the ground. Walking to the base of the tree I stretched out my wings. They were one eighth the size of a normal fae's wings, and they were covered in the soft downy black feathers that the fae are normally born with but shed when they grow into their adult wings. Mine had always and would always remain black. "How much do you need?"

Dooley hopped down to the ground.

"Whatever you can grab," he said.

He was staring at me, making me even more self-conscious about my pitiful wings. "What is it?"

"It's just that...I...you're beautiful."

"You wouldn't say that if you saw a true fae. Their wings are amazing." Despite my words, I felt a tiny glow inside at Dooley's compliment.

"I think I have a true fae standing right here in front of me." Dooley smiled again and checked his watch. "But we do need to get going."

"Right." My wings beat at the air around them, and I rose up to the thorny branches. I was not able to fly for any distance, but I could hover damn good. I rose several feet into the air and lifted my arms to cover the rest of the distance. I gathered the leaves and flowers into my satchel and floated back down to the ground. My wings returned to their resting position atop my shoulders.

Dooley looked at the fading light as the sun dropped down to the horizon in the west. "We don't have a lot of daylight left. We may need to make camp somewhere close. If this works maybe we can stay here for the night and go to the clinic first thing tomorrow morning to allow us all some rest. But I'll need to do this now. We could go back to my cabin, but it would be a waste of time. Do you mind sleeping outside?"

I laughed and hefted my satchel up. "Nope. I'm actually pretty used to it. Got everything we need in here."

"If you continue down the path you'll come to a zig zag bridge that crosses over to an island. I think we will be undisturbed there for the night. I just need to talk to them, and then I'll bring Franca." He handed me his backpack. "I've got some supplies in here. I don't think anything is made of iron. Can you get a fire started?"

"Sure."

I turned and followed the path across the zig zag bridge which was lined on either side with tall grasses. I remembered the ginger grass in my pocket and pulled out a piece, chewing on the tasty pith.

I crossed over to the island and kept going until I found a small area tucked off the path. The ground was littered with rust colored leaves that crackled under my feet. Bright red leaves splashed bursts of color between the deep evergreens.

If I squinted and let the lines blur around the edges of my vision I could almost pretend I was home during a much better time. A time when the ice fruit trees wore their lush purple leaves proudly, and the sparkling blue fruits were so heavy on the branches I could reach up and pluck one down without the need for wings. A happier time.

The sun was making its final appearance, and I knew I had little time to get a fire going and a shelter put together before we lost the light completely. The blackened boughs and branches of the trees were naked of their leaves and covered in bright green patches of moss forming a natural canopy.

I pulled some rope and a large piece of tarpaulin from my satchel and set to work on a makeshift shelter using the natural canopy of the trees as my frame. I then turned to Dooley's bag. I dumped the contents onto the ground in a neat pile, not wanting to risk sticking my hand into something made of iron by accident. A small clear plastic pouch contained some matches. I gathered as much dry tinder and wood as I could find and struck a match, starting the fire ablaze. Dooley had a few wool blankets that I spread out around the periphery of the fire.

As I was shoving the rest of the contents of Dooley's backpack back into place, a glint of light caught my eye. Inside the pouch with the fire-making materials was a small mirror.

The last sliver of the sun dropped out of the western sky.

Aric. He would be waiting for me to contact him. At least I hoped he was. I held the mirror at a small distance in front of me until the whole of my face was framed and tried to catch as much of the light from the fire as possible as I touched the stone of my ring to the mirror.

❧

Again I saw the vision of the same room as before. Kali rushed into view. "Valora! Oh, my gosh, are you okay?" She looked relieved and terrified all at once.

"Kali! For now I am fine. I am working on finding a way home. Thank you for bringing the mirror to the King."

"No, Valora, you don't understand." Just then the door burst open. Siam stormed into the room followed by Aric and the rest of the Royal Guard.

Aric quickly positioned himself in front of the mirror. Through the space in his body between his back and his arm I could see them dragging Kali out of the room. She was shouting as she was pulled out of the room. "Liar! Traitor! We had a deal!"

"Take her back to the Soulstealers' cells and make sure she is properly secured this time. I don't care if she was a Hunter. You understand me? She is not to be trusted," said Siam. "All of you. Go back to your posts around the periphery of the temple. I need a few words with the King." He shut the door behind the last of the Guard and faced the King who was still blocking the mirror.

"Sire, we are losing them. We have more fae in the hold than we do above. They are bound to find a way to escape. I am not sure how much longer we can hold them. What is your plan?"

"Leave that to me, Siam. Soon we will have everything we need to put things back into order."

Siam drew his eyebrows together but said no more as he exited the room.

Aric turned around to face the mirror. "Valora. I am sorry you had to see that."

"But what have you done to Kali? She is my friend. She would never be a Soulstealer. She would never betray the people of Dell'Aria."

"But she has to. Don't you understand? It is either her or you."

"What do you mean?"

126

"The other fae think that you are the Soulstealer. But Kali was with you that night by the Portal. She was the only other one. She must have been the one to sneak through with you and kill Brokk before you were able to get there. Who else could it have been?"

I sat back on my heels, waves of disbelief crossing over me. I had lived with Kali for years. How could I have missed that she was a Soulstealer? I could not believe what he was saying, and yet his explanation made sense. "But then why was Kali here just a moment ago? I saw her in the mirror before you got here. And what did she mean by you having a deal?"

"What did she say to you?" Aric's eyes blazed with anger.

"She only wanted to make sure I was okay. It seemed like she was about to say something else, but then you all burst in."

Aric's face relaxed. "Good. I was hoping she had not upset you. Are you alone?" Aric raised one eyebrow.

The woods were still. There was no sign that Dooley was coming this way as of yet. "Yes."

"Good. Tell me you still have the amulet."

"I do. But what exactly is this? An ogre almost took my head off today when he saw that I had it."

"What?"

I gave him the quick rundown of what had happened that day. He was silent for a moment. "I never thought they could use it to track you."

"Who are 'they'?"

"Valora, I believe there are those in Underworld who seek to dethrone me. There have been rumblings of another attack on Dell'Aria now that they know we are weakened.

Make no mistake, our troubles are no secret through the Realms."

"Then why not call the fae to arms? Send the birds of the aviary to the other colonies of Overworld and ask for their assistance."

"No, they will not help us, not as long as the Queen is missing. They will never answer to me." He reached into his shirt and pulled on a chain revealing an amulet which was the twin of the one around my neck.

"You have one also?" I pulled the amulet from my bodice and held it in my hand.

"Yes." He put the amulet into the palm of his hand and traced a circle with his finger around the glittering red stone in the middle. As he did so the stone on my amulet began to pulse. "Place the amulet against your chest, Valora."

I tucked it back inside my bodice and felt the tracing of Aric's finger around my breast. I looked up into the mirror, and my breath caught in my throat.

"I see you have discovered one of the many things I can do with these amulets." His fingers trailed over the jewel and with each light touch came a twinge of pleasure in my nipples.

"Aric." My voice was barely above a whisper.

"Until I can hold you in my arms for real, this will have to do, my love." He drew his tongue across the surface of the jewel triggering a moist caress between my legs.

Footsteps echoed from down the path. "They are coming. I have to go."

"Don't stray from me, Valora. I need you now more than ever."

I watched as Aric tucked his amulet back into his shirt, completely hiding it from view.

"You don't have to worry about my loyalties. Will I be able to talk to you again?"

"Yes, in two days. Then everything will have come together, and I will come for you, my love. Don't worry. I will make sure that we are together again. Next time, flesh to flesh."

❧

Just as Dooley entered the clearing, I looked back into the mirror which now only held my flushed reflection then turned my attention to him. He had Franca draped around his shoulders, and I sprang to my feet to help him lay her on one of the wool blankets by the fire.

"We are fine for tonight. No one will bother us. Do you have those pieces of the Hawthorn tree we collected?"

I retrieved the Hawthorn bits from my pocket and handed them to him. Dooley took a stone mortar and pestle from his bag and began to grind the leaves and flowers together into a paste. "I know she normally eats these things whole, but we need to find another way to get them in her."

Franca's condition was rapidly deteriorating. Her breathing had become shallow and I was having difficulty recognizing the rise and fall of her chest. "We have to hurry."

Dooley nodded and pulled a plastic bottle of water from his bag. He took the paste and added it to the water, giving the bottle a shake to mix it up. "Hold her head up."

I cradled Franca's head in my hands and Dooley put the bottle to her lips. "You need to drink this Franca. Please."

Franca was barely responsive, but gradually she began to swallow the mixture until she was gulping it down. After draining the last drop, she sat up straight, the color returning to her cheeks. "Wow, that was a great brew, Dooley, thanks.

You have not only saved me, but you have saved us the trouble of a day's journey."

"What do you mean?"

She looked around. "We are halfway to the Portal back to the Realms. The one I came through."

CHAPTER SEVENTEEN

I wasn't sure if Dooley's expression was one of relief or sadness at the thought of being rid of us in the near future. "We'll be out of your hair soon, Dooley. Then you can get back to your normal life."

"I'm not sure that after the last few days I could ever view life as normal again." Dooley half-heartedly shoved his belongings into his satchel. Night time had taken hold. The burps of small frogs sounded off in the marshy banks of the island. Lights twinkled in the sky, a mixture of stars and flying transports. Silence fell over our way-worn troupe, broken only by the crackling of the fire.

"I know I have been doing a lot of lying about lately, but if you two don't mind, I think I will turn in early tonight. The next leg of the trip won't be any easier than this one." Franca bunched a blanket underneath her head and was giving off a low snore before my eyes had left her.

"I suppose the poison gave her system quite a workout." Dooley stared into the fire, transfixed by some thought.

"Do you think she will be okay?" I asked.

He turned his gaze from the fire to me. "Yes, I think she

must have shaken it. We'll be okay here for the night." He cocked his head to the side. "But how are you doing?"

A sudden chill passed over me as the wind blew through our little clearing and I pulled my coat tighter around my shoulders. "I'm fine. What do you mean?"

"Want to do another session before you leave?" My face must have given away my reaction because he hastily added, "You would be doing me a favor. I don't get many chances to channel my energies like that."

"But you don't have any of your equipment out here."

He rubbed his finger around the lip of the mortar, bringing up a blackened tip. "There's enough of the mixture I made for Franca."

"But it is cold."

"If you don't want to, you can just say so." He dropped the pestle back in the mortar with a thud and rested his head in his hands, drawing his fingers through his hair. Flames reflected off his eyes as he focused again into the fire.

I imagined Dooley back in his mountain cabin all alone. Brokk had probably provided him with a sense of belonging and family he wasn't even aware of.

I had heard stories of Earthside fae who had lost all sense of who they were when they were not around their own kind. They roam the Earth with absolutely no idea that they are fae. This world is so hungry for magic that after time the land sucks the magic right out of you. But no one can take the spark. The only time the spark leaves you is when you pass on from this plane to the next. To the fae that meant spending eternity under the service of the Goddess Varuna.

With the current state of affairs at Dell'Aria I was beginning to wonder if she had abandoned us altogether.

I pushed aside those thoughts and decided to let Dooley

practice his channeling on me. Maybe this time it really would be healing. I stood, retrieved my satchel and dug around until I found a smaller piece of tarpaulin. "How about I set up another smaller tent over this way, and we can perform the ritual out of this drizzle?"

Dooley perked up. "Are you sure?"

"Yes, though I admit the whole thing makes me nervous. What could these memories mean?"

Dooley crossed over to me and took my hand. "I'll be there with you." Something about Dooley made me feel safe. He drew from some inner well of strength that shored me up as my doubts crept in. He had much the same effect on me as Pryn did. Pryn had told me I would save the fae, but I was having a hard time now even believing I could save myself.

We set up the small lean-to against a wall of poplar trunks. The front entrance faced the fire and funneled the warmth inside. It quickly became hot enough to shed our coats. I sat down and pushed with my feet to scoot further into the tent, and in doing so bumped up against a bare chested Dooley. He had removed his shirt along with his jacket.

"Whoops." I blushed, turned around and immediately faced forward again after getting another glimpse of Dooley's dark and hard muscled chest as the light of the flames danced across it. My memory quickly went back to the moment in time when he had dropped his towel, but then just as quickly reverted to Aric. My King. I had to remain true in body and spirit. In only two days he said I would see him again, and I was definitely ready.

Dooley pushed my hair aside, his fingers barely grazing the tips of my wings. "I need a bigger canvas this time."

I reached back and pulled at the clasps holding my

bodice together, letting the back fall open while clutching the front firmly to my chest.

A shiver ran down my spine as Dooley began to draw the symbols on my back. "You seem to shirk from any kind of nudity. Is it really so uncommon where you're from? I don't mean to embarrass or offend you."

I gave a chuckle. "No, really it's just me." And it was. Underworld was full of beings that didn't believe in clothing at all. And it was not uncommon for there to be rituals in the fae temple and during our midsummer festival when nudity was not only common but encouraged. No, it was just that I was not used to participating in these rites. No one wanted to see my misshapen wings and be reminded that the fae were sometimes imperfect. "I'm fine."

"Good. I was hoping to have you lean back against me during this next session. I think if we were in better contact I could be more present in your memory."

I was leery of his suggestion, but what did I have to lose? Dooley's last probe into my memories had brought me to tears, but it had also made me feel even more connected with Aric.

"Okay, just lie back and I'll begin."

I leaned back onto Dooley's bare chest. The symbols he had traced on my back were still moist, and I could feel them transfer to Dooley's warm skin. My wings fluttered against him, and he gently lifted them to spread over his shoulders. I gave an involuntary shudder. No one had ever touched my wings before. No one except me, that is. There were nerve endings within the wings that played directly into fae magic, a different kind of sensation which could be painful or pleasurable on a whole different level.

"Are you chilled?"

"No, I'm okay."

"Good." Dooley reached out his hands and let them hover about two inches above my chest, moving them over my stomach and back up towards my chest again. "I pulled on a life line before. I am going to work on a heart line this time."

A sudden wash of fear spread through me, but Dooley's soothing voice was there, ringing through my mind. "It will be okay."

The sounds of the forest surrounding us began to drift away, replaced by a rhythmic drumming which I slowly recognized as a heart beating. Two hearts beating, separately at first, and then drifting together into an intense whooshing that carried me into another memory.

It was two weeks after my mother had succumbed to the Blight. I slowly dragged my hand across the same stone hallway that I had used to guide myself to my mother's bedside the night the first wave hit. I stared into each room as I roamed the halls of the Court, capturing all of the memories I had of her.

The time she spent sitting on the dais knitting woolen shawls for the cold winters that blew through Dell'Aria. The times I would find her in the Court kitchen, stealing away a corner and rolling out the most delicious butterbread cookies in all of Overworld.

I then found myself staring at an empty kitchen. King Aric appeared alongside me in the doorway, startling me with how close he was.

"What are you doing down here? You know the cooks don't come in for another few hours," he said to me, a look of concern on his face.

It was strange to see King Aric all alone without Siam, Captain of the Royal Guard, or some other uniform behind him though with his stormy blue eyes and his eyebrows shaped like small lightning bolts, you wouldn't think he needed anyone to come to his defense.

My voice caught in my throat and tears came to my eyes. In all my years at the Court I had barely said two words to King Aric, though I had always held a lustful heart for him.

He gently reached out and took my arm. "Come in and sit. You know my home is yours. I am sure they have some of my favorite sweets in here."

I took a seat on one of the stools in the middle of the kitchen and watched as King Aric searched the cupboards. He took down a brown ceramic jar and set it on the counter as he took a seat on the stool across from me.

He looked deep into my eyes, and his gaze froze me in place. "You know your mother was strong with magic. That is why she took ill so quickly."

I was shocked he knew so much about my mother and about the Blight that had rocked through our colony. But then again, he was the King, he had access to all sorts of information I had no clue about.

He waved his hand over the jar and muttered a few words under his breath then lifted the lid, reached his hand inside and pulled out a small candy wrapped in a bright yellow wrapper. I had never seen anything like it. He placed it in my upturned palm. "My favorite from when I was a child. My mother's favorite as well. She was also taken from me too soon."

Before I could ask him anything about his mother he quickly replaced the lid to the jar and put it back in place in the cupboard. "You really ought to be getting to your chambers. It is late."

I scurried to my room and shut the door behind me, looking down at the strange candy in my palm.

Again I awoke. This time I was shaking, but it was not

from the cold. The memory of my mother's death was fresh in my mind, and the sobs broke forth from me uncontrollably. The only thing keeping me from falling apart was the grip of Dooley's arms around me. I felt at once silly and vulnerable yet strangely relieved. This was something I had not had the leisure of doing in the last five cycles since I became a Hunter. When you were sent out on a hunt at a moment's notice, you did not have time to sort out emotions about your past.

Even now I knew that I was indulging in a dangerous pastime. Making it through the Portal with Franca would be only the first challenge. After that I would have to make it home and hope that my world was still standing. I sat up and tried to scoot away from Dooley, closer to the fire, letting its warmth dry my tears as fast as possible. I hastily reached back to refasten my bodice.

Dooley pulled his coat over his shoulders leaving it open at the front. The muscles in his chest flexed under the flecks of paint left on him as he searched through his bag for something.

"What are you looking for?"

"Oh, it's nothing really, it's just—found it." He turned to me with a smile. "Close your eyes for a second and hold out your hand."

Without any energy left to dissuade him I did as he asked. He placed a small object in my hand which gave forth a crinkling sound as I closed my fingers around it. My eyes flew open. I couldn't believe what I was holding. "How did you get this? The King's favorite treat. I haven't seen anything like it since that day."

"They are very common here. Butterscotch candies. I have a whole bag of them with me. It's one of my weaknesses."

"The King's favorite treat is a candy from Earthside?" I clutched at my breast to press upon the amulet beneath my bodice. The only connection I had to the King. The amulet connected us on some kind of physical level, but at the moment I wished it also let me read his thoughts.

CHAPTER EIGHTEEN

My sleep was fitful, and all sense of time would have been lost to me if it hadn't been for the bright ball of light in the sky beckoning me awake.

When I finally got my eyes to open I saw Dooley was stoking the fire and talking with Franca whose color had returned.

"Look who decided to join the land of the living." She handed me a mug full of steaming brown liquid.

"Look who's talking. What is that?"

"Dooley says it is called coffee and apparently very common here on Earth and very common in the colony of Seattle. If you want to blend in as we get closer all you need to do is drink this stuff. No one will think you are from out of town." Franca winked and went back to drinking her own cup. "Whew. Good stuff."

Dooley chuckled and raised his cup to me with a smile.

I sniffed at the drink. It sloshed around the cup like dirty bog water and one whiff of it quickly wiped all sensations of other smells from my nose. I took a gulp and immediately gagged on the bitter, strong, acidic brew as it slid down my throat. "Are you trying to kill me?"

Dooley and Franca fell over each other laughing.

"I'm glad you two find it funny."

I was about to pour it out on the ground when Franca reached up, wiping her eyes with the back of her sleeve. "It's an acquired taste. If you don't want it I'll take it."

I gave her my cup and sat back down on the log. Dooley handed me a cup of water. "What is the plan for today then?"

"I have to go back to the visitor center and see if I can reach Ralph. I tried calling him last night, but I only got his answering machine." Dooley shrugged. "Then I guess you two can go wherever you need to go."

The thought of leaving Dooley here without an explanation as to his fae bloodline seemed wrong, but I knew it was no business of mine to tell him his ancestry, especially when the revelation of that information might cause Dooley to have more questions than answers. No, it was probably best I keep it to myself. It was better to let the Earth take his magic and let him forget there was ever anything different about him.

Dooley threw another log on the fire. The mist of the morning had started to burn off, but the air still chilled to the bone. "I'm going to go make that call. I'll be back in a little bit."

Franca stared at me over the fire. The dwarf was feeling better and likely thinking of what favor she was going to ask me for. But after what Aric told me, maybe I should stay put and wait for him.

"I am not sure I am going to be taking you up on that offer to go through your Portal after all."

"What is it, Valora? After all we have been through, you still don't trust me? Or should I say, you don't trust a dwarf?" She slammed her cup down on the log beside her. The hot coffee sloshed out over her hand, but the heat didn't seem to bother her.

"What do you expect, Franca? I was raised my entire life that the only goal of any creature in Underworld is to steal the magic of those in Overworld. I want to believe you want to help. But all my training is telling me that I should not trust you." I couldn't tell Franca the real reason I needed her to leave me behind. She was safer not knowing.

Franca crossed her arms as she glared across the fire at me. "Did you seriously just imply that the dwarves are the one stealing the fae magic? You are a Hunter. Do I need to remind you what your whole purpose is? If you will not even listen to yourself, I cannot help you."

"King Aric, you know the one who is back home in Dell'Aria trying to hold our colony together, gave me one task. He told me to return one of the Soulstealers, and I couldn't even get that right. Now I have myself trapped Earthside, and for all I know, all of Dell'Aria thinks I am a Soulstealer now, too."

Franca continued her quiet stare. "You have only ever been taught that which your elders deemed fit for you to know. You say your training tells you not to trust me. But what does your heart tell you?"

I deflated a little at Franca's question which was more like advice because I knew there wasn't any way I could follow it. "I stopped listening to my heart many years ago. My training for the Guard taught me to put all my emotion aside. It was the only way I could move past my mother's death."

Franca's stare softened, and she walked around the fire to sit by my side. "Sometimes I forget that for a creature so rich in years, your kind spends those years in such isolation that in many ways you are much younger than I am."

"What is that supposed to mean? I'm not naive. I've travelled the Underworld. I have explored outside of Dell'Aria."

"Yes, but not enough to know that in order to tackle your feelings about your mother you will need more than battle training. And that tackling those feelings about your mother will be the only thing that brings you to the greater truth."

"I felt sorrow over my mother for ten cycles. Ten cycles is long enough."

Our conversation was interrupted as Dooley came running down the path towards our camp. "We need to get going immediately."

I rose to my feet. "What is it? Did you reach Ralph?"

"Yes. I got him on his cell phone. He has no idea what's been happening the last few days, and he had no idea his cruiser had been taken. He's been sitting outside the clinic since yesterday in an unmarked car."

I pulled down our shelter, shoving it back in my satchel. "What is he doing there?"

"What do you think? He's casing the joint. He's desperate to get medicine for his daughter. Apparently she's under observation at Harborview Medical Center in Seattle. Incidentally, he also mentioned one other thing that might be of interest to you. Brokk's body was just transferred to the King County Medical Examiner's Office for an autopsy. They're worried that it might have been some kind of animal attack, and Ralph couldn't convince them otherwise."

Franca gave me a smug look. "I don't suppose you will need my help with this one."

There was no way I could leave Brokk's body here to be taken apart. Aric hadn't said anything to me, but I was sure he wouldn't want that to happen. And I couldn't do it by myself. "Are you going to make me beg?"

Franca hopped to her feet. "Of course not. What do you take me for? A monster?"

Franca could have left me at any time. There was nothing making her stay and help me and nothing making her help me through the Portal. No matter what my training had told me, I had to admit that I could think of no reason Franca would stay other than she wanted to help me. She didn't need to help, she wanted to.

We decided that we would go to the clinic first. It was best to derail Ralph from this mission he was set on, because the last thing his daughter needed was for him to get arrested. We were also hoping he could help get us into the coroner's office somehow.

❧

Back on my bike, I followed Dooley and Franca in Ralph's car up the highway towards the clinic. I had to admit I was curious about this place. Apparently they had medicine that could sustain Kit even though she would likely have died many cycles ago without being able to return to the sea. I hadn't realized there were any Earthside medicines that would do such a thing. Maybe I could even find something that I could take back with me to my home world of Dell'Aria to help those afflicted with the Blight.

I was still having a hard time believing that Kali was involved with the Soulstealers. She had said the priests were interested in taking over the remainder of her ice fruit fields, and Brokk was surely some kind of priest.

Dooley brought the cruiser to a stop across the street from a brick building with many storefronts. Set between a licensed massage therapist and a chiropractor was a clinic with a sign above the door that read "Alternative Health Care Center." The place was unobtrusive and wouldn't attract attention at all had it not been for the blacked out windows and doors. If it weren't for the neon "Open" sign on the outside, you might question whether it was still in business. I could tell as we drove up that there was no back alley. It seemed the front door was the only one way in and out.

I stopped my bike behind the cruiser and followed Dooley over to a blue sedan which was parked across the street from the entrance. Dooley tapped on the driver's window, and Ralph quickly rolled it down. "Get in here. All of you. I don't want to attract attention."

I wasn't sure that we hadn't already done that, but we all complied with Ralph's request. Franca and I slid into the back seat, and Dooley got in the front with Ralph. As soon as I sat down I could smell stale coffee and sweat. Ralph had been here awhile.

"So, Ralph, what's your plan, man?" asked Dooley.

Ralph eyes were wild. "I can't lose her, Dooley. They don't know what's wrong with her. Of course they don't. I have to get that medicine." Dooley pointed across the street to the clinic. "But I don't have enough money. I went in there yesterday. I told them about my daughter. I told them Kit needs help. I begged them. But they don't care. They only want the money."

He lifted a pair of binoculars to his eyes and looked across the street at the clinic door. "The sign never turns off.

They're always open. Sometimes I see people go in, but I don't see them come back out. I have been around the back. I don't see any other way in or out of there except the front. I haven't seen any employees come out since I've been here. It's like they never leave."

"Let me see those binoculars." Ralph handed them to me. I had my fair share of experience in doing surveillance as a Hunter. It wasn't often that we went in cold. It was easier if you got to know the habits and routines of your target. That way you could extract them with the least possible resistance. I scanned the entrance and saw something that made my blood run cold.

CHAPTER NINETEEN

"What is it? Let me see?" Franca caught the binoculars as they dropped from my hand. She scanned the entrance just as I had. "Is that what I think it is?"

"Yes," I said. I didn't need to ask her what she saw. I didn't need to ask her if she knew what it meant because in all of the Realms, all of Overworld and all of Underworld, all creatures knew that symbol. They all knew the symbol of what was once the most powerful of all the fae colonies.

"What in the heck is the symbol of the King of Dell'Aria doing on the front of this clinic?"

I now had the attention of everyone in the car. "Ralph, you have been inside with your daughter right? What is in there?"

Ralph shook his head. "Brokk always went in and got what Kit needed and came back out. The only thing I saw when I just went in there was a waiting room. I couldn't tell you anything else."

"Brokk took you to the clinic? I thought you went there yourself and then came to Brokk when they stopped helping you?" asked Dooley. He faded back into his seat and

146

pinched at his brow. He was likely trying to come up with a justification in his own mind for Brokk's actions, something I was becoming increasingly familiar with.

"And Brokk never told you anything else? He was bringing medicine that you gave to your daughter and you didn't question it?"

I knew I had crossed a line as soon as the question left my mouth. Ralph leveled his gaze at both Dooley and me. "I don't expect you to understand, seeing as how you don't have any kids. Brokk gave me something that kept her alive and asked me not to ask questions. After he couldn't get her more medicine here he found another way. He earned my trust."

My mind was reeling. I couldn't tell anyone about my recent relations with Aric. There had to be a reasonable explanation for all of this. He had even told me that he would see me in a few days. Perhaps he was planning to tell me then. Or maybe the symbol meant something entirely different on Earth.

"Maybe it is just a coincidence," I said.

Dooley's brows knitted together. "You really think so? After all that has happened recently? Brokk mentioned this clinic to me a few times. He said they had great power to help people, but the ways they did so were questionable, and they were only in it for their own gains. It seemed strange to me to associate an alternative health clinic with money hungry medical practitioners, but I never had cause to question him. I've only seen the waiting room myself."

"I just can't see how anything here on Earth could be associated with Dell'Aria. It's impossible. Since the Queen disappeared, King Aric has been under constant watch by the Royal Guard. The closest Portal to Earth is a day's journey away. There is no way he could be involved with this, whatever it is," I said.

Dooley put his hand on Ralph's shoulder. "Buddy, is there any way we can talk you into driving away from here? We can all go visit Kit together. What do you say?"

"I say that if I drive away from here, it's going to be with a vial of that medicine. I won't go to see Kit empty handed. I told her Daddy would make her better. I told her I would get her the medicine. I promised. I can't break my promise. I won't." Ralph clutched at the front of Dooley's shirt, his eyes filled with desperation.

Dooley gently released his shirt from Ralph's grasp and turned to me. "I've been in there before with Brokk. They could recognize me. Is there any way you two can go in and see what you can do?"

"Seems like if we are going to get moving, we will need to go in and see if we can charm them out of some of that medication," I said to Franca.

"Okay, but you sure are racking up the favors." Franca gave me a smile. "You know I am joking?"

Franca suddenly reminded me of Kali. I wasn't sure if she was still alive. Franca, Dooley and Ralph might be the only friends I had left. My father always wanted a way to write me off, and now he had it. I wouldn't expect any help from him.

"Be careful in there," said Dooley.

Franca and I quickly conjured up a story about her being ill which wasn't too much of a stretch since she still had the wounds to prove it. We walked across the street and were hit with a wall of energy, thick as tar.

"Holy Mother, do you feel that?" Franca struggled forward as I did.

"Yes, the magic is pouring forth from that place. I don't know how the heck we are going to get in there."

Dooley jumped out of the car when he noticed the trouble we were having. As he reached me he grasped his head.

"Dooley, you should get back in the car," I shouted.

"I've been here before and I never felt this much energy." He reached his hands forward and swept them slowly through the air. "I think I can disperse what is between us and the clinic."

"Yeah, but what if we get inside and have the same problem? You are going to need to come with us," said Franca.

"I am sure that seems like a good idea, Franca, but Dooley might be recognized, and, besides, he needs to stay in the car and make sure Ralph stays put." There was something supernatural inside, and we had to go in without weapons. I didn't need to worry about Dooley getting hurt.

"I think I can help you from out here." Dooley moved his hands through the air quicker and quicker as he dispelled the magic that was preventing us from getting any closer to the clinic doors. "You should be able to get in there now."

I took a step forward and, although there was still a leftover tingling sensation, I no longer had to struggle. "Okay, stay out here. We can't afford to have them see you."

As Franca and I got closer to the door I wrapped my arm around her waist. "Are you ready for this?"

Franca gave a few forced coughs. "I think so."

I pushed open the clinic door, and a bell above the door tinkled to announce our entrance. The front area was stark and consisted of two metal chairs between which sat a small table and several battered copies of free magazines. There was a window cut out in the wall and a door which I assumed led back into the clinic.

A woman appeared at the window, presumably alerted

by the sound of the bell. She had large round glasses with a beaded chain attached on the ends that looped over her ears. Her hair was brown and cropped short. I sensed nothing supernatural about her.

Franca nodded, and I could tell she had come to the same conclusion.

"Do you have an appointment?" the lady asked.

Trying to think of an excuse which would get us past this woman's obvious sense of duty, I helped Franca up to the window. "Sure we do. I believe if you check the schedule, we will be the next ones on your list."

The woman looked from me to the paper calendar in front of her and frowned. "Well, it is highly unusual that someone is a day early for their appointment, but I will see if you can be seen now. How about I escort you and your friend back to a room?"

Something didn't sit well with me. I would have expected her to turn us away if the only appointment they had on the books was the next day, but I wasn't going to protest if it meant getting in and out without causing a scene.

"We must have mixed up the dates. I really appreciate you fitting us in," I said.

The lady hopped down from her stool and depressed a button that made an audible buzz. A mechanism in the door unlatched and swung in allowing us a view of a hallway. White doors lined the white hallway, all of them closed. A dark wooden door, ornately etched, framed the entire end of the hall and was very out of place with the starkness of the office.

We followed the lady down the hall, and I glanced back. The desk the woman had been sitting at had only the paper calendar. No telephone. No paperwork. No little cup of pens. The only other thing at the desk was latched to the underside. A gun.

A bad feeling settled in my gut. She led us to the first room on the right. "Please wait in here." We went inside, and she left, closing the door behind her. Franca took a seat on the exam table, the white crepe paper crinkling under her as she sat.

"So what exactly was the plan?" she asked.

"Honestly I was hoping it was some kind of dispensary, and that we could just gently suggest she give us whatever medicine they are handing out here."

"You do know that they are handing out magic right?"

"That much I had figured, though since Dooley did his little ceremony outside I haven't felt anything."

Nothing in the exam room was of much help. There was a small sink which had a bar of white soap, a wastepaper basket and a cupboard which was empty save for a stack of paper towels.

Franca jumped down from the table. "I don't like being stuck in this room without our weapons."

I placed my ear to the door and heard nothing. "We need to check out the rest of the rooms. I would especially like to see what is behind that door at the end of the hall. But how are we going to get past that front desk gal? I don't suppose they gave her a gun without training her how to use it."

"I could explore the rooms if you could keep her occupied."

"It's as good a plan as any," I said.

I walked slowly back up the hall to find the woman again perched on her stool, staring blankly out the window. I noticed that the blackened windows we had seen from the outside were completely clear to her. Not only had she observed Ralph casing the joint for the last day, but she likely saw that we had been talking to him beforehand and had to struggle to get inside.

She turned but did not make a motion for the gun latched to the underside of her table. "Is there something I can help you with? The technician should be here shortly. I had to call him in. He wasn't expecting you."

Stitched in red thread into the woman's starched white blouse was the name "Maria."

"Sorry, Maria, I just realized I needed to use the bathroom." I heard the click of a door. Franca had opened one room.

"We don't have any bathrooms." She tipped her head down, her gaze level with mine.

"Really?" Another click. "Must be a tough place to work. So, you just man the shop here, I guess?"

Another click. "I am not used to so many questions Miss...what did you say your name was?"

She turned to look at her schedule just as a peal of bells rang through the clinic.

She grabbed the gun under her table and raced down the hall. I dove towards her and caught her by the ankle. She turned the gun towards me and fired off a shot which fortunately went over my head.

Franca appeared in the hallway behind her and delivered a quick blow to her head, knocking her out cold. She kicked the gun away from her hand and hopped over the unconscious Maria.

"Let's go." Franca held her hand down to help me up, and we raced outside the clinic towards Ralph's car.

"Go, go, go." Franca and I hopped inside as Ralph began to drive away.

"My bike!" I shouted. I should have felt more unease at putting my fate entirely into the hands of those with me, but

I didn't.

"We can come back for it," said Franca.

"Didn't you two hear that alarm or the shots?" I tried to catch my breath.

"What?" Dooley looked thoroughly confused. "Everything was quiet out here. How could there have been an alarm and shots fired in there without us hearing it out here?"

Franca reached into her pocket and pulled out a thin vial filled with a swirling copper liquid. "Magic, that's how."

CHAPTER TWENTY

"You got it. You got the medicine for Kit." Ralph swung back onto the highway. "We have to bring it to her right away."

"Franca, let me see that." Franca handed me the glass vial. "Where did you find it?"

I tapped at the cork on the top. The liquid had a life of its own, roiling as if heat were being applied to it.

"It was in that room at the end of the hall. I pushed the door open, and it was pretty dark in there, but from the light in the hall I could see that there were stands with rows and rows of these vials. And there is one other thing, Valora."

"What?" I pulled my gaze from the copper brew.

"I think they have a Portal in there."

"What makes you say that?"

"I saw a faded shimmer of light, and there was a faint afterglow that I could sense. Like I said, I can't be sure. I couldn't even see that far into the room. The alarm went off, and I just grabbed what I could before high-tailing it out of there. And there was one other thing I grabbed." Franca pulled some scrolls out of her cloak and handed them to me.

"These and many more were in one of the other rooms. It was set up like some kind of lab."

I turned the scrolls over. "They are all sealed. I'll need a seal breaker to open them. I know where one is, but it's nowhere near here now." I tucked them into my pocket alongside the grimoire, thankful that the seals were blank and did not contain the King's mark. Justifying to myself again that he had nothing to do with this.

I gave a small pull on the cork in the vial. "I think I can pop this cap off."

"Don't spill any of it. Kit will need it all." Ralph sped down the highway, tires sliding against the wet pavement as the rain began to fall, veering in and out of traffic which thickened as we headed north of the city proper.

"If you stop driving like a crazy person, I won't."

Ralph eased off the gas a smidgen and moved the car into the far right lane.

I tugged the cork from side to side, slowly working it out of the vial. As soon as I got the cap off the other two supernaturals in the car sat up and took notice. Dooley and Franca leaned into me, both uttering something to the effect of "What is that?"

"Guys, give me some space." But I was also drawn to whatever was inside. The magic in the vial was strong. The container must have been reinforced to keep it from losing too much of its power, because it was definitely concentrated. I took the cork in my hand and dabbed the inside of my wrist, letting the remnants of the copper liquid on the cork touch my skin before placing the cork back in place. As I watched, the liquid seeped into my skin. An immediate infusion of power and tranquility revitalized me.

"This is from Dell'Aria. This magic. I know it." The amulet at my chest grew warm, and I pulled it from its hiding place. The red stone was pulsing. As it did, the overpowering effects of the magic wore off, and I felt balanced again.

"What is that?" Franca grabbed at the amulet, and I quickly shoved it back into my bodice.

"A gift from a friend."

"You don't think that Brokk had anything to do with this, do you?" asked Dooley. He hung his head.

"Dooley, you know I was sent here by my King to bring Brokk back because he was a known Soulstealer." I held the vial up. "This only goes to prove that he was probably as dangerous as Aric thought."

"You don't know Brokk. He would never be involved in killing people like you claim. He was all about healing and helping." Dooley turned and faced forward again, his steely gaze focused on the rivulets of rainwater that trickled down the window.

Ralph pulled the car off of the freeway and headed through side streets. "I have to agree with Dooley. Even after I couldn't afford the medicine anymore, Brokk was able to somehow keep Kit alive. It wasn't as good as the medicine, but it kept her alive and happy. He cared about people."

"But he didn't care about the fae. He took this and the rest of it and in doing so killed my mother. Do you even understand? He took everything from me." The blast of emotion that poured forth from me was sudden, and I knew immediately I was wrong about them not understanding. I wasn't above realizing that these people had their own sorrows, but I still wasn't able to control my feelings.

Franca whispered to me. "The truth will free you from these demons."

"Fact is, we don't know who did what, Valora," Dooley said, his voice firm. "But I sure as hell intend to help you

156

find out. I intend to clear Brokk's name. He is the reason I am the man I am today. I can't let his last memory be that of a destroyer of worlds. I know it's not true, and I'll prove it to you."

Dooley's abrupt pronouncement cut everyone short, and we drove for a few blocks in silence. I was entranced by the swirling liquid in the vial. For all I knew, it was magic that had been drained from my mother. Magic she had needed to survive. But there was nothing that would bring her back. Not even all of the vials in the clinic. She had passed on to the Goddess Varuna. If her magic could help save the Selkie child I knew she would wish it so. She had been a healer herself, like Dooley. I suddenly felt like the rear end of a troll.

Ralph pulled in to the parking lot, and we decided to split up. I handed the vial to Ralph and gave him a quick hug. "I really hope this helps."

I saw the crinkles at the corner of Ralph's eyes and realized he had spent the better part of his adult life worrying about this child. He didn't care whether or not she was fully human, or even if she would ever make anything of her life. He only wanted to make sure she lived it.

Dooley and I headed to the morgue. Brokk had no relatives Earthside, but Dooley and he had been roommates these past few years, and we hoped to be able to convince someone that he wanted one last visit with his friend.

Franca went with Ralph to visit with Kit. Ralph would need someone to help him distract the doctors and nurses while Ralph slipped Kit the vial of magic. According to Ralph it would likely last her for a few days. It used to last longer, but she had lost too much of her own magic to this world, and she would need much more than the vial to survive.

Kit was being held in the special diseases unit under quarantine. The doctors did not know what was wrong with her, and they never would. There was no instrument on Earth that I knew of that would find a difference in her DNA or blood which would tell them that she was anything else but human especially since she was half Selkie and not yet showing any of the signs of her Selkie heritage except for her inability to live on Earth without magic. That was not to say that she wouldn't eventually show more signs. Sometimes even full Selkie children didn't go through the change until after they started to reach adulthood. Kit was rapidly approaching that time.

I thought perhaps that was why she needed increasing amounts of magic, but I didn't dare tell Ralph that possibility. I wasn't sure if he could handle the news that his little Kit was turning into a woman by the fae definition. I wondered how many other children the Selkie Queen had abandoned to die. King Aric was right in not allowing our kind to go through the Portal to Earth. We only caused pain and misery.

Dooley and I wended through the wide hallways of the hospital made narrow by the gurneys that had been placed along the sides and the nurses and doctors that scuttled back and forth. I followed him as he exited from the stairwell onto a floor which was very different than the one we had come from. The halls were dimly lit and barren.

"The dead don't need fancy lighting," he said.

The echo of our footsteps sounded as we walked down the hallway towards the doorway marked "Morgue." We pushed the door open, and the fae at the desk inside looked up at us.

"Valora, my dear, I haven't seen you since you were a wee sprite."

CHAPTER TWENTY-ONE

"Uncle Artemus? What in the Realms? Why are you here?" I had not seen my uncle since, as he said, I was a wee sprite. My mother had once told me that her brother had fallen for a fae on another colony and had gone to live with her somewhere else in Overworld.

I quickly caught my uncle up to speed on what was going on in Dell'Aria and pressed him for information as to his whereabouts in the past several cycles.

"Your mother was correct in telling you that I had fallen for a fae on another colony. The only thing was that that colony was not in the Realms," said Artemus.

"You mean you came to Earth against the King's orders? King Aric says that the fae who have left are the ones responsible for the magic leaving our colony."

"Valora, do you think I would do anything to hurt your mother, my sister?"

"No." My mother had often spoken about her brother. Although I only had a few memories of him from childhood, I knew he could be trusted.

"I cannot tell you why Dell'Aria is losing its magic. But I can tell you that the Realms have magic enough to sustain any colony, even the barren ones. The fae have been coming to Earth for many millenniums, Valora. There has never been a Blight such as you are describing in all the histories I have read."

"Nor the ones I have read."

Dooley rocked onto his toes and back to his heels while giving a slight cough.

"Oh, I am sorry. Uncle Artemus, this is Dooley. Dooley Fays. He was friends with a fae that was recently brought into the morgue here. His name was Brokk. Have you seen him?"

Uncle Artemus grinned. "Why do you think fae are here on Earth Valora? I have already taken care of what is needed to mask his true nature. When the medical examiner does review his body it will be just as they suspect, an animal attack, which is not hard to fathom considering where he was living. It is hard to lose Brokk though. He was such a champion for the cause."

I was shocked that Uncle Artemus would be involved in this treachery. *Hadn't he just assured me he knew nothing about the problems in Dell'Aria?* "So you admit there is a cause you are fighting for, and that Brokk was involved?"

"Oh, yes, but it is not as devious as your King would make you think. Brokk and I were here to help those that are of this world and also of the Realms to adjust to life. You see the half-fae...or in the case of your friend Kit, half-Selkie...are not fully equipped to live in this world or within the Realms, but they are powerful. And that kind of magic should not go unmanaged if we are to keep the balance between our worlds."

"And the fae you fell in love with, where is she now?"

160

"My Liliana." Uncle Artemus's gaze turned to the ceiling. "She is with the Goddess Varuna now. At least that was what she told me she hoped for her future. You see, she was half-fae, also. I tried to convince her to come back with me to the Realms so she could prolong her life, but she was too stuck on her life here as a human. I lived out her years with her until her passing. And I guess you can say I am now stuck on this life as a human."

"So what do you know about the natural health clinic that is selling fae magic?" I asked.

"I don't know what you're talking about," said Artemus.

I quickly filled him in on our recent dealings with the clinic and Brokk's apparent involvement.

"Sometimes I feel like I spend so much time down here that I don't actually know what is going on up there in the real world. Valora, you must know that I had no idea. Brokk never said anything to me about this clinic. I just assumed he was helping the others as I have been."

"And how is that?" Dooley stepped forward to stand beside me.

Artemus pulled back his sleeve to reveal dozens of small slashes along his arm. "They aren't healing as quickly as they used to. Brokk told me that I needed to be careful with how much magic I shared."

"How in the world did you share your magic that way?" I pulled back and tried to hide my squeamishness. I had seen all sorts of blood and guts in my work as a Hunter, but never had I seen a fae so wounded by his own hand.

"Brokk showed me how. He developed a machine that allows you to collect magic from the bloodstream in small quantities. Of course, I do have to be careful since if too much is taken, I would be struck dead. But I am one hundred percent fae. My magic recharges after time."

Artemus pinched at the bridge of his nose and looked puzzled. "How do you suppose the fae of Dell'Aria weren't able to recharge their magic? With all the copper imbued in the foundation of the city —it just doesn't make sense."

"Someone or something is stealing it faster than we can recharge. You said that Brokk had a machine, some kind of device. Do you have it?"

"No. Brokk kept it with him."

I turned to Dooley. "Is there such a device back at your home?"

"Not that I've ever seen," said Dooley. He was obviously intrigued with what we were saying, but detached at the same time. I suppose the influx of information was starting to wear on him.

I had also learned much in the last few days, but was feeling lost in all the bits and pieces that were being thrown at me. I could only hope that I could bring it all to Aric, and he would know what to make of it as well as be able to protect me from those that believed me to be a Soulstealer. Someone was stealing the magic of Dell'Aria, that was certain, but I still had no idea who. Brokk was the only name that kept coming up, no matter what Dooley wanted to think.

❧☙

We said our good-byes to my Uncle Artemus, giving many promises to keep in touch, and headed to the ward where they were keeping Kit under observation. As we entered I saw that Franca was sitting on a bench in the hall outside Kit's room. The door to the room was closed.

"Is everything okay?"

"Yes, I was able to get the vial to her. But now we have another problem. As soon as we slipped her the magic all her vitals shot up to normal."

"Why is that a problem?"

Franca shook her head. "Oh, that wasn't the problem. It was the development of the webbed toes that now have the doctors shaking their head."

I took a deep breath. "Oh, Goddess, she is going through the change. We need to get her back to the Realms. She will never survive it here." The Selkie were born to the water and lived their time there. Although they sometimes ventured onto land for periods of time, they always had to return. I wasn't sure what to expect of a half-Selkie, but if Kit was showing signs of becoming more like her Selkie heritage, there would come a time that, if she was unable to breathe the waters of the Realms, she would perish. I knew of no other way.

As I entered Kit's room the sound of a dozen various beeping machines masked my entrance. Ralph was standing near the back of the crowd of specialists that had descended upon Kit. Their green garments created a wall around her. I motioned and was able to get his attention.

"Valora, I don't know what's happening. Was there something wrong with the medicine?" whispered Ralph.

I quickly explained to Ralph what I thought was happening. A cold sweat broke out across his forehead. "So she has to go with you and Franca through the Portal?"

"I don't see any other way. I can promise you we will make sure she is delivered safely to one of the Selkie colonies. It is the only way she stands a fighting chance. Do you have any ideas on how we can get her out of here?"

"But you say you aren't sure? Maybe if we just get her more medicine. Maybe if we brought her back to the lake where I met her mother." Ralph clutched at his jawline and stared up at the ceiling, the rims of his eyes full of tears. He took a sharp intake of breath and let it out in a quick puff.

I put my hand over his arm. "Brokk asked you once to trust him and not ask any questions. I'm asking you to trust me and you can ask all the questions you want, but first we need to figure out how to get her out of here. I'm afraid of what they will do if she undergoes any more changes."

Ralph stood stock straight and looped his fingers through his belt loops, the tears disappearing from his eyes. "I'm still a sheriff. There's nothing that can keep me from taking her home since she's stabilized. But I don't want to cause a scene when all of them are here. When are you and Franca planning on leaving?"

"Tomorrow morning. Let's go talk to Franca."

Franca and I spoke to Ralph about where the Portal was in the park in West Seattle, and Ralph agreed to meet us there the next morning. Franca said that the Portal would be open for a short time, and we should all be able to make it through if we were there on time.

Ralph looked over my shoulder at Dooley who was patiently waiting a few feet away while we spoke. "I need to have a word with you before you go. In private."

"I'll go see what kind of greens they have at the salad bar," said Franca.

"Listen, Valora, I know you came here for a purpose and that didn't include us. But you need to know something about Dooley. Brokk meant a lot to him. I've known Dooley a long time, and the past few years he's finally found focus in his life. You need to ease up on him a little with your accusations about Brokk, no matter how strongly you feel."

"I can appreciate your concern for Dooley. He is lucky to have you."

"No, I'm lucky to have him. We all are. He's special. It's what I've been telling him ever since they put his mother in a home. He wouldn't listen to me, but something made him listen to Brokk, and for that I am grateful."

"His mother is in a home?"

"Has been ever since he was five years old. She has early onset dementia or Alzheimer's or some kind of senility. Basically she forgot who she was and who Dooley was. He was put in foster care, and he didn't do too well with it. He had a lot of run ins with me through the years."

Franca popped back around the corner. "I hate to break up the conversation, guys, but we should get moving."

Ralph gave me a curt nod before returning to Kit's room.

Dooley fidgeted with the hem of his t-shirt. I still had not been given the chance to tell him what he was. And even though his mother was alive, she wouldn't ever be able to tell him, either. But perhaps that was for the best.

I walked over to him. "I guess this is where we part ways."

"You know, you never did find out who killed Brokk. Do you even care?" asked Dooley.

"Dooley, we are not going to come to any agreement on this, that much I can tell. I have information that you could not possibly understand." I tried to choose my words carefully. "Information that tells me Brokk was in over his head."

"Your own uncle had dealings with him."

"Yes, and my uncle also had no idea what Brokk was really up to. Brokk knew about the clinic, Dooley. He told Ralph about it. How much more proof do you need?"

"My proof is down in that morgue. Brokk's dead body. You think he up and slit his own throat out of an extreme feeling of guilt? You may think that your boyfriend, the King, has all the answers, but he doesn't. No matter what Brokk's involvement in all this, I know one thing for certain. He was good to me and to all those he dealt with."

My pride flared. "The King is honorable. You have no idea what he has done for me and for the fae of Dell'Aria." I grabbed at Franca's arm and started to pull her away. "I think Franca and I will be going now. I am sorry about your friend, Dooley, but my mission is not to find out who killed him. It is to save my home and the thousands of fae who are depending on me to find an answer. Tell Ralph we will be taking the car and leaving it in the park. He can pick it up when he meets us there tomorrow morning. I'm sorry for the trouble I caused you. Feel free to have the bike I left at the clinic. I don't think I'll need it anymore and I think Franca's hotwiring will allow it to work for you."

Dooley crossed his arms over his chest. "Don't worry yourself over me."

❧

I let Franca drive the car to our next destination while I stewed in the front seat. "What the heck is he talking about? It's not like we didn't risk our neck with the demon at the clinic to get that medicine for Kit."

"Yes, well, technically that was for Ralph and Kit, not for Dooley," Franca said.

"What? Are you on his side now? Since when did it become my job to help Dooley figure out who killed Brokk and to help Dooley figure out he is half-fae?" I clasped my hand over my mouth.

"So you noticed something funny about him, too? I couldn't quite put my finger on what, but it makes perfect sense."

."How do you suppose?"

"You said that your Uncle and Brokk were here helping other half-fae and other supernaturals adjust. Maybe Brokk helped Dooley without having to tell him. He doesn't have wings, so there would be no need to make him deal with the idea that part of him belonged to a whole different world."

Franca turned the car onto a bridge which spanned a small bay from the main city of Seattle. We passed a sign indicating that we were headed into West Seattle. We were rapidly losing daylight.

"Any idea where we are going to sleep tonight?" I asked.

"Tonight we camp in style. I already had reservations for a cabin at Camp Long. I guess I don't mind sharing it with you."

"Reservations at a cabin?

"Valora, I don't know how many ways I can say it or how many times you have to see it to realize that the creatures of the Realms have travelled back and forth through the Portals to Earth for ages. We are discreet in our travels as we have seen the basic human nature that says to take all natural resources and squander them, but it doesn't mean we bar any interaction with humans." She paused and gave me a wry smile. "I made the reservation when I first came through the Portal. Thought after a few days of collecting I would want a proper roof over my head, especially since it tends to rain a lot here this time of year."

I sat back in my seat. The edges of my anger faded, replaced by regret. My mother had always taught me that I could do anything any other fae had ever done. But all I had focused my energy on was doing what others expected of me. It was a hard feeling to shake. I had been outcast because of my wings for so long that I only wanted to belong. I was certain that Dooley wanted to belong, too, and he thought he did once he found Brokk. And I had all but told him that his best friend and mentor was a fugitive and a murderer.

"I have kind of been an ass, haven't I?"

Franca patted me on the leg. "Don't worry. I won't hold it against you."

We rode the rest of the way in silence. I was alone with my thoughts, and I didn't like it. If I stopped ignoring everything that was surrounding me, then I was left with a lot of questions. The only answer I wanted was that Aric would answer those questions for me and that he would protect me. The amulet pulsed against my breast. Perhaps Aric was trying to reach me again. I had to trust Franca with something. She was the one who was going to get me back to him.

"Franca, what do you think Dooley meant when he said that the King was my boyfriend?"

"Just angry talk. He has a bit of a thing for you, in case you hadn't noticed, and all you seem to talk about is the King. It probably got under his skin a little."

To say I hadn't noticed Dooley would be like saying I had a paper sack over my head the last few days. I had noticed him, more than I wanted to admit. If Franca was right, and she seemed to be very perceptive, it was probably best for Dooley and me that I was going back home tomorrow. My heart belonged to the King. I couldn't let a few whisperings in my head, my mother's words, and some chiseled abs change that. *Oh, dear Goddess, I'm in trouble.*

Franca pulled the car through the winding dirt road up to the area of the park where the cabins were nestled into a corner. We walked up a path that was covered in overgrowth until we reached a small cabin that had seen better days. Massive pine trees bent their heavy branches, tickling the roof with their needles and threatening to smash the tiny hut at the slightest provocation of the wind.

"I hope they didn't charge you much." I walked onto the small porch, and the boards creaked below my feet.

"No, no. It is the off season, and I come through here enough that they let me stay here for free if no one else is asking. It saves me from trying to track down the money they use here."

"So where is the Portal located?"

"In an interesting location."

I followed her into the cabin.

Franca shirked her satchel off her shoulder and onto the small wooden table in the middle of the room. She pulled a match from the interior of that satchel and lit a small lantern. The warm glow barely reached past the edges of the table. In the corner of the room was a wooden bunk, each bed having recently been covered in fresh straw. My eyes started to feel heavy at the thought of a soft place to lay my head, even if only for a short while.

We sat in the wooden chairs across from each other, and I was reminded of my friend Kali. We had spent many nights at the table in our hut telling each other the stories of the missions we had been sent on. My heart clenched painfully as I recalled the last time I'd seen Kali. *What had happened to her? Would I ever see her again?*

"Sometimes I think that the humans can sense more about the Realms than we give them credit for," Franca said, interrupting my thoughts of my other friend. "Honestly, I don't know how else to explain it. The Portal is centered at the top of a twenty foot high climbing structure that they call Monitor Rock. Inscribed at the base are the words 'warn, remind, advise and instruct.' Of course it was built over 50 years ago. It could have been another one of us."

"Speaking of warn and remind, exactly where does this portal dump out?"

Franca reached into her bag and pulled out two small wooden cups and a glass bottle. She poured a deep red liquid into each cup before sliding one across the table to me. "You might want to drink that first."

"Seems like we are skipping right to advise and instruct." I downed the drink in one gulp, barely tasting the end of the brew as it travelled down my gullet, warming me instantly. A tingly happy sensation radiated through me. "Is that mead?"

"That it is. Want another?" Before waiting for my answer she had filled my cup again and pushed it back towards me.

As I downed the next cup, albeit a bit slower, Franca returned to warn and remind. "It brings me to the heart of Mount Elbrus."

I was mid swallow as she finished her words, and not everything went down the right tube. I choked and coughed on the last bit of mead. Franca jumped up and struck me on the back, a little harder than I was expecting, and I went sprawling onto the floor. My coughing fits were replaced by laughing fits.

"Are you okay?" Franca stood before me with one hand still on the neck of the bottle of mead.

I lifted my cup up to her. "After I get another cup of that I will be."

"Are you worried about how you will be received by the dwarves?" Franca finished pouring and took a sip from her own cup.

"You might say history dictates that if I was in the heart of Mount Elbrus, I would not be alive."

Franca smiled. "We can learn from our history, we don't always have to let it repeat itself. Don't worry about my people."

We continued to trade stories all night just as I did with Kali. Franca assured me that traveling through the Realms to reach Dell'Aria would not take more than a few days. She promised she would go with Kit and me as soon as her clan had given her leave, which she was sure wouldn't be a problem.

"I have gathered more on this assignment than all the other Collectors put together. Plus, the clan leader has a crush on me."

I perked up when she said this. "So is the clan leader like our King?"

"With a whole different set of politics, but basically, yes."

"How is it that you know he likes you?"

"Really, Valora, you only need open your eyes. Wait, are we speaking about me or you and the King?"

Again the warmth from the amulet permeated through my bodice. I had forgotten all about the signal from earlier. I clutched at my chest and pushed myself up off my seated position on the floor.

"Excuse me, I need to use the bathroom again."

CHAPTER TWENTY-TWO

The only door in the sparse cabin was the one we had come in. "Where is the bathroom?"

Franca eyebrows knitted up her forehead. "Are you serious? You are. Okay, there is an outhouse around back. Did I mention this cabin was free?"

"Yeah. Heh. Well, I'll be right back." I grabbed my satchel and hurried down the squeaky porch. The cabin had a small window on the backside which looked out into the forest. The soft glow of the gas lamp that Franca had lit showed a short well-worn path that ended at a rickety outhouse. The smell that emanated from it forced me back towards the front of the house. "Ugh."

I pulled out the amulet, and the stone in the middle pulsated erratically. *Where was I going to find a mirror in the middle of the woods?* My gaze came to rest on the car parked down the path from the cabin.

As I settled into the driver's seat I positioned the rear view mirror down so that I could see it best. I set my ring to the mirror which struggled to switch images, and when it came into focus I realized why. Across the middle of the mirror was a jagged crack. In one panel I saw the King's chamber, which was empty. In the other I saw my friend Kali.

"Kali, what is going on?"

Kali was somewhere dark. Her face was strewn with dirt and blood, but I could not tell where the blood was coming from. She was walking somewhere, carrying a piece of the mirror in one hand, her eyes constantly darting from side to side as if she thought she was being followed.

Kali's mouth opened in surprise. "It still works. I wasn't sure if it would." She hurried along whatever dark path she was on, only looking down at the mirror briefly. "Valora, you don't see any other image on your end do you?"

"Well, I do. The King's chamber. But it is empty."

"That's probably because he's among those who are chasing me down right now. I don't know exactly where I'm going," she said, a note of desperation in her voice. "But I escaped, along with a few others, from where they were holding us. I was able to break into the King's chamber and smash off a corner of the mirror."

I heard shouting in the background. Tears streamed down Kali's face. "Valora, I don't think they'll leave me alive if they catch me."

"What's happened, Kali? What's going on there?"

"Someone is stealing the magic, Valora, and from what I can gather it isn't any of those I was imprisoned with. But no one will believe us. It's a horrible mess. The King was infuriated. He claimed that I was to blame for your disappearance. He was going to put me to death. I had to escape."

The sounds behind Kali were getting louder. I could hear the shouts. "She must have gone this way!"

I watched in horror. I could hear Kali's breathing become more and more labored as she continued to race down the hall. She had given up talking to me, and all I could see was a jumble of dark shadows as she pumped her arms fiercely up and down while traversing the passageways. I had always heard that there was a labyrinth of tunnels below the city, and just where they started and ended, I had no idea. Until now I was uncertain that they even existed.

A blink of light passed over the mirror, and Kali raced towards it. As she got closer she slowed down and I could see that she was in front of a door that had light coming from the bottom. She reached for the knob without hesitation and burst forth into the room. A fresh batch of sobs poured forth from her. She set the small section of mirror down on something that allowed me to see her and her surroundings. Surroundings I was very familiar with, having seen them only a few days before. The King's chambers.

"Well, I guess we now know where all the tunnels under the colony lead to. Whatever happens, Valora, know that I never betrayed you. I am not a Soulstealer."

The tears poured down my cheeks as well. I touched my hand to the mirror. There was nothing I could do to help her.

Seconds passed, and the door that Kali had come through burst open allowing a contingent of the King's Guard to burst in. The main door to the chamber opened, and in walked Siam followed closely by the King.

I watched, aghast, as the King's Guard pounced on Kali, throwing her to the ground and kicking her in the side. I heard the sizzle of her flesh as they tossed iron chains atop her to keep her from escaping.

Aric looked straight at me and put his finger to his lips in a shushing motion. I quickly removed my ring from the mirror, and the image dissolved. A short rapping on the window startled me. Franca was standing there looking in at me.

⊱⊰

"You know you didn't have to come to the car to have a nervous breakdown." She stood with the car door propped up against her hip.

"I...I need to tell you something," I managed to say.

Franca helped me back to the cabin. My last nerve had been frayed, and I wasn't sure how much more of this burden I could take alone. Aric's message to me just then had been clear. He wanted me to continue to keep quiet. But what was that getting me? My friend Kali would likely be executed. All of Dell'Aria thought I was a Soulstealer. I had no home and no friends.

I proceeded to tell Franca everything I knew to that point. About the strife in Dell'Aria. The Soulstealers. About Kali and, lastly, about my pseudo-relationship with the King. I left out some of the more personal details. When I finished, I set the amulet on the table.

"And this seems to be how he contacts me. Though I am not sure how it works exactly. There was the time that it healed my blistering hand just with a touch. It's all more than I can wrap my brain around."

"May I?" Franca gestured to the amulet on the table.

"Of course."

She picked it up and studied it carefully. "I was fairly certain you had some dealings with your King. And I don't want you to take offense, but what do you think is in it for him?"

"I don't understand."

She turned the amulet over and ran her fingers around its edges. "I mean, I told you about the dealings I have had with the leader of my clan. I am no ninny. I know exactly why he targets me. I am a Collector. I share things that I bring back from Earth with the entire clan. But it is up to me to divvy up everything when I return. Mostly I give it to the medicine men and the priests."

Franca studied the markings on the back of the amulet, running her fingers along the grooves and squinting her eyes as she spoke. "Now, you would think that the leader of the clan has everything he could possibly want. But I know that's not true. And one of the things he wants is a certain herb I have brought back with me on occasion. It's not easy to come by, not even here, and the medicine men have decided that they don't need it. But he really wants me to bring it for him even though there is no greater purpose for it. No reason to take time to collect it when he only wants it for his own personal pleasure." Franca smirked and turned her eyes to me. "If he can make me believe he cares for me, then perhaps I will do as he wishes. I know I am not the only one he tried to ply with his affections."

"I don't know what I could possibly offer the King."

She pushed the amulet back towards me. "That's not to say that his intentions are not genuine. I just find the entire thing somewhat strange. I would be careful with that if I were you. It may connect you to him in a way you're not aware of." She pointed to the carvings along the edges of the amulet. "The markings are some kind of binding magic. Bind what to what, I have no idea. And the stone definitely channels energy somehow."

I wasn't sure what to think or who to trust. Aric wanted me to trust him, but then again he had never really told me what the amulet could do. Normally I would just do as he asked, but I was past taking things for granted anymore. Nothing was what it seemed. Once I would have given anything to be bound to Aric without question, but now I wanted to know for what reason he would want to be bound to me. And for once, that question wasn't born of my own self-doubts.

"That much I already figured out. I'll keep it put away until I know more about it." I shoved the amulet into my satchel.

Franca reached across the table and put her hand on my shoulder. "There is a shaman in my village. We can ask him what he thinks. We need to get some rest. The journey home tomorrow will not be easy, and we will need to make sure we have time to prepare Kit for the journey."

For the first time in many days I stripped from my dragon leathers and pulled on a long soft linen nightshirt I had tossed in my bag for extra layers. The night was cool, but living in Dell'Aria had steeled me against it. I slowly faded into dreams for the first time in weeks, but they were not pleasant. That night I fought every battle I had ever fought my entire life. I awoke suddenly in the middle of the night wet with my own sweat and shaking from head to toe. I searched out some water and fell back into the wooden bunk.

CHAPTER TWENTY-THREE

When I awoke I felt like I had been hit with a sledge hammer. Franca was dabbing my head with a cool cloth. "Oh, thank the Goddess you are awake. How are you feeling?"

I went to sit up and fell right back down again. "I feel sick."

"I'm so sorry, I had no idea the mead would affect you this way. The fae drink, don't they?" Franca darted around me nervously.

"We do. Plenty. This is not from the mead."

I was completely drained, fatigued from head to toe. I remembered those in the colony who had been stricken with the Blight. They were generally quarantined from everyone else, but I had heard what the symptoms were — everyone knew. And since there were no natural illnesses to fae, I could only be experiencing one thing.

"This is the Blight, Franca. I don't think I will be able to make it through the Portal with you."

"How is that possible? I thought you said this was an illness that infected the fae in your colony on Dell'Aria. How could it have followed you here?"

There was a knocking on the cabin door.

Franca peeked out the front window. "We have company."

Kit walked in, a baby seal stuffed animal clutched to her chest. She was followed by Ralph who gave a small salute to Franca. And lastly, in walked Dooley carrying Brokk's copper chest.

Kit pointed to me. "Daddy, she has wings."

Their mood, unexpectedly jubilant, turned quickly somber as everyone took in my appearance.

"Is it that bad?" I asked.

Dooley dropped the chest on the table and dashed to my side. He held his hands above my body.

"Strange." With eyes closed, he tilted his head to the side and passed his hands over me several times. "It's as if the energy within you is no longer bound to you, and it's slipping away. I can't possibly catch it all."

Franca rushed over to my bag and fished around until she found the amulet. "Put this on."

I shoved her hand aside. "It might not be safe."

She shoved it back at me. "Humor me. Remember what I said about the binding runes on this? Give it a shot."

I nodded, and Franca slipped it over my neck. I grasped the amulet and warmth returned to my body. The red stone pulsed like a heart beating. Each rhythmic throb pumped more life and energy back into me.

Franca spoke before I could say anything. "Getting her to talk is like pulling teeth. I just found out some important things last night, and let's just say it's a long story and we don't have too much time until the Portal opens." She paused and gave a knowing look at Dooley. "So, what exactly are you doing here?"

Dooley rose to his feet. "I'm going with you."

"You're what?" His conviction quickly sobered me.

"And so am I," said Ralph. He stood behind his daughter with his hands on her shoulders.

Franca approached Ralph. "Have you thought about this? You need to know that there may be no way for you to come back after you have lived any time in the Realms. And you must know that not all beings in the Realms think very well of humans. Your life could be in danger."

"Daddy!" Kit turned and wrapped her arms around her father's waist.

Ralph bent down and put himself eye level with Kit. "Sweetheart. I told you we're going to another world. A world your mother is from. I can't promise that I'll fit in like you will. But I will do my best, and you know there is no other way for you to survive, Kit. You need to go home."

Kit stared into her father's eyes. "But you could stay here, Daddy. You don't need to come with me. You would be safe here."

A tear came to Ralph's eye and to my own. "And here I thought I was protecting you all this time. My little Kit. There are many things that could cut my life short here. I would rather take my chances by your side then to never see you again. I don't think I could bear that."

Kit and Ralph turned back to face us all. "So will you take us through?" he asked.

Franca nodded. "I suppose you have made a pretty good case. Although I'm not sure how I'm going to explain bringing you all back through with me. I don't think that batting my eyelashes and saying 'But I am a Collector' is going to get me very far this time." She breathed a heavy sigh. "Ah well, I suppose it's good the clan leader has a crush on me."

I gave a short giggle, and Dooley looked from Franca to me. "Another long story," I said. "So why do you think it is a good idea for you to come through the Portal?"

Dooley walked to the table and set his hand on the box he had brought in. "This."

"Brokk's chest is the reason you want to come back? I don't understand."

"I had a late night visitor last night. Your uncle. He brought me Brokk's effects from the morgue which included this key." Dooley pulled a copper key from under his black t-shirt. "He said that this key would open this chest. But only in the Realms."

"So it's a treasure hunt then?" I looked up at Dooley and gave a smirk. He immediately returned the smile and I felt my cheeks flush, embarrassed at my reaction and for the argument we had the last time I saw him.

"A hunt for the truth," he said. "And I think the answer lies on the other side of that Portal."

"Ah, right," Franca said. "Everything is in order, folks. I'd love to stay and chat more about all this, but we really have very little time and a bit of a climb to make. Valora, you might want to get your clothes back on." She ushered Ralph and Kit out the door.

I looked down and realized I was still in the almost sheer linen top I had gone to bed in, the sweat from my illness having done its job in assisting it in clinging to my body.

Dooley gave me a quick wink. "I'll wait outside for you."

❧

I quickly pulled on my leather skirt and bodice and laced up my knee high boots, shoving the dragonskin pants and coat into my satchel to allow my wings to stretch. My wingspan was only slightly past my shoulders. It felt nice to know I was going back to the Realms and that, in a way, I would not need to hide who I was anymore. But I still had to worry about what everyone back home thought. Aric said he would come to me tomorrow. How or why, I didn't know. But I was hoping he would finally give me the answers I needed. And I hoped he would tell me that Kali was okay.

I hopped down the stairs to find Dooley leaning against my motorcycle. "Hey, how did you get it here?"

Ralph patted the large rusty truck they had apparently arrived in. "I gave it a tow."

"Exactly how are we going to get it up into the Portal?" asked Franca.

"I meant it when I said I wanted you to have it," I said to Dooley. "Maybe we can stow it here for when you return?" I had taken my bike with me through the Portal because I thought I needed it. I realized the only thing I needed now were the people around me. I could trust them. The motorcycle was something that kept me isolated from others, I wouldn't let that happen again.

Dooley's jaw dropped. "Geez, I wish I had known that before I wrestled that thing into the back of the truck." He rubbed at his shoulder.

"I'll make it up to you," I said. I was glad that Dooley was coming along. He had always made me feel safe. I figured it had something to do with his fae energy. And we were about to go into a territory with barely any fae, Mount Elbrus.

Franca led the way to Monitor Rock. Ralph and Kit followed behind her, and Dooley hung back to walk alongside me.

"I know we have had our differences," I said.

Dooley held up his hand. "I think what we both really want is the same thing. We both want to know what is happening in our world. Brokk was really important to me, and I would sure as heck love to know what happened to him. I realize that's not your mission, but it is mine."

"Dooley, there is something you should know." We kept walking side by side as the twenty foot high human made mountain came into view. "You aren't just human."

He stopped and stared at me. "What? What are you talking about? Are you trying to insult me or something?"

"No! You're not human in a good way. Look at how you can manipulate energy. Well, you call it energy. Back in the Realms we would call it magic. But it is more than that, Dooley. There is a pull I feel towards you that is common among many fae." Even as I said it I knew part of what I was telling him was a lie. My attraction to Dooley was different than what I felt towards my father or to Kali. But I couldn't put my finger on it.

"So because you are attracted to me that means I am fae." Dooley raised his eyebrows at me.

I gave him a smack on the shoulder. "Part fae, and I didn't say I was attracted to you."

"Okay, but since I have no little wing-things...I am going to have to reserve my belief in your 'feeling' for a little bit."

Franca called from the front of the line. "Okay, we are burning up time here. Let's get climbing."

Before us stood a squat, man-made structure about twenty-five feet high. The walls were constructed with smooth granite stones. As we ascended we could see Camp Long which was dotted with cabins. Franca had obviously come this way before as she quickly climbed a pre-planned path. Ralph pushed Kit up the rock face, and Franca reached down to help her. I happily grabbed onto some of the thinner outcroppings on the more difficult face of the rock. I was excited to be climbing again, something I had not done since I took my last lone journey through the Realms.

Dooley quickly passed me and held his hand down to me. "Can I give you a hand?"

I pushed away from the rock face, my wings beating furiously to keep me aloft. I could hover for a short bit of time, but not long.

"Okay, show-offs, the Portal is opening. All who are going better get up here," said Franca.

I pulled myself up the side and accepted Dooley's hand. As I got to my feet I got a short jolt from the amulet and stumbled backwards, almost falling off the edge. Dooley grabbed my hand and pulled me forward into the safety of his arms.

The heat from his body permeated through my bodice. Neither of us let go. We stared into each other's eyes. I felt a different pull from him this time, something so deep it both threatened and thrilled me. I tried to shake it off, but I couldn't.

A light tapping on my arm brought me back to reality. Kit smiled up at me, the long strands of her faded blond hair wrapped around her shoulder and her deep blue eyes beaming.

"The lady says it is time to go now," said Kit as she pointed back to Franca.

Franca smiled and wiggled her finger at me. "Good thing we have this one here to bring you two out of that trance. Now everyone, you will be a little disorientated when you come out of the Portal. Just make sure you stay still and don't get too agitated. My people will be waiting on the other side, and I will have to do some quick explaining so that they don't think a bunch of trespassers hitched a ride through my

Portal opening. I'll go through first, and you all follow behind me. Quickly. Ready?"

Franca turned, and the Portal opened in front of her. The white light that emanated forth from it was brighter than the daytime sun on Earth. Woven through it were red swirls of light to indicate that this Portal belonged to Mount Elbrus whose depths were filled with red hot lava. Franca stepped forward and disappeared.

Ralph squeezed Kit's hand and they both stepped through.

Dooley took my hand. "Ready if you are." We both stepped through the Portal simultaneously.

CHAPTER TWENTY-FOUR

The pressure on my body was immense, as was the heat. I knew immediately why the fae only used certain Portals. We were now being accosted by the fires only found deep within Mount Elbrus. I lost contact with my body. My mind floated through the arid atmosphere as it built to a crescendo. Through it all I felt two things, the amulet against my chest and Dooley's hand in mine.

We collapsed hard onto solid ground. My vision was hazy, and I saw everything through a film of steam that hung in the air. It quickly settled against my skin, mixing with my sweat. Ralph was cradling Kit in his arms. Her eyes were closed. She looked like a limp, wet noodle. A vision of my mother's lifeless form careened into the forefront of my mind. I opened my mouth to yell out for help, and only a barely audible gasp escaped my lips.

Hard rock pressed into my back. Dooley turned onto his side and smiled at me in a way that made me think he might have hit his head too hard.

The sound of voices mixed with the clatter of weapons echoed around me. I reached down and felt the hilt of my blade.

Franca was already up and talking to the first of the dwarves to meet us in a cavern which seemed to have no ceiling, the walls extending up into a dark nothingness. Small pools of water bubbled forth from the ground around us — burbling and boiling. There was no plant life, only rocks and steam and heat.

I sat up and tried to suck in some air, but nothing came. Dooley's breath was labored, but not as bad as mine. I gestured towards Franca. She gave some instructions to someone near her, but I couldn't make out what she was saying. Then the room went black.

I sat up and drew a breath of crisp air deep into my lungs. I opened my eyes, and the first thing I saw was Dooley.

"Here, drink this. Should make you feel better." He handed me a glass of water.

I greedily gulped it down. Water spilled out the sides of my mouth and down my cheeks.

"That does feel better. Where is everyone else?" I asked.

Gradually my vision adjusted to the outside light. Dooley held me in his lap, his back resting against a large boulder. Lush green vines wrapped around an arched doorway that was carved into the side of the mountain. We were at the base of Mount Elbrus.

"Franca has them inside. Everyone else was okay but you. Apparently the fae can't handle the temperatures in there. Franca didn't think you would succumb to it so quickly, but I guess since you just got over the sickness you may have been more sensitive than she thought."

"Kit? Ralph?"

"There are doctors here. I guess they call them medicine men. Anyway, they were able to give Kit something to revive her until we can get her home. But we won't be able to wait too long. Franca says she needs to get there soon."

I gazed up at the sky. My sky. The Realms. "It seems like we landed here near day's end. Did Franca say when we should get going?"

"Apparently there's some kind of feast tonight in her honor. She thought it would be safe to wait until morning. And it will give us all a chance to recover from the portal crossing."

So we'd be here all night. I wasn't sure if Aric had meant he would contact me tonight or not. The time was all messed up between Earth and the Realms.

"Is Franca coming with us?"

As if answering to her name, Franca exited from an archway cut in the side of the mountain. Her yellow hair was adorned with a crown woven with bands of metal and glittering rocks.

"There you are. Finally decided to wake up from your nap? I have an elixir for you to take. It cost me an arm and a leg to get it, but I thought that after all we have been through you deserved a good dwarven meal. I promise you'll like it."

She handed me a vial with thick red liquid inside. "Drink this and you'll be able to stand the heat inside for a day. No more, though. Of course we will be long gone by then. And, yes, I am going with you, so don't give me that look. I am a Collector. Just out on another collecting mission and letting you all tag along as far as I am concerned."

I knew in my heart that Franca was only trying to help me. That was what made it all the harder. She had asked for a favor in return for her help, but now she asked nothing.

Franca's words about Aric came back from the other night, about what he might want from me. But love was different, wasn't it? Love. Was that what it was?

I had wandered off into my own thoughts again. Dooley broke the silence. "Sounds great." He handed me the vial. "Drink to...happy trails?"

I winked at him. "Yes, happy trails, indeed." I downed the thick brew. It was like swallowing taffy and tasted strongly of elderberries, a sweet medicine.

"You have Brokk and his gardening skills to thank for that. Sticks to the insides. Let's go." Franca pulled me to my feet, and I followed her back inside Mount Elbrus.

The night was spent in various stages of celebration. The dwarves certainly knew how to throw a party. Dish after steaming dish was served with every dwarven delicacy . Skewers of roasted roots and the bright purple pods of the nightshade swimming in a gravy of devil's milkwort. Veiny stalks of saltbrush coated in silver lettuce seed pods. Thick hardy bread made with narrowleaf nettles.

I was pretty sure the elixir she gave me was what made their food palatable, because I knew that usually I wouldn't be able to eat that sort of food.

Kit and Dooley were part human, and thus they were able to tolerate many other types of conditions and eat many types of foods. As strange as humans were I had learned that they were much more adaptable to change than any of the fae I knew in the Realms, both emotionally and physically.

Ralph was entirely human and seemed quite comfortable, especially after he'd had a few glasses of the dwarven mead.

When the music and dancing finally died down, Franca dismissed herself to bed.

"Been right nice celebrating with you two, but I have to get myself to bed if I am going to keep my short legs up with you giants." She gave a hearty laugh followed by an audible belch and tottered down a side tunnel.

❦

Ralph and Kit had fallen asleep in a hammock strung up in the corner. More dwarves raised their glasses to Dooley and me as they passed by and disappeared down other tunnels. Soon we were alone.

"You want to take a peek?" Dooley gave me a wry smile and raised his eyebrows.

"What?"

He pulled the copper key from his shirt. "Brokk's chest. What did you think I was talking about? Follow me."

He got up and went down another side tunnel. He twisted left, right and then left again before coming to a small arched doorway which was covered with a tattered curtain. He swept it aside and ducked into the chamber which had a dwarf sized ceiling.

"We may need to get down on our knees."

I followed his lead and knelt down as we hobbled into the chamber and towards a soft pile of blankets which had been laid out on the floor. The warmth in the chamber was fed by a blazing fire that crackled away in the corner of the room. The dwarves liked their fires, and I probably would have objected had it not been for the elixir Franca gave me and the sudden shiver that ran down my spine as I watched Dooley crawl into the room.

Set atop the blankets was the chest.

"You haven't opened it yet?" I tried to remain focused on the chest, but Dooley's dark eyes were only focused on me.

"No. I wanted us to do it together," Dooley said softly.

Something inside me clicked. It was like a whirring in my chest, a steady thrum. A beat I was meant to follow. Abandoning all thought I let myself be pulled into Dooley's gaze, closer and closer until there was no space between us but our lips. Moist soft lips that reached out for me. Caressed me. Teased me and soothed me at the same time. I let the heat coursing through me control me in this moment. My lips teased his as well, and when his lips parted, the bottom dropped out from under me. The taste of him evoked the scent of Winter Haven. Cool, rainy days. Damp dirt and wet tree bark. A hint of flowers and the sweet earthy scent of truffles.

I pulled back from him just as we were both drifting deeper into the illusion.

"What was that?" Dooley sat back wide eyed. He searched for the source of what we had just experienced, and his eyes came to rest on me.

The dam broke on the tears I tried to hold back. I choked on my words, unable to form a clear sentence.

"It was Winter Haven."

He waited for me to explain. Waited for me as he also searched my face for a hint as to what my next comment would be.

It took a moment, but gradually my voice returned to me. "My mother told me the story when I was a young girl. I asked her when you would know that someone was right for you. When you knew you had met the one. She told me two things. She said that your other would be able to speak to you in here." I raised my finger to my head as my mother had done. "And she said that when you tasted his nectar you would feel the power of Winter Haven surround you. Winter Haven is one of our most sacred places. For those who have not been there we only have the stories from others. Stories about the ripe and green forested land that our forefathers came from. Cool and wet. Damp and lush. Sweet and strong. I had no idea what she meant until now." I reached out a hand to touch his cheek, and he put his hand over mine.

A sudden pang of energy ripped through me like all my nerves had gone alight at once. The amulet throbbed against my chest. I now wore it on the outside of my clothes, having no need to keep it hidden. The stone flamed red and then faded. Dizziness threatened to overcome me. Dooley put his hands on my shoulders, and I wavered slightly.

"Are you okay?"

I now knew why my feelings for Dooley had been so strong and so conflicted at the same time. A leftover crackle from the amulet sent a pulse of energy bristling through my spine. I was now connected to two men, one in a very real way through the amulet hanging at my chest. I was not sure to what extent it bound me to Aric, but there was no question that it did. And I was also bound to Dooley through the magic of Winter Haven.

"Yes, I'm okay," I answered as I wiped the sheen from my brow. "I'm probably just still feeling a little woozy from that mead. Let's open that chest."

I tried to push back the feelings that had risen to the surface after Dooley and I had kissed. I tried to keep my mind clear from thoughts that would be a betrayal to my King, to Aric. I would have to wait until our next meeting to fully understand why Aric had chosen me to be bound to him in this way.

Dooley spent a moment looking into my eyes before he pulled the copper key from his pocket. "Okay."

He rocked back on his heels creating a distance between us. As he pulled away I returned to a more level headed state of mind.

He inserted the key into the lock and turned until I heard a mechanical click. As Dooley lifted the lid we saw three things resting inside. A journal held together with a piece of cloth that had been tied around it, a faded photograph, and some kind of contraption made with copper.

Dooley reached for the photograph and stared down at it.

"Do you know who that is?" I asked.

"Yes. It's my mother."

"She is very beautiful. I can see where you got your dark skin."

"How is it you come to that conclusion? What if my father had dark skin?"

It all made sense to me now. I had wondered what horrible thing Brokk had done to drive him out of the Realms. But what if he had gone of his own accord? "Dooley, I have told you before, I believe you are half-fae. The only reason I can see that Brokk would have your mother's picture in a locked chest is..."

"...he was my father." I could see the wheels in Dooley's mind were turning as he finished my sentence. "But how is that possible? He was the same age as I was. He never said anything to me. Heck, I don't even have wings."

"The fae age at a different rate than humans, and I am sure he was only trying to protect you. If those who were out to harm him ever knew that you were his son, that could put you in danger. But he obviously desired to be close to you. As for the wings, not every child of a fae and human pairing ends up with wings. The range of differences is as varied as the differences between human children. I mean, look at me. I am full fae and I don't even have the full wings that all normal fae are born with. It's what you would call a birth defect. There are a lot of fae who think the whole idea of pairing with humans is wrong since you are bound to have offspring who have what some fae would consider a defect."

Dooley hugged the photo to his chest and then looked at it again. He set it down and turned his arm over, tracing his finger over one of the black tattoos etched on his forearm.

"What does it mean?"

Dooley looked up at me. "It's the first tattoo I ever got. I was pretty young. Still wanted to seem tough. I choose the symbol for mother in Japanese." He gave a short laugh. "Got my street cred without the kids thinking I was weak. Funny how none of that matters now. Hasn't mattered in a long time."

"I wish he could have told me something about her. I wish he could have been the one to tell me about all of this." He brought his arms up in a sweeping gesture and just as quickly shook off his reaction before reaching back into the chest for the journal. "This must have been his." Dooley untied the strap of fabric from the journal and laid it to the side. He flipped through the pages.

Something about the fabric caught my eye. I reached out and ran the white silk strap through my fingers, feeling its unnatural softness. Its edges were frayed, but otherwise it was still brilliantly white and clean despite having been used to hold the tattered journal together.

Dooley tossed the journal back into the chest. "He wrote nothing about me or my mother."

The fuzziness from the mead was beginning to wear off. I crawled around the chest and closed the distance between us once more. I tucked the curly locks of his hair behind his ear and placed my finger under his chin.

"Some stories and memories we keep locked deep inside us, Dooley. You should know that more than anyone. He had you in front of him. He was not expecting to die on the day that he did. Perhaps he had planned to tell you himself one day."

Dooley closed his hand around the amulet and slowly pulled me towards him. I wondered for a moment if his contact with the amulet would put either of us in danger, but when his mouth closed around mine all my fear faded away. I fell down beside him on the blankets and he wrapped his strong hand around the top of my thigh, pulling my leg over the top of his. I snaked my arms up his chest and around the back of his neck, pulling his tongue deeper into my mouth. His hand caressed the top of my thigh and found the crease there. He trailed his finger across, gently stroking me as the frenzy of energy built within me.

I moved my hands down his spine and grasped at the small of his back, pulling on his shirt with frustration at the fact that I could not get any closer to his flesh with all these clothes between us. I kicked my leg back over him and sat up to try and loosen his shirt. As I did, the chest behind us fell, and we both froze in place as a mechanical ticking came from inside it.

"What is that?" we both said simultaneously.

I turned the chest over and pulled out the journal. The copper contraption was the source of the noise. I reached inside and brought it out. The machine consisted of a copper rod which had a glass bulb at each end. Inside one bulb were cogs and wheels that were spinning at a pace so fast you only saw them as a blur. The other bulb was empty.

"It must have turned on when I knocked it over," I said.

A small ripple of energy burst through the air, and my knees weakened. My hands clasped around the copper rod, and I was unable to let go. I felt it pulling the magic from me just as the amulet heated up against my chest. The red stone pulsed brightly.

"What are you doing?" Franca shouted from the doorway.

The sound of the contraption had reached a fevered pitch along with the loud, low humming that came from the amulet around my neck. Franca grasped her hands over mine and pulled at the contraption pitching us both over to the ground. The machine rolled to the side, and the bulb which had once been empty was now full of the same coppery liquid magic we had stolen from the clinic. I collapsed to the ground, and the humming of the amulet continued until my strength returned.

I turned and saw Franca sitting on the stone floor in shock. Dooley rushed to my side and helped me sit upright.

"Are you okay? I'm so sorry. You were right. Brokk must have been one of these Soulstealers you were talking about. That looks like the same stuff Franca got from the clinic. Doesn't it?"

Franca nodded. "Yes, but that is not the only thing that can take magic."

"What do you mean?" Dooley picked up the contraption and held the bulb to the light of the fire. The coppery substance swam around inside.

"That amulet. It just stole magic from me to replace what you were missing. We are going to need the shaman to examine that before we leave tomorrow," said Franca.

The amulet rested silently against my chest.

"Stole magic from you? Are you okay?" I asked. Franca winced slightly as I tried to help her up.

"Yes, just don't touch that thing again. Stick it back in that chest, lock it up, and we'll see if we can figure this out in the morning." Before I could say anything more she hurried from the room.

"I think you may have scared her a little," said Dooley.

"Damn it." I wanted to tear off the amulet and throw it into the fireplace. But I knew the last time I had been without it I had almost died. And I wasn't planning on dying today.

"Dooley, I think that was the contraption my Uncle was talking about." The conversation I had with Kali about Brokk came back to my mind. "He was a Builder. That's what my friend Kali said. He must have invented that himself."

"Invented for who? Maybe he was stealing the magic of Dell'Aria. Your Uncle said it himself, you couldn't use that thing too often or you will die." He pushed the base of his hands into his forehead and shook his head. "Just come to bed. Franca will help in the morning. I'm sure everything will be fine."

Dooley leaned back on his elbow and patted the blankets beside him. The glow of the fire behind him cast him in shadow, and I gazed down the outline of the length of him before shaking myself out of reverie.

"Sure, I just need to get some air. I'll be right back."

⊷⊷

I walked towards the entrance we had come from, turning right, left, right down the hall and back towards the outside. The sun was gone, but the stars twinkled. One of the several moons of the Realms shone brightly. Night was never as dark here as it was on Earth. I blinked and rubbed my eyes as an orb of light came through the trees in front of me. As it got closer I saw that it was not an orb of light, but a man. King Aric.

I instinctively dropped to my knees. He walked slowly through the brush and came to stand in front of me. His wings covered his back, and he was dressed all in white, wearing the same shirt and pants I had seen him in back on that first night in his chambers.

"Please stand, Valora. You don't need to give praise to me."

I took one shaky step and then another as I stood to face him. My small wings fluttered. "How is it that you are here?"

I took another step forward to place a hand on his chest as if I was being drawn to him by some unknown force. My hand passed through the illusion.

"I am in here." He placed his finger to his temple. "In your mind, Valora. And I suspect in your heart. For you certainly have found a place in mine."

"So how is it that I can see you?"

Aric tugged at a chain at his neck and pulled from his shirt an amulet identical to the one I had around mine.

"Through these. Magic that binds you to me. We are never far apart with these."

"But why is it that when I take it off I get sick?"

Aric bowed his head. "I had hoped you would not find that out. You see, you were affected by the very first wave of the Blight. When I found you with your mother, I knew you, too, were infected. I had the priests forge these amulets from the metals found deep within Dell'Aria. They blessed them with a binding ritual. It was the only way I could make sure you stayed well. The copper draws magic to you, Valora. So you are safe."

"Why can't you do this for everyone else? Why can't all the people of Dell'Aria be saved?" For the first time the amulet, which once held romantic notions attached to it, suddenly felt heavy.

"The metal and stones in these amulets are like no other, Valora. It is a limited resource. Not enough for anyone else." His arm reached out, and a ghostly caress passed over my skin. "The bond between us is strengthening. Before I could only come to you through the mirror. But now you are able to see me even without it."

"But why me?" I was pleading with him now. None of it made sense, and I desperately wanted it to. I wanted everything to intersect. "There are dozens of fae more worthy of your affections. And what of the Queen?"

"This is what I like about you. Even though you have been kicked down all your life, even though no one has ever considered you their equal, let alone a threat, you still strive to live within the boundaries of societal rules. Why is it that you do this, Valora?"

He looked at me with curiosity. He honestly did not know. "Everything I have ever done in my life I have done to please you my King." And the moment I said it, I knew it was true. Whether or not it was right, it was true. The only time it had not been so was moments ago in the bed chamber with Dooley.

"That was what I had thought. There is no one with as much devotion towards me as you. You may not believe it, but I have spent my days watching you through the halls of the Court just as you watched me, Valora. But it was those rules of society that prevented me from showing my love to you. The Queen has abandoned her people. She has abandoned all of Dell'Aria. Come back to me, Valora. Come back and we will perform the ceremony to make you Queen. No one will ever look down on you again."

Aric's image wavered. "The Guard approaches. Make it back here, Valora. Come back to me, and we shall be united forever. And you will bring Dell'Aria back to its former glory." His image faded.

"But wait, I need to tell you what happened on Earth. There is something important you need to know about the Soulstealers."

The image disappeared as soon as it had come, and all I was left with was the luminous glow of the moons and the offer from my King to become Queen of Dell'Aria.

CHAPTER TWENTY-FIVE

I passed through the dwarven halls deep within Mount Elbrus with impunity. I had to thank Franca for that. I would never have thought it possible considering all I had learned growing up. From the time I was a small child chasing the sprites down the hallways of the Court I had been taught that we were only safe from the other creatures of the Realms because they were in Underworld and we were in Overworld. Otherwise they would like nothing more than to take everything from us.

It is a funny thing about all that you are taught as a child. As you grow older you question everything except those things that have become the solid foundation for who you are. You can question everyone else's ideals and everyone else's reasons for being. But question your own, and you risk shaking your very foundation, all that you are and all that you have come to be.

Foundation. The word struck me with a sudden thought. I raced the rest of the way back to the room Dooley and I shared. He had fallen asleep. "Dooley, I need you to get up. It's important."

Dooley opened his eyes sleepily and looked up at me with the casual air that abounded around him. Even when I was keyed up to a screaming pitch, his affect slowed me down to the point where my thoughts formed cohesively. "What do you need?"

"I need you to take me back again. There is a memory I need to see. I need to see it again to know if what I am remembering is real. It was from when I was a child."

It took Dooley a few minutes to set up his tools. His actions would have made me squirm a week ago. The thought of being so close to magic and to the thing that had caused my mother's death had always kept me from the practice. But now all I wanted him to do was hurry.

He set a pot on the hook above the fire. The black tar liquid inside quickly came to a boil.

"That pot. What do you suppose it is made from?"

Dooley gave the brew another stir and flicked the side with his finger, returning a dull thud. "Some kind of iron."

"And you are able to handle it without a problem?"

"Yes. Oh, that's right, the iron burns you. But I am half fae, and it doesn't do anything to me. Why?" He went back to stirring the pot and motioned me over towards him.

"Like I said, I know very little about half fae. It is interesting though. Do you want me to sit or lie down?"

"No, you'll need to stand. If we're going to access a memory deep in your past then I'll need to trace the distant symbol on you. You'll need to be patient with me. There's a lot involved in this ritual."

I nodded. Looking into Dooley's eyes I was ashamed to hide from him my meeting with Aric, but before I decided anything there was something I needed to know, one last thing that I needed to confirm. I hoped this memory would do it.

Dooley drew the curtain across the entrance to our room. He crossed over to me and swept off his white t-shirt in one smooth movement, tossing it to the side. My eyes travelled down his chest, over his hard muscles to the lines at the bottom of his stomach that led to other things below his waist. His khaki green shorts were loose and held by a thick brown leather belt. It was hard not to imagine taking my knife to that belt, which would be the only way I could loosen it since it had an iron buckle.

Dooley took the pot from the fire and set it near my feet. "You trust me." His words were both a question and a statement at the same time.

"Yes."

He circled around behind me, and I took in a sharp breath as he untied the top lace that held my leather bodice firmly together. One finger at a time he pulled the lace through each eyelet until the only thing holding it to me was my hands which had instinctively come up to hold the last of my modesty firmly in place. My mind and my actions were not yet on the same page.

Dooley put his hands on top of my shoulders and traced down the length of my arms until his hands came to rest over mine. He took my hands in his and placed my arms at my side. The bodice dropped to the floor at my feet, and the warmth of the fire licked at my bare breasts.

With his finger he began to trace the symbols. My back acted as his canvas. Each of his touches sent pulses through me, and I could feel his magic beginning to take hold. He crossed in front of me and began to paint symbols along my chest, being careful to trace around the fullness of my breasts which were aching for his touch.

Dooley bent down on one knee before me and finished tracing the last of the symbols along my waistline. The fire reflected in his dark brown eyes with a promise that there would be time for us to quench the fire burning deep within both of us, but not now.

He stood fully erect and wrapped his arms around me, holding me tightly. The paint on my chest transferred to him and acted as glue between us. He bent forward, touching his forehead to mine. I closed my eyes and allowed myself to be drawn into his magic. Dooley no longer needed to move his hands over me to gain access to my thoughts. I had opened myself up and allowed him in freely. I only needed him to be the guide and bring me to the moment in time I was trying to recall, a moment for which I had lost the details I needed.

I remember the first time I saw him. He was only a prince then. King Aric's father, King Alastair, had announced the birth of his son on his eighteenth cycle then kept him in hiding until he had been taught the refinements of the Court and could present himself as the next King of Dell'Aria should.

I was only in my eighth cycle, considered a child among the fae who typically lived one hundred or more cycles. I stared out of my bedroom window down into the main Courtyard. My father was right hand to King Alastair, and our family lived within the Court walls. But it wasn't my first view of King Aric that day that would leave a lasting impression. It was that evening.

Mother was sound asleep, and father was missing from bed. I heard a scuffle in the courtyard below my window. I crawled from the downy blankets and peeked out the window. The King's Guard had a prisoner in iron chains, and they were bringing him towards the entry of the King's Keep. The prisoner struggled against his captors. The night flowers were beginning to bloom and a small sneeze escaped me. From below the prisoner looked up to my window.

In the dim light I saw the small lightning shaped eyebrows of King Aric, only a prince then. Mother explained that Aric was sick with a fever and had run off, however, there was one other thing that went unexplained. A small detail which until now had been erased from my mind. As the iron chains touched his flesh they did not burn. The weight of the chains was heavy no doubt, and the fae guards who struggled against him wore full protective gear, but the cold metal sat against his flesh and did nothing to him.

As I came back to reality I did so with complacency. If I came back all at once I would have to face the truth — many truths. I opened my eyes at the same time as Dooley. He still had his arms held tightly around me.

"So he's like me? He is half-fae? How is it possible that he is your King?"

"I don't know. But I do know that it means he has lied to me and to all the fae of Dell'Aria."

I wondered at how much my father must know and how deeply he had knit his life and mine into this disastrous scandal.

"But you don't know the worst of it," I said.

I detailed to Dooley all that had come to pass between Aric and me in the last week and the intensity of feelings I thought I had for him my whole life. And lastly I told him of the vision I had of Aric just moments ago. Dooley hung his head. I feared he would pull away from me not only in that moment, but forever.

"Please, please say something to me," I begged.

He raised his head. There was no sadness in his eyes, only a ferocity I had never seen in Dooley before.

"You seem to fear that I will leave you."

"Why wouldn't you? I have basically told you that I have feelings for Aric, and that we have been together, in a way.

And, of course, that I entertained the idea of being his Queen." I choked on my final comment. "I was weak."

Dooley was the one to place a finger under my chin this time. "You forget. I have been inside your mind in this and other moments. I know that even though you've been drawn towards the King, he doesn't lie in your heart."

He drew a finger down my chest and touched the amulet that hung between my breasts. "This is the way he has gained access to your mind."

Dooley took the amulet, moved it so it was hanging down my back and proceeded to place his lips where it had been. He kissed at the space between my breasts which was free of the Reiki markings and moved his lips around the flesh of my left breast to place gentle kisses over my heart as it pounded in my chest. He reached down and unlatched the iron buckle making his desire all the more apparent as he stood naked before me. But he was calm in that moment and fully focused on the memory he had shared with me. He drew back and placed his finger over the moistened flesh that covered my heart.

"This place is only for me."

I let Dooley lay me back onto the blankets which were warm from the heat of the fire. "It's too hot," I muttered feeling half in and out of consciousness.

Dooley left my side for a moment and returned with a bucket of water and a cloth. He sat me up and pulled me to sit between his legs.

"I'll cool you down."

He reached the cloth into the bucket and wiped away the markings. The water was ice cold, and by the time he was finished with my back I shivered slightly. But it felt good.

"Turn around."

I did as he bade me and gathered my knees between his

legs. He washed away the paint on my chest, brushing the washcloth over my breasts. The chill of the water sent a rush into my nipples pulling them taut and hard as he continued to rub them back and forth with the damp cloth. The longing in me peaked to a point of no return.

I could smell his longing as I leaned closer into him, a strong musky scent that told me he was ready for me. He reached out and cupped my breast, using his thumb to pinch at my nipple, and waves of pleasure coursed through me. I wanted him just as he wanted me.

I wrapped my legs around his waist and came down upon the erect length of him which slid into me as smooth as silk. We unleashed the intensity of our feelings and quickly let the magic that had been flowing all around us channel into our sex. I lost touch with my surroundings as I clutched his body and we rode each other deeper and deeper. My wings beat the air at a stallion's pace, and slowly we rose from the floor. We hovered above the ground as I came to my peak. My body shuddered, and he grasped me tighter as he also released the torrent from within.

We slowly glided back to the ground and, wrapped in the embrace of my new lover, I fell asleep knowing that in the morning I would not be alone. I said a silent prayer to my mother's spirit to let her know that the one thing she had always hoped for me had finally happened. I was sublimely happy.

CHAPTER TWENTY-SIX

The morning came all too quickly. I pulled tighter against Dooley and listened to the beating of his heart.

Franca burst into the room. "Hey we need to get go...whoa. You two need a little bit more time to get ready, since you also need to get dressed."

She waggled her finger at me as Dooley had just begun to open his eyes. "You have very little time before that elixir wears off, and we will need to take advantage of all the daylight we have if we are going to make it to the nearest Selkie colony before dark." Franca gave me a wink as she turned around and closed the curtain behind her.

I brushed my fingers through Dooley's hair, which was much longer than my own, and tucked it behind his ear. "I suppose I have you to thank for keeping me warm last night."

For so many cycles I had dreamt about waking in the arms of the King. I had never thought any other man would be able to take his place in my heart. Dooley had surprised me at every turn.

Dooley stared at me, and his eyes softened. His gaze

went from Brokk's chest and back to me.

"I know that contraption in the chest is some kind of proof that Brokk is involved. But how?" he asked without expecting me to answer.

The press of the day was again upon us. I got up and gathered my clothes from where they lay in piles around the room. I slipped my arms through the sleeves of my bodice and turned my back to Dooley. He deftly laced the ties into place. *What that man could do with his fingers.*

Dooley finished lacing the ties and pulled the top knot tightly as he secured the bow in place.

"There are still his journal entries. They must hold the key to something," he suggested.

The dwarves hosted breakfast for us outside their caverns in deference to me. Franca and I huddled together at one of the tables while Dooley and Ralph played a game of catch with Kit.

I had filled Franca in on my midnight visitor and my midnight romping with Dooley. "What am I supposed to do?"

I watched as Kit threw the ball to Dooley and he pretended to collapse on the ground at her display of strength. I couldn't help but let my eyes linger on the patterns traced up and down his arms, the same arms that had held me tight the night before.

"It seems like you have already made your decision."

I turned back to Franca and she gave me a small wink.

"But Franca, Aric asked me to be his Queen and told me that these amulets link us and are the only reason I am alive. I can't just ignore that."

"I have been meaning to talk to you about that. We need to have you see the shaman before we leave. Maybe he can help us with this."

Franca lifted the amulet from my chest and let it fall with a thud. The longer I had the amulet the heavier it became.

I followed Franca over to a small tent from which the scent of fire, earth, and old magic emanated. As we got closer I stopped, unable to will myself beyond the threshold. Franca ducked in then ducked back out again when she realized I hadn't followed her inside.

"What's wrong? The shaman is inside. We need to go to him, he does not come to us."

"There's something dark inside there, Franca. I would say evil but I don't want to insult you."

"Too late. Come on in, girl. I promise not to bite yee." The head of a wizened old dwarf had popped out of the tent behind Franca. He had a beard that was longer than he was tall. He wore an elaborate headdress of sorts that seemed to function both as an ornament and also as the place he stored his various herbs and potions. It was stuffed with springs of elderberry and beesroot amongst other things. I recognized the plant life that Franca had collected when she was on Earth. There was a slight clinking as the jars atop his head swayed slightly. He pulled his head back inside.

"Will you get in here?" demanded Franca.

"He said he promised not to bite. He didn't say he didn't bite."

"A promise is a promise." Franca grinned. "Look, the shaman is very old, Valora. His magic is tied directly into the powers that flow through all the Realms. Do you want his advice or not?"

I nodded and passed through the heavy burlap flap that covered the entrance to the tent, being careful to pull my wings close to my body so that I would not snag them against anything lurking within the darkness inside. As I entered I saw a small fire smoldering brightly. A hole at the top of the tent let the smoke funnel out of the top, but even so, it was so thick it did not allow for much light.

I tried to stifle a cough but I couldn't help it. "How do you breathe in here?" I instinctively began to wave my hand in front of my face.

"Don't disturb the veil. How do you expect me to see if you mess about in it like that?" the shaman croaked. His voice warbled like a broken record.

I leaned over to Franca as the shaman rocked back and forth in some kind of meditation. "Do you want to explain to me what is going on here?"

"He is connecting to his...um...guide through the spiritual world in order to find some answers for you."

"You hesitated, why did you hesitate?"

"Well, when you said you felt something evil in this tent you were partially right. The shaman's guide is a demon."

Before I could bolt out of the tent the shaman reached across the fire and grabbed hold of the amulet around my neck. His eyes flew open and stared at me with a red glow. The corner of his mouth turned up in a wry half-smile. "Clever, clever magic we have here. Damned if you do, damned if you don't. But damned, that's for certain." There was a slight twitch of the shaman's face. "The shaman tells me I shouldn't scare you. Sorry, it comes naturally." He ran his finger over the amulet.

"Can you tell me more about it?" I asked.

He continued to trace his finger around the center stone. An aching pulsed between my legs where Dooley had so recently been.

"Oops. Sorry about that."

Looking at the demon through the shaman's eyes I seriously doubted that.

"Seems like this is the work of another demon. Someone has employed a demon to enchant this amulet. You already know that you need to wear it in order to stay alive, and likely you know that you are tied to another through it."

"But how do I break the enchantment?"

"Sorry, that I cannot tell you. That would be something known only to the demon that created it and the one who employed him."

I sat back, and the amulet slipped from the shaman's fingers. "It's been a real pleasure, Valora. I shall look forward to seeing you again, for I am certain there will come a time when you will seek out my counsel in the future." Another smile, and the eyes of the shaman returned to normal.

"I trust he was able to tell you what you needed. I am sorry but his methods are not always very polite. He is a demon, you know," said the shaman.

"How is it that you are mixed up with a demon?" I asked.

"My dear, not all demons are bad. Just as not all fae are good. I do not ask the demon to perform black magic for me. But someone certainly had a demon perform black magic when they created that amulet you are wearing. I knew it the second Franca told me of the binding effect it had over you. No, the only power that comes from is dark magic, and the only ones that know anything about that are demons and those that call upon them."

"But Aric was trying to save me. Perhaps that was the only way."

"Didn't he also tell you that it was forged by priests?"

I sat back as far from the fire as I could without exiting the tent. Everything inside me wanted to run away from this place and all the other things I had learned in the last few days, but to do so would also mean running away from Dooley. He was the only thing I was certain about at this moment.

The shaman sat back and plucked some beesroot from his headdress then packed it into a pipe. "Stay for a smoke?"

"Sorry, no." I started to crawl backwards out of the tent, but Franca snatched my ankle.

"We don't want to be rude." The way Franca looked at me I knew there was no use refusing. The only way I was going to get out of this dwarf demon shaman's tent was to smoke a pipe.

"Sure."

I gave a hesitant nod and reached out to take the pipe offered to me by the shaman. He lit the pipe, and I took a deep inhale. Beesroot was produced by winged creatures that liked to burrow into the sides of the mountains to make their homes. They coated the tunnels they made with pollen which at times would become so thick you could pull at it taking the root from the shaft.

The dwarves were known to harvest it for its sweetness and for the root which could be smoked. I leaned back and let the wave of beesroot waft through me. It had certain numbing properties which I was all too keen to take advantage of in this moment. It was something I had done a few times after losing my mother and so many others during the Blight.

Wave. Blight. I sat up and studied the pipe in my hand. At one end was the bulbous bowl of the pipe set atop the stem. "Franca, what does this remind you of?" I stood the pipe on end.

"A pipe that is about to lose its beesroot?" Franca giggled. The beesroot had definitely had a quick effect on her.

"No, the contraption. Brokk's machine. I don't know how I missed it before. I need a writing instrument. A pen, something." Franca looked at the shaman's hat and pulled a quill from it, quickly handing it to me. I took out Brokk's journal from where I had stashed it in my satchel.

"Does Dooley know you have that?" asked Franca.

"I was studying it. I just need to find a blank page." I flipped through the book and stopped. Looking back at me was exactly the picture in my mind.

"This is it. This is what is causing the Blight!" I exclaimed. I handed the book to Franca and set my pipe down. "I need some air."

Again the walls closed in on me. I crawled out of the tent on all fours and saw Dooley making his way towards me.

His calm demeanor turned to concern as he rushed to my side and helped me to my feet.

"What is wrong? What happened?"

Franca burst out of the tent after me holding the journal. "Valora, what is this picture of?"

"It's the great temple of Dell'Aria."

CHAPTER TWENTY-SEVEN

"You're crushing my wings." Dooley and Franca had immediately sandwiched me between them as much to give me their support as to support me since my legs had suddenly turned to jelly.

Franca spoke first. "How could this possibly happen under the nose of the King?"

The picture showed it all. Hidden in plain view. The top of the tower was a huge copper antenna. And somehow Brokk had been involved in making a contraption that turned it into a divining rod for all the magic of the fae of Dell'Aria.

"That's just it, Franca. I don't think it is. I think he must know about it. I am not sure to what extent he is involved. Maybe the Royal Guard is forcing him to comply. But he must know somehow."

I told them about my friend Kali and how the last time I had seen her she was traversing between the tunnels that led from the great temple to the Court.

"Maybe Aric was trying to divine some magic to supplant his own since he is only half-fae. I don't know. I can't imagine he would ever do anything to hurt anyone."

"Really, Valora?" Franca pointed to the amulet.

"I can't explain it." *Not to her or even to myself.* "I grew up with him. For many cycles he was the only other fae in the Court who even approached my age. And he has never been anything but kind to me and my family. He has never shown me an ounce of anything but good intentions."

I ceased arguing my point to Franca and turned to look at Dooley. He was staring at his feet, a pained expression on his face.

"Dooley, you must be happy. This clears Brokk's name. I am sure he was only doing what his King asked of him. He was loyal."

He cut me off before I could say anything more. "I don't need you to tell me Brokk was loyal. We really need to get going if we're going to bring Kit back to the Selkies. I'm not sure how much longer she'll last without an infusion of the waters."

I watched Dooley stalk off towards Ralph and Kit. *Why would he be upset? I thought this was what he wanted.*

We quickly packed up our supplies and said our good-byes to the dwarves of Mount Elbrus. The clan leader shouted out to Franca as we left, "Don't be too long, my little collector." Franca smiled and waved.

"Wow, you weren't kidding. He really has a thing for you."

"Shut up. Speaking of, have you figured out how you are going to fix that tremendous blunder of yours from earlier?"

"What blunder? What are you talking about?"

"You can't tell Dooley's upset?"

"Yes, but I don't know why." It seemed I wasn't able to read any of the men in my life at the moment.

Dooley walked, his hands thrust deep into his pockets,

alongside Ralph and Kit who sat atop one of the squat beasts of burden that the dwarves used in their mountain mines.

"Are you kidding? Let's back this up. He knows you are connected to Aric with this amulet and that you have a thing for him. And now you are defending Aric despite all the evidence. Exactly what does that mean for Dooley, Valora? Will he ever win your heart so long as you are still attached to Aric?"

"That's just it isn't it? I will always be attached to him through this thing."

I wanted nothing more than to pull the amulet from my neck and toss it to the ground. But it only took the memory of all the magic draining from my body to stop me.

"I can't rid myself of my connection to Aric even if I wanted to. And Dooley is going to have to deal with it because I can't change that."

I kicked at the dry dirt as our caravan continued up the dried river gorge we had been told to follow.

"He hears exactly the same things I do, Valora. You said 'even if I wanted to.' The point is not whether or not you can rid yourself of the connection to Aric. What will matter to Dooley is that you want to be rid of it."

We continued to walk in silence as I muddled over Franca's words. I had yearned for so many years to be important in the eyes of the King. I wanted him to see me as valuable as the other fae. And now I was not only important to him, I was his confidant, his sole supporter amongst my company, and personally requested to be his Queen. Not to mention I was already bound to him.

I hadn't been given a choice in that matter.

"I am going to catch up with Dooley, okay?"

Franca gave me a wink as she took the reins of the other beast from my hands. I hurried to reach Dooley and the others.

"Valora!" Kit squealed. "Isn't he fuzzy soft?" She nestled her face into the woolly brown beast who gave a grunt in response. The animals were very docile and happy to walk in any direction you pointed them.

"Yes, he is. It seems you have found yourself a good pet there."

Kit squealed again. "Oh, can we keep him? Can he come with us?"

I didn't know how much Ralph had or had not told his daughter about her future home. Ralph raised his arms professing ignorance. He had just as little idea about what he was getting into as Kit did. He only came because he knew that was what she needed to survive.

I paused a little too long in my response. I looked over at Dooley as he turned his head from the dirt he was kicking up to look at me and then to Kit. He put on a smile, which at first didn't reach his eyes, but the excitement on Kit's face was infectious.

"Maybe Valora can tell you a story about your new home." Dooley wrapped his hand in mine and gave it a quick squeeze of encouragement.

I tried my best to charm Kit with all the magical tales I had heard about my Selkie brethren, the fae of the waters, leaving out as many of the scary parts as possible. I honestly was not sure if they would accept Kit into their world. But I had made Ralph and Kit a promise that I was going to try to help them, and I had no intention of breaking my word.

CHAPTER TWENTY-EIGHT

By mid-day we had reached the end of the dried river gorge and had come to the beginning of the estuary. Beyond the banks we could see the seas and rivers that fed into the estuary providing a mix of sea water and fresh water that stirred up into a deep torrent of water.

"How do we let them know we're here?" asked Dooley.

"Easy, we knock. Kit, put your finger to the water," I said.

Kit turned to her father, asking for permission. Ralph nodded and stood by his daughter as she knelt down to place a finger to the murky edge of the water. As she did, a pulse flew over the surface. Kit jerked her finger back and held it to her chest.

"Are you okay?" Ralph pried Kit's finger from her chest and inspected it. "There's nothing, hon. It's okay."

"I felt them, Daddy. All swimming around down there."

The answer to our knock was not far behind. A half dozen selkies breached the surface with their heads scouting about then quickly swam under again. The surface of the water burbled as a small, ornate black carriage rose up and rolled out of the water to rest in front of us on the banks. There was no driver to the carriage and no creatures to pull it. It simply moved on its own. The door swung open, and for the second time I saw the Queen of the Selkies. The first time I had seen her had been in a drawing in a book I studied at Court.

"Your majesty." I gave a respectful bow. The selkie were our brethren, but they're known by our kind to be much more vicious than we are. Nevertheless, the Queen that stood before me had entered into the pact with King Aric to siphon off some of their magic to prevent Dell'Aria from falling down into her colony.

"How is it that you are here? We are at least a day's journey from Dell'Aria," I asked.

The Queen turned and I watched as her lower half morphed from fins to legs. She stepped down from the carriage to stand before us.

"You Overworld fae should really walk around down here more to learn about your own world. Silly child, all of the Water Realms are connected. Now, what is it you are doing here?"

Her presence commanded attention. Her eyes and hair were a sparkling deep sea-green. I had no doubt that she had used them many times to enchant. I was already feeling her pull. The only thing that broke the spell was the spiked teeth I saw peeking out from beneath her red half-smile.

"Elemi?"

The Queen turned as Ralph called out to her. She walked towards him, her pointed gaze going from Ralph to Kit. She stopped in front of them.

"I cannot possibly explain to you all you want to know," said the Queen.

Ralph's jaw set firm, and he stared her directly in the eyes as he said, "Kit, meet your mother."

Queen Elemi tore her gaze from Ralph. She smoothed her hand over Kit's head. As she did so, Kit's hair turned as brilliant blue as her eyes.

Kit grabbed fistfuls of her hair. "Wow, I have blue hair! Valora, I have blue hair."

"Blue as the ocean, little one. I have much to talk about with all of you."

Franca chimed in, "I can watch Kit for a while if you want to talk to Ralph." The Queen gave a slight nod and Franca motioned the girl to sit where we had laid all our supplies. "How about I put that pretty blue hair of yours into braids like mine?"

Kit squealed with delight and ran over to Franca. I had never seen her have so much energy.

∂∘∾

"Why don't we make some lunch?" asked Doolcy.

"Are you speaking to me now?" I foisted my hands onto my hips with as much attitude as I could muster.

Dooley gave a chuckle. "I never stopped speaking to you, Valora. You give yourself so much punishment I would never need to add to it."

"But Franca said — and Aric — and..." Dooley put a finger to my lips. "Then why were you upset before?"

"Even the most confident man can be a little jealous sometimes. But I promise I will try not to forget I have been in here." He pointed to my heart. "And here." He pointed to my temple.

"And other places." I winked as I placed my arms around his waist and gave him a squeeze. I tilted my head down. "But I would be lying if I said I didn't also think of Aric."

"Of course you do." He lifted the amulet. "And we will find a way around that eventually."

I nodded and sank into his embrace. How could I explain to him that I thought my feelings extended beyond the amulet? I wanted to contact Aric again. I needed him to know what we had discovered and have him give me a rational explanation for how he was involved.

That night we set up camp on the banks of the estuary. Ralph and Elemi had spent a majority of the day talking, and we had eaten up all our daylight. Franca began to cook a rich stew over the fire, and Ralph and Elemi rejoined us. Ralph sat down, but Elemi did not.

"Fae of Dell'Aria, we must speak." The Queen's eyes shot daggers at me. If I had real wings, I would have used them to fly far away from that look.

Dooley perked up. "Hey, why don't I come along?"

"No. We talk alone," she said without moving her eyes from me.

I pushed myself to standing. "It's okay, Dooley. Sure, let's talk."

The Queen strode over to her carriage and opened the door. "After you."

I stepped into the carriage which had two bench seats facing one another. It was very similar to the carriage I had found myself in with Aric when he took my first kiss from me. But I had a feeling this ride would be a lot less pleasant.

"We will be back by morning." Before anyone could react, the Queen stepped in and shut the door behind her. The carriage jerked forward. Elemi handed me a vial of deep blue liquid. "Drink this or you will drown before we get to where we are going."

I quickly downed the potion as water poured in from all sides of the carriage. It swirled around my feet and rose higher and higher as the carriage sank deeper into the water. Instinctively I tried to keep my head above the water level, and panic set in as only an inch of space remained for my lips to suck what was left of the air. A hand shot out and pulled me under.

Through the blue water, the Queen leveled her stare at me. Her hands quickly slid under my ear and placed something that allowed me to hear her speak in the murky depths.

"Just breathe, for the sake of the Goddess. I didn't give you that elixir so that you could waste it on holding your breath and cause your own death."

My lungs gave up, and I sucked in the icy cold water surrounding me. I was instantly at peace. Surely I had died. Bubbles floated around my field of vision. I surrendered to another power. All that was left for me to do was to go on this ride.

"Snap out of it. I brought you down here so we could talk. You are a fae of Dell'Aria, are you not?"

"Yes." I was surprised to hear my own voice come back to my ears as clear under water as it did above.

"Then it is true. Aric has sent spies to seek out my secrets. I thought we had an understanding." Elemi broke the distance between us and placed a hand next to each side of me on the bench.

"You tell your King that if he wants to continue to take my magic, then he will back off. Now that Kit is here. I will not let her go. I will let all of Dell'Aria fall into my home of Mavrovo without a second thought."

I was confused. "But I was the one who brought Kit to you. I was hoping that you would take her in. She was dying."

"Dying? No, that was not the arrangement. Your King was to supply her with the magic she needed to stay alive and well. There was going to be no harm brought to her."

I explained to the Queen all I knew about the clinic, Brokk, and the Blight that was affecting Dell'Aria.

She seemed to take the news incredibly well. "So you have kept her alive. I am forever grateful. I can only hope that Ralph can forgive me. It is difficult to explain to a human how things work in the Realms."

I gingerly placed my hand over hers. "If there is anything that I have learned in the last few days, it is that, if someone loves you, they work to come to an understanding with you. I am sure if you keep talking to Ralph he will understand. Why is it that you hid Kit on Earth all these years?"

The Queen sank back into her side of the carriage. A small brightly colored Basslet swam inside. It had a brilliant purple head and body that contrasted with its yellow tailfin. It took a small bow for the Queen and continued on its way through the other side of the carriage.

"My Kit meant everything to me. The story itself is too long to tell in the space of time we have. But trust me when I say that, had I not been persuaded to do so, heavily persuaded, I would have claimed her for my own true daughter and heiress the second she was born. As you know, half-breeds are not allowed in positions of power. I knew she was one who could have hid her human side, just as the King does, but he forced me to give her up. He said he would expose my dalliances and threaten my crown if I did not do as he asked. I only agreed to his demands if he would keep her safe. I could only take his word on it. And now I find out that he has lied all along." She twisted in her seat as if she was looking for someone or something to take a swing at.

I swallowed hard. "You are certain this is all the doing of King Aric?"

The Queen noticed the amulet around my neck. "You carry a piece of him with you? I sent an ogre after this." She pulled down harder on the amulet than was comfortable for me. "This would have kept Kit safe. This would have kept her whole. But instead you use it as a whore would. A whore!" She pulled down harder on the amulet, but the chain held. "Don't think I can't see right through you. That man up there is foolish if he thinks he will ever truly possess your heart."

I kicked out at the Queen and put her off balance as I struggled to pull myself out the window.

The weight of the water threatened to drag me down. I turned to see if the Queen was coming after me, but the carriage was lifeless and still. I stopped fighting and let my body gradually float to the surface. As I came up I saw Dooley waist deep and soaked to the bone. He rushed towards me and put both his arms under my shoulders as he pulled me back to shore.

Franca and the others came to my side. "Are you okay? What the hell happened?"

Before I could answer, the Queen surfaced from the water and walked calmly up the shore. "Ralph? Kit? Are the two of you ready to go?"

Ralph turned to me.

"I'm fine. You know Kit needs to be home, Ralph. You should go," I said.

Ralph leaned in and placed a kiss on my forehead. "I really appreciate you keeping your promise. And I hope you find what you're looking for."

Ralph and Kit walked towards the Queen who stared down at me. "Being Queen is a lot harder than you know, fae. Think hard on that decision."

I reached up behind my ear to pluck the charm which apparently allowed the Queen access to my thoughts and tossed it towards her.

"Thanks for the advice."

The Queen pulled another vial of the blue elixir from her robe for Ralph. Elemi spread her arms around Ralph and Kit and brought them close to her as she dove into the water with a splash. The surface of the water returned to its normal motions, controlled by the tides and the breeze.

Something inside me split in that moment. Even I wasn't sure what it was. I had hoped that my tears would be covered by the fact that I was soaked from head to toe, but the harsh sobs that jagged out of my throat in an untimely rhythm made it all too obvious. For a while I was thrown back to those days at my mother's tomb when my crying was all I heard for days on end. Then there was no one to hold me, but now Dooley would not let go.

He drafted Franca into his employ, casting her about for blankets and water and other things he thought might soothe me. But when one doesn't even know why one is crying, the only thing that will help is the crying.

༷

At some point I must have fallen asleep because I awoke with Dooley curled around my back, his arm heavy across my side. The fire crackled faintly, and Franca was curled up not too far from the both of us.

My muscles ached from being curled into a fetal position most of the night. I eased away from Dooley and tried to walk the cramps out of my legs. My wings flitted in a sudden breeze that came from the trees, and I turned to see a familiar glow. The amulet pulsed, and I knew what was coming. My King was coming.

Aric stepped from the tree line. His form more clear now than it was when I saw him before. His white blond hair billowed about his wings as his steely blue eyes cut across the darkness and pierced straight through me. He stood before me and I could feel the pulse of his heart beating in my own chest. He reached out to me and his luminescent hand became solid as he grasped his arms around my waist and pulled me towards him, sinking his face into the crook of my neck and folding his wings about my body.

Caught off guard, I pushed away from him. "How is it that you are more than an image? I can feel you."

Aric smirked. "Yes, of course. Now that you are back in the Realms I am able to trace you and appear to you. I have missed holding you, Valora, my Queen." He reached out again, and I took a step back, holding up my hands.

"Wait. There is something you need to know. I don't think I can be your Queen."

"And why do you think that?" asked Aric with amusement in his voice.

"Dooley and I have been together." I spit out the words so fast I wasn't sure that Aric had heard me, especially since the next moment he moved to embrace me once more. This time I did not back away from his advances. Aric had not done anything to harm me. I was sick with guilt. Guilt for betraying him with Dooley. Guilt for yielding to Aric's embrace. Guilt for not knowing what to feel guilty for.

Aric brushed his lips against my ear. "I know all about that, Valora."

I blinked away the tears forming at the edges of my vision. "How is that?"

Aric kept one hand about my waist as he took the other to pull the matching amulet from around his neck.

"There are powers within these amulets. I won't bore you with the details. I should have known the last night I visited you and offered you the position of Queen that you would fall into the throes of passion with another. I blame myself. You have nothing to worry about."

"What do you mean?" I pushed away slightly from Aric.

"The stones." Aric rubbed his finger over the protruding nub, and again a longing was triggered within me. But this time I failed to fall under his spell.

"Do you think I don't care about Dooley? If that's what you think then you're wrong. I mean you no disrespect, King Aric, but I cannot, I will not, be your Queen. But you don't have to worry. I will still work to find these Soulstealers. When I was Earthside I found the clinic where they are storing the magic of Dell'Aria. And I know how they are stealing the magic. I just need to get back to the city to uncover who is behind this."

Aric backed away from me. "Very well. You cannot come back to Dell'Aria."

"You said that before. Don't worry about me. I will be safe. I can help." I took a step towards him, and he backed away again.

"No, I am telling you I do not want you to come back to Dell'Aria." He turned to walk away from me.

"I know you are part human," I said. "I know that and I don't care. Aric, don't forsake the entire colony because I can't return your affections. I know you care more about Dell'Aria than that."

He spun on his heel and bent over me. I had never before realized his full height. "You say you can't return my affections, but there will come a day when you won't have any choice. Don't think I let go of what I want that easily. And you may think you know about me, but you are wrong. You will not come back to Dell'Aria, and I will handle this myself. If you enter the colony I will have you arrested."

My breath caught in my chest, and I fell to my knees as the image of the King before me dissolved into nothing. All I was left with was the amulet which had gone still.

I heard a shuffling in the dirt behind me and turned to see Dooley standing there with his hands thrust in his pockets.

"How long have you been standing there?"

"Long enough. I'm pretty sure your King there wanted me to see the whole act, but he wasn't expecting it to turn out the way it did."

We walked together back to the fire where I curled up and Dooley held his arms tightly around me. I knew that I had made my decision, but that was the easy part. Now I would have to find a way to sneak into Dell'Aria and save the fae.

CHAPTER TWENTY-NINE

I awoke as daybreak crested on the horizon of the Realms, spreading the first fingers of light across the estuary. The surface of the water glittered brightly, and I could only hope that we had done the right thing by bringing Ralph and Kit to the Selkie Queen. I was certain she would not hurt them, but I was uncertain about her arrangement with the King.

Franca stoked the fire back to life, and Dooley slept soundly. I couldn't help but smile as I traced the line of his jaw with my gaze.

"So, are we going to talk about where we are going from here?" Franca threw a side of meat on the fire, and it sizzled in the pan.

I described to her my interaction with the King. "I think he is hurt because I refused to be his Queen. Honestly, it's not something I ever anticipated I would do." I absentmindedly stroked my short wings, plucking at the loose feathers. "If he had asked me even last week I know I would have said yes without hesitation. But now that I have experienced Winter Haven, I know what my mother was talking about all those years ago. I can't let that go."

"You don't have enough vanity within you for any of that queen stuff to matter. You know it as well as I do. However, I think perhaps your King is different."

"The Royal Court is used to getting what they want. But his offer was more than that. The Queen hasn't been found. Technically she is still the Queen, and he is not allowed to take another until the former Queen has been declared dead. This is not an easy task without proof. Also, he would have to make the people fall in love with me and accept me as their Queen. I have no idea how he was planning on doing that."

Franca reached her hand out to my arm. "Has it not crossed your mind that he never intended on having you be beloved by the people? If you were only Queen in word, he could rule without your input. He could put the orders to your mouth. He could control it all."

I poked a stick at the fire. "I suppose you're right. I have let myself be far too vulnerable."

I stood up and strode over to where my satchel and my belongings lay strewn about the ground. I bent over and clipped my scabbard back into place, feeling comfort in the weight of it.

"The plan is that we are going to go into Dell'Aria, find out who is behind the plot to steal the magic, and stop it. With or without the help of King Aric we will make sure that not another fae dies because of this Blight. That is, if you're still with me?"

Franca's normally bright yellow braids looked a little worse for wear. Her hair and her face were covered with a thin layer of the dust and dirt we had endured over the past week.

"It is time for me to ask you the favor you promised to me," said Franca.

I sank down beside Franca and took her hand in mine. "I don't know what I could possibly offer you. I am a crippled exile of my homeland. My only hope is that Dell'Aria be returned to its former glory. I have no assets to offer you, though I wish I could."

"Again you underestimate yourself." She gave a small smile and squeezed my hand in return. "I believe you will be successful. It has been written into your future since the moment I saw you. And if it is to come to pass, I wish an alliance between the fae of Dell'Aria and the dwarves of Mount Elbrus. If we are to move forward from this time in history it must be together."

"My beautiful Franca. You have my word." I brushed the stray hairs from her face and bent forward to place a kiss on her grimy cheek.

"Wow. Hot," Dooley murmured as he rolled over and spied Franca and me though half-slit eyes.

I reached over to grab his satchel and tossed it at him. "Hurry up and get ready. We are set to ride to Dell'Aria today."

❧❦

I greedily shoveled a portion of spicy meat into my mouth, taking very little time to chew and even less to devour. The juices vented out the sides of my mouth, and I took no care as I swiped them from my face with the back of my leather bracer. Dooley peered over my shoulder as I sketched the route for the day into the sand with a blackened stick from the fire.

"So how many miles is that, exactly?" Dooley swallowed hard on the lump of meat in his throat. "I'm not really conditioned for long distances."

Franca pitched backwards off the log she was sitting on as her laughter took over. Tears streamed down her face as she righted herself. Dooley's face was blank.

"Are you kidding me, Dooley? You just traveled from Earth to the Realms. I would say that is longest distance any of your kind has ever travelled," said Franca.

"So are we going to use a portal then?" Dooley's eyes filled with hope at his request.

"No. Besides the fact that I have no idea where they are located between here and Dell'Aria and have no idea how to control them, they are ruled by powerful magic. No. We have to sneak up on the colony if we are to have any chance of accomplishing this mission," I said.

I was comfortable talking like this, finally back in my element as a Hunter, except this time I was hunting an unknown prey.

"Don't worry. You will be fine." For the first time as I reached out to Dooley I felt as if he needed me instead of the other way around.

He nodded and motioned for me to continue. "So how are we to make it up to this cloud city of yours?"

"For that we will have to rely on another friend of mine, Kali. In spirit anyway."

Saying her name again brought a pain to my chest. Kali was the only fae in Dell'Aria, besides my mother, who never once judged me based on what I was born with. She was a true friend and a dedicated Hunter. I still could not believe that she had anything to do with the Soulstealers. But whoever was pulling the strings had definitely set it up to make it seem like she was.

I held the image of my mentor in my mind, the swarthy piratess. I could only hope that Aric would not take his anger at me out on her.

Without an airship there was no hope of my friends and me making it up to Dell'Aria. No doubt the ships would be searched and I still had the heavy weight of the amulet around my neck. I tried my best to keep Aric out of my mind, hoping that if I did not reach out mentally to him, he could not reach out to me.

"I will need to get the two of you on an airship without the others noticing. They are probably looking for me. Kali told me that I was an accused Soulstealer. If I can get them to land, maybe I can get them to take me aboard as a prisoner." I shuddered at the thought of the iron cage, but with my useless wings I needed the airship to get all of us up to Dell'Aria.

Franca leaned forward. "Don't worry about us. You get that ship to land, and I will make sure that Dooley and I are on it." I saw the warrior within Franca flash for a second. "Plus, I am sure I can do some great 'collecting' onboard. It's bound to be worth the trouble."

I nodded. "Once we are inside I will need the two of you to try and find a place to lay low until nightfall. We can rendezvous on the outskirts of the ice fruit fields. It is far enough out of town that hopefully no one will notice."

Franca began to pack up camp, and Dooley took me aside.

"I can't help but feel like I would just be holding you back on this mission. Wouldn't it be safer for you and for Franca if I just found a place to lay low?" asked Dooley.

I reached up and took his head between my palms. "You know, I find it very funny that I am now in the position of making you feel needed." I touched my lips to his, lingering a bit longer than I should.

"Your world. Your rules." Dooley smiled broadly.

"Yes, but you forget. This is your world, too."

He was right. I would worry about him, though if he were to stay in Underworld I would worry no less.

"Besides, you're here to find out who killed Brokk, your father, and I think that whoever was responsible for that is also the one who is responsible for stealing the magic of Dell'Aria. Our goals intersect and, therefore, so do our paths. You are meant to be by my side during this mission, Dooley Fays. I can feel it."

"I will call upon every power I have, and they will all be at your disposal." He gave a dramatic bow.

With that the three of us set out towards the edges of the Riparian forest where I thought I might be able to get a signal to an airship, and where I hoped I would be captured just as Kali had been.

CHAPTER THIRTY

We spent the day trekking through the Realms in a much slower manner than I was used to. Usually I would take my bike out and ride as fast as I could until I could get to an area with some cover, but I had left it behind for a reason. I would rather have Dooley and Franca by my side than my bike.

Franca was our guide as we made our way through the long grasses of the plains that skirted the Riparian Forest. She pointed out to Dooley all the various plants and animals that crossed our path, giving him a quick lesson in the plant life that abounded in this region. I listened as much as I could. Franca was a better teacher than any of the books I had read in Court as a child.

I passed my hands over the tops of the soft tufts of ginger grass which grew so tall and thick that we could not see anything in front of us as we walked.

"Are you certain this is safe, Franca?" The soft grasses transitioned to harsher reeds, and with each step there was a sucking sound as our feet pulled in and out of the mud that had replaced the dry ground.

Franca beat back the plant life encroaching onto the path with a short blade. I could see our destination ahead, but this was not a way I had come before.

"It should be. Your landing point is not too far ahead," she shouted back to me.

As soon as we got to the place the ship could land I would be able to send a signal to the airship from a device I had taken from my bike. I only hoped it still worked.

The water that pooled around our ankles rose higher as we walked further into what had become a marsh.

"Franca, I don't think this is a good idea. I think we should find another way." The water had reached my waist.

Franca turned around, and just as she was about to answer me something pulled her under the water. Dooley was first to rush to her aid.

"Franca? Franca? He splashed around where he had seen her go down, and I struggled to catch up to him.

Up from the reeds rose a viciously beautiful creature, an echidna. Her long dark hair draped over her shoulders, barely hiding the fact that she wasn't clothed. The beast was beautiful from the waist up and deadly from the waist down. Dooley hesitated, caught in the gaze of her violet eyes.

I heard a thrashing in the reeds behind her and saw Franca struggling against the squeeze of the lower half of the echidna's serpentine body which had curled around Franca's mid-section. As if in a trance, Dooley stepped forward towards the echidna who smiled revealing sharpened teeth.

"Hey, bitch, that one is mine."

I pulled the silver blade from my scabbard and struggled to free myself from the sticky mix of water and mud that impeded my path. I beat my wings as fiercely as I could and charged the echidna with my sword.

"Dooley, snap out of it and get out of the way." I pushed Dooley to the side as I swung at the echidna who tossed Franca to the side so she could use her tail to swipe at me. The end was barbed with sharpened spikes which held a deadly poison.

"Dooley, check on Franca!" I hoped my plea would snap him out of his trance.

Dooley regained his senses quickly and gave the beast a wide berth as he made his way over to where Franca lay limp on the ground.

I slashed at the echidna, dancing about her from the ground and the air as she tried to spike me with her tail. I cut into her side, and the beast let forth a roar then disappeared back under the water.

I flew over to Dooley who held Franca's head in his lap. Tears filled his eyes. "She's dead, Valora."

"No, no, she can't be dead." I dropped down next to them and wiped the dirt from Franca's face, brushing it off her thick yellow braids. I searched her body and found the fatal wound. The spikes of the echidna's tail had made its way through the chink in her armor delivering the toxin which had likely brought her a speedy death. Dooley reached behind my neck with his hand and hugged my forehead to his.

I saw the fear in his eyes before I heard the rustling. I also saw the reflection of the echidna rising in the water behind me. I slowly set my hand over the hilt of my sword which lay on the ground next to me.

"Down!" I yelled as I saw the spiked tail swing towards us.

Dooley threw himself to the ground, and I quickly turned with the blade of my sword in the air to catch the echnida's tail on the back swing. The sharpened edge of my sword cut through the scaly flesh like butter and lopped off the most dangerous part of the echidna.

I jumped up and flung myself at the echidna, my sword clasped in both hands before bringing it down into its chest. Again. Again. The beast's blood splashed up onto my face, mixing with my salty tears. It had no fight left and I had more than enough. I continued to slash at it, wishing I could have done this only a moment ago. I stopped when the body fell over with a splash into the murky bog.

Dooley pushed himself up to sit on the spit of solid ground Franca had landed on.

"We were so close to land. So close to being safe," he said.

I looked around and realized that we had reached the shore, and less than half a mile away was the landing pad for the Peixes.

I cradled Franca in my arms, willing her to come back. I remembered how I had done the same thing with my mother. It hadn't worked then, and I knew it wouldn't work now. I was determined not to lose my focus. It would not be what Franca would have wanted. I knew what she wanted.

I bent down to whisper to her before the last of her spirit left her body to travel up with the Goddess. "I will find out the truth, Franca. And I will bring our people together. I promise in the name of the Goddess Varuna. Your life and death will not be in vain."

Dooley helped me carry Franca's body to higher ground. "We will come back for her. I will make sure that she is returned to Mount Elbrus to be buried with her ancestors."

I brushed the stray blonde hairs from Franca's eyes and pressed the lids closed. "I need a knife, get me a knife."

Dooley pulled a small blade from his pocket and flipped it open before handing it to me. "Is there anything I can do?"

I slipped the knife under one of the two yellow braids of Franca's hair and sawed back and forth until it released into my hand. I brought her hair up to my nose, taking in the smoky scent of Mount Elbrus mixed with the flowers she had woven in her hair only a few days ago.

Dooley's arms wrapped tightly around my shoulders. There was nothing he could do besides hold me. His grip pressed my mother's grimoire into my chest. I pulled away gently and retrieved the small volume from my pocket.

"We are running out of options," I said, rocking back on my heels.

"We could take Franca's body back to Mount Elbrus now. I'm sure the dwarves will help us get back through the portal." Dooley brought his hand under my chin and turned my face toward his. "I can't lose you, Valora."

"I have to shut down the machine, Dooley. No one else knows about it. Kali is imprisoned. Aric won't let me get involved because I hurt him. The only solution is for me to go back there and fix this myself. If I don't many fae will die, including my father."

Dooley's gaze rested on the grimoire in my hand. "Then I will help you figure out a way to fix this. You won't be doing this alone."

"No, she certainly can't do it alone, but I don't think either one of you are quite ready for what you are going up against."

We both turned in time to see the careworn face of an old friend and said simultaneously, "Pryn!"

❧❦

"How did you escape the King's prison?" I asked.

"You were being held prisoner by the King? Pryn, Brokk is dead and I am here to find out who did it," said Dooley.

"I'm sorry to have surprised the both of you with my presence at such a sorrowful time." He gestured to Franca's body, and I tightened my grip around the length of her braid I still held in my hand. "But it seems that there is no hiding from what is happening any longer. And now is the time to fight back."

"But you still haven't told me how you escaped."

"I saw an opportunity, and I took it." Pryn's golden eyes sparkled just as they always had.

Pryn was as cryptic as Aric. I was beginning to wonder if it was a genetic trait in all men.

"I am guessing you visited with Brokk and Dooley on Earth?"

"Yes, he did," said Dooley.

"I had to visit with Brokk after the King first declared I was a Soulstealer. I had to know what he knew about all this."

"Did he tell you?" I asked.

"His knowledge was limited. He only knew what he needed to in order to create his machine. After that he was exiled to Earth so as to keep the truth from the fae of Dell'Aria," said Pryn.

"So he wasn't a Soulstealer?" asked Dooley.

"No, he is not the one responsible for bringing death to the fae of Dell'Aria," said Pryn. "But I have been unable to discern exactly who is. Of course, I am not the one who is supposed to find out."

Pryn shifted his gaze from Dooley to me. The words he whispered into my ear when he saved my life echoed back to me. *I save you because I know in the end you will save us all.*

"How do you know I am the one who is supposed to save the fae of Dell'Aria?"

"You didn't hear me right, Valora, I said you would save us all."

Again, he was cryptic. "And exactly how am I supposed to do that?"

"You have always had the answer to that question. But I realize that time is short. I need to assist you in your preparations as I did your mother. Do you have your mother's grimoire?"

With the lock of Franca's hair safely stashed into the pocket that had once held the grimoire, we sat down and began to turn the weathered pages one by one.

That afternoon Pryn set about teaching me all he had once taught my mother. Several cycles of training were crammed into several hours. When he rose to leave I was exhausted and I still had no idea how all of it would help me.

"How can you leave when I still don't know what it is I am supposed to do?"

Pryn's golden eyes glinted in the setting sun. "Some lessons cannot be taught. Go with your instincts. You have always had the balance of your father's good sense and your mother's way with magic. I know you will find a way."

Magic, the one way I had ignored since mother's death. Opening her grimoire was like ripping the bandage off a weeping wound, each spell like pressing salt into it. But something in me knew that it was only through the hurt that I would heal.

He disappeared into the Riparian, and I knew there was no use in following him. He had given me the tools. I had to figure this one out on my own, but it didn't mean I had to do it alone.

I feared for Dooley, but I also knew that without him I would lose my nerve. I was entering back into Dell'Aria and there would be no Hunter's welcome this time. In fact I was hoping to sneak in unnoticed.

"I think I know how you can help."

CHAPTER THIRTY-ONE

By the time we had made all our preparations the sun was low in the sky. I hoped that the evening light would make this easier. Dooley and I had just learned how to use a glamor spell and I wasn't sure how good we were yet. I was impressed by how easily Dooley slipped into Brokk's skin. The wings he had produced were brilliant.

I used the communicator I had ripped from the mechanism inside my motorcycle to signal a return call to the Peixes.

It did not take long before I saw the bird of passage descend from the clouds which were collecting low and dark in the sky. Perhaps the Goddess Varuna was helping me in my efforts of subterfuge. The large floating fortress came down gently to the patch of ground we had cleared, gently bobbing above that ground. Its belly was lined with thin sheets of copper plating that conducted the magic that allowed the craft to fly. The gangway shot out from the side and landed with a thud on the ground.

I tried to hide the look of shock on my face as Kali hobbled towards me. Her tattered wings looked just as they had the last time I saw her.

"What the hell are you doing out here?" said Kali. She may have been surprised, but I was more so.

"I was sent on a mission by the King. I am not allowed to speak about it."

Kali bent to take a closer look at the body lying at my feet.

"Did you kill her?" There was anger in Kali's voice, and as much as I wanted to trust her, I also didn't want to put her in any danger.

"That is no concern of yours. I had my orders, and now I need to bring this Soulstealer to face the King."

Kali scratched her head and stood to face me. "Might I ask who it is you have here?"

"His name is Brokk. Apparently Valora Delos had been sent by the King to retrieve him and instead she fell under his spell and I found her assisting him. She gave me no choice."

"I find it hard to believe King Aric would have sent you out on your own? "

"I am Siam, Commander of the King's Guard. I do as I see fit."

"Yes, I know who you are. Shall we depart?" asked Kali.

I pushed against the ties that bound Dooley's hands behind his back. The glamor that he and I were putting forth with our combined energies was holding, but I wasn't sure how long it was going to last.

Kali's eyes shot daggers at me. "I won't leave one of my own out here. We take Valora's body back with us."

"Whatever. It is no matter to me." I tossed the communicator to her and pushed Dooley up the gangway, towards the holding area in the bottom of the ship.

The fae who were aboard did not seem to take much interest in another Soulstealer. A few of them hurried down the gangplank as Kali barked the orders for them to help her with the body. I turned and saw them carry what looked like my lifeless body onto the ship. Kali signaled for them to put it in the holding area. She watched me from across the deck. I could not read her face. Kali and I were like sisters. If she thought Siam had killed me, perhaps I had put myself in danger yet again.

I took Dooley down to the holding area and cut the ropes binding his wrists. I carefully donned the gloves that would protect my hands from the iron of the holding cell and swung open the door, shutting it as Dooley walked inside.

"There is no lock on this cell. The iron is meant to keep fae inside. When we land you need to find a way to sneak out of the ship and find my hut like I showed you. I will be there are soon as I can. The seal breaker, we need to get it."

Dooley nodded, and I turned to make my way back up to the main deck.

"Valora, I love you."

I turned back and in my mind's eye I saw through Dooley's glamor. There were no shields between us. But that didn't mean that nothing was hidden.

"I love you, too."

I shed the gloves and took the steps two at a time towards the upper deck. I had to do all I could to keep this plan from unraveling, at least until we made it to Dell'Aria.

❧

When I reached the deck I could see that the ship had lifted and turned back towards Dell'Aria. Kali sat on a bench mid deck drawing smoke from a pipe perched between her dried lips. Her arms were dotted with purplish bruises, and she had a scratch down the side of her face.

In her other hand she held a bottle of mead. The rest of the crew had gone below deck. The ship had been set on its course back to the docks of Dell'Aria, and they were not needed.

She turned to me as I exited from below deck and chomped down on her pipe as she patted the bench next to her.

"Have a seat. The winds might kick up a bit as we enter the cloud bank, and you'll want to be holding onto something."

Heavy gray clouds bore down on the Peixes as she ascended willingly into their clutches.

"Why don't we go below deck with the others?" I asked, not entirely trusting what she might want to do to the person she believed murdered her friend.

Kali patted the bench beside her again. "It's a little crowded down there, don't you think? Don't tell me a member of the King's Guard is afraid of a little lightning. You can't end up any worse than me."

Kali's broken wings fluttered involuntarily as the winds picked up. She took a long swig on the bottle and held it out to me.

"Get over here and take a drink, soldier. Don't refuse my hospitality aboard my own ship. It is considered rude." The last comment she said with a downward tilt of her head, and I suddenly had a feeling she could see right through me.

I straightened my shoulders as I sat down next to her and took a swig of the mead. It was much stronger than I was used to and I sputtered a little as the heat of the brew trickled into my stomach.

"So, Valora was one of your own? Ever think she would help out a Soulstealer?" I asked.

"Never, but it seems there are a lot of surprises for us all these days." Kali snatched the mead from my hand and took a long pull from the bottle. "Nothing is how it seems to be now, is it?"

The Peixes broke through the clouds, and the deck filled with a rolling fog that made it impossible to see more than a foot in front of me. I knew that if I moved now I might be tossed off deck, and since the wings on my back were only a glamor it would mean my death.

The first thunderclap shook the deck followed by a lightning strike that sheared off the port bow. The Peixes was magically protected from the strikes, but it was still unnerving. We typically didn't fly in this weather if we could help it, especially with magic in such short supply these days.

"I want to thank you for bringing me back Valora," Kali said. "She was special to me. It's really too bad things did not work out for her. But I am having a hard time believing the King sent you out to bring her back dead when I had a deal to bring her back alive."

Kali puffed on her pipe, swirling the smoke of her tobacco with the tendrils of thunderclouds that passed around us. She set the bottle of mead down on the bench, but not before giving it one last swig, then reached into her pocket to pull on a set of protective gloves. Kali reached into her pocket again and this time pulled out a set of irons. I shivered slightly.

"You don't have to worry about the prisoner," I said. "I put him down in the cell myself."

"Oh, I know you did. These are not for him."

Kali lunged towards me, and I rolled away from her grasp into the mist enveloping the deck.

"Come back here, coward," she yelled.

Kali's experience on the deck of this ship greatly outweighed my own. I jumped to my feet and became immediately dizzy with the disorientating drink drowning the depths of my vision. The floorboards creaked under my feet, and I heard Kali run in my direction as she heard the sound.

I fell to the floor again and rolled as the deck of the ship tilted. It was turning towards port. I could only hope that the cloud layer was thick enough to hide me. I fumbled my way to the edge of the ship and bent over it. A jet of hot air blasted me back as the landing struts pushed their way out of the sides of the ship, readying it to be clamped into place at the port of Dell'Aria.

I fell backwards with the force of the blast and locked eyes with Kali who held a silver blade above her head ready to take a downwards stab at me.

"Wait, Kali, it's me."

I pulled the amulet from under my shirt and shed my glamor as I held the necklace in front of me like a shield.

Kali's blade landed with a thunk into the wood of the deck beside my head, and suddenly I was pulled to my feet.

"Dammit, girl. I was going to kill you for killing you. Do you know how stupid I would have felt?"

Kali put her arms around me and gave me a quick vise-like squeeze. She released her embrace and gripped me by the shoulders.

"Why would you do something like that? What is the point of playing dead?"

"I wasn't expecting you to be onboard. I didn't want to put you in any danger since I didn't know what happened to you, and I figured all of Dell'Aria thinks I am a Soulstealer. I thought you had been captured. What happened?"

"I was able to talk my way out of it. As far as you are concerned, you're right, you won't be safe in Dell'Aria. But Aric certainly will help you, won't he?"

I had never known Kali for her powers of persuasion. My thoughts returned to her desperate cries as she was fleeing down the corridors and into Aric's chamber. She had claimed they had a deal.

"I am not so sure he will."

"You may be right. It's hard to get close to the King these days, the Guard have him under constant watch. Since you told me that Brokk is dead, I assume the person in my hold below deck is someone you can trust? More than me, I am guessing."

"It's not that at all, Kali. He has his own interest in this situation."

The deck of the ship vibrated as the clamps locked into place on the dock. The rest of the crew came up the stairs from below deck.

"I don't have time to explain. I just need you to trust me. I am here to save Dell'Aria, but the King cannot know that I am here. Will you keep the secret for me?" I swept the glamor back across me as the first of the other Hunters appeared above deck.

"Yes, I suppose I could do that. Do you know where you will be staying?" Kali spoke softly.

"The less you know, the better. But I will do my best to keep in touch, okay?"

I headed towards the gangway, and Kali grabbed my arm.

"Wait."

Before she could finish, shouts came from below deck. "He has escaped. The Soulstealer is gone."

CHAPTER THIRTY-TWO

"I tracked him down before. I will track him down again," I shouted to the fae. "Kali, please do me one favor. That body is a dear friend of mine. One I intend to bring back to her family. Please keep it safe."

"You know I won't be able to keep the other Hunters from talking. Soon word will reach the King that you came back dead. Don't you think your father will want to see your body?"

The thought had not occurred to me, but I knew Kali was right.

"Yes, and if he does, that's okay. It's probably better that he thinks I am not alive anymore. There is a good chance that soon it may be true in any case." For that matter, I wasn't even sure how long our glamor would last on Franca's body. The goal was to get to Dell'Aria, and we were finally there.

"May the Goddess be with you," she said.

I patted Kali on the shoulder and bounded off the ship. I had wanted to hug her for all she had done for me, but I had to remember that I was still parading around as Siam. I

searched the crowd for any strange activity, any sign of
Dooley, but I saw none.

What I did see shook me to the core. I had to keep a
grip on my emotions to control the glamor. Lining the
streets of the Port was a queue of coffins awaiting their final
send off to the Goddess Varuna. It was so unusual to even
have one fae die in a single cycle, to see fifty or more coffins
awaiting their final send-off was unheard of. This last wave
had done massive destruction.

The usually busy port shops were all but closed down.
Only a couple of them remained open, and they had very
few patrons.

I turned to go towards the hut I shared with Kali where
I had planned to meet Dooley but suddenly stopped dead in
my tracks. My first stop would have to be the temple where
the machine that caused the Blight was held. I needed to
somehow shut it down. I couldn't let this happen again, and
I couldn't endanger Dooley any further.

After I found the machine, I would need to figure out
who was responsible for it all.

I had some idea who it was. The Queen had disappeared
and left behind her Guard who ran everything in her stead.
King Aric had recommended me for the Guard yet I had
been denied entrance by Siam, Commander of the Guard.
He was no doubt hiding something. He knew my loyalties
were with the King, and he had never intended to let me into
the Guard. If I could find the proof that the Queen was
responsible and bring it to the King he could shut down the
Guard and save Dell'Aria. And maybe he could forgive me.

I rushed up the cobble stone streets, now covered in
thin wisps of the high storm vapors. The lights of the great
temple bounced off the blue veined white marble making it
shine like a beacon in the darkness that was rapidly

descending as the clouds surrounded the colony.

The thunder ripped through the sky overhead, and a wicked bolt of lightning struck down onto Dell'Aria causing a rumbling through the city. Screams rang out, and there was panic as fae ran for cover. Another rumble of thunder, and the peal of an alarm sounded through the air. I had only heard it before during the drills I had gone through as a child. It had been decided back then that there might come a time when we would need that alarm, and now that time had come. The magic of the city had become so weakened that we were no longer protected.

The panic was made worse by the darkness and mist that trailed through the city making it almost impossible to see where I was going. But I knew where I was headed. The temple lights were still strong, and I wended my way through the narrow streets towards the entrance.

As I approached I saw that many others had the same idea. Dell'Aria was ripping apart and there was nothing to do other than to pray to the Goddess Varuna. No one would be able to fly away from Dell'Aria in this storm. We would all have to ride it out together. Throngs of fae pushed against each other as they tried to force their way into the entrance. The King's Guard had spread out across the tops of the marbled stairs leading up inside the temple and had formed a line keeping everyone outside.

I could tell I wasn't going to get inside this way. I circled to the other side of the temple where I knew there was another entrance specifically for the Guards. It was not common knowledge, but I had been taught about it during my training.

Finding the yellowed marble that acted as the alternate entrance was not easy in the darkness, but another streak of lightning lit up the sky and bounced off the wall in front of me, and I was able to make out the edges of the false door. I knocked on the door, hoping that they had left someone inside to guard the entrance. A small window slid open, and two eyes peered out at me.

"Hey, it's Siam. Let me in," I said.

There was a pause, then the window slid back into place as the door opened inwards into a darkened hallway.

"That's funny. I just had to see who it was who thought they could get away with being me."

The fae stepped into the light and I was looking straight back at Siam, the fae I happened to be impersonating. My glamor immediately dropped as Siam countered it with his own spell. Glamors were easy to break if you knew what you were dealing with.

"Valora! You are wanted by the King!" Siam was standing half behind the semi-open door.

"Believe me, I know."

I shoved my entire body weight against the door which pushed Siam back into the marble wall behind him, knocking him out cold. I stepped over his legs and pulled him the rest of the way inside the corridor before letting the door ease closed behind me.

I couldn't help but feel a small feeling of satisfaction. I had always wanted to give Siam a shiner. I passed my hand over his body to hide him in the shadows with another glamor and suddenly felt light headed. The glamor flickered in and out and finally took hold.

Restoring my own glamor so I could continue to be Siam took an extra effort. The amulet at my chest trembled. Obviously my powers would be limited in here. I was headed into the lair of the beast, the contraption that was sucking the magic from Dell'Aria. The only thing that allowed me to continue the glamor was the amulet. I couldn't stretch my powers too thin especially since I didn't know what I was up against, and I was alone.

A foot stuck in the door before it closed. I flattened myself against the wall, trying to stay in the shadow. The door slowly pressed open and a figure stepped inside, flickering before my eyes.

"Oh, crap." Dooley passed his hands over his body, and I stepped from the shadow. "Am I me again? I was trying to focus really hard."

I practically knocked Dooley over as I jumped into his arms and folded myself around him. "What are you doing here?"

Dooley laughed. "You'll have to forgive me, Valora. You still look like a man, you know. And not even a very cute one."

"Oh, that's right." I slid off of Dooley and tried to clear my mind. "What are you doing here?"

"I want to help you. I can't just hang around in your hut until you come and tell me the coast is clear. And don't think I don't know that was what you were doing. I know you don't want to put me in danger, but I don't want you to worry about that. Let's just say that I have gotten over my culture shock and I'm ready to do battle. These fae go down as easy with a right hook as humans do. I think I can handle myself."

"You seem to forget about the wings and the magic, a few things that humans don't have."

"Yes, well, I thought I had the glamor thing down." Dooley shut his eyes and clenched his jaw in an effort to bring the skin of Brokk back around him.

I reached out and took hold of his clenched fist. "Don't bother. It won't work here."

"But you still look like that Guard."

"It's only because I have the amulet. I can't pretend that I am not glad you are here, but you need to be careful." Siam's unconscious body lay still on the ground, the glamor I had put on him obscuring his form but not completely hiding him. "You need to switch clothes with him. If you are wearing the uniform and his outer cape then maybe the other fae won't notice that you are missing your wings. Did you bring the seal breaker?"

Dooley pulled the seal breaker, wrapped in cloth, from his coat and handed it to me.

"I won't have time to use this now, but soon."

I pulled Siam's clothes off him as Dooley stripped down in the hallway. I stole a quick glance at the tanned muscles of his thighs. Focus. I handed him Siam's pants and shirt and tossed Dooley's clothes on the sleeping Siam. I wouldn't leave him with nothing, but if he woke up sooner than I wanted him to, he would have to take time to get dressed.

Dooley fastened the clasp of the cloak at his neck. "How do I look?"

"You may not want to ask me that. I need to keep my mind straight."

It really didn't matter what Dooley wore, but seeing him in the clothes of the fae I was used to seeing every day made the jump between falling in love and falling in love with a half-fae a shorter distance.

"Right. I'll follow behind you then. Just tell me the plan."

"I need to get up to the highest point of the temple. The spire must be where the machine is kept. We need to shut it down somehow."

"Sounds like a good plan to me."

Dooley and I made our way up a spiral staircase which emptied into the choir area of the temple. I could hear the

257

shouts and cries of the fae echoing through the nave from the outside the main door of the temple which was vacant with the exception of Dooley and me.

"We just need to go up that staircase, and I think we will make it to the spire," I said.

Dooley followed behind me, our feet tapping out a hurried rhythm on the stone floor. By the time we got to the top of the stairs my lungs were burning. Behind me Dooley clutched at his chest. He gave me a wry smile, trying to hide his discomfort.

Facing us at the top of the stairs was a large bronze door that had no handle or hinges. I pressed my weight against it but it did not budge. For all I knew it was a dead end except that there would be no reason to construct a large stairway to nothing.

"Let me try." Dooley pushed his full weight on the door, and it gave way with too much ease. He fell, knocking his head on the stone floor. I dropped down to help him and saw my reflection in the shiny black boots of my King.

CHAPTER THIRTY-THREE

Standing behind Aric was my worst nightmare, Orris, with his sword drawn.

"Seems as though your brother has brought us an intruder," Aric said as Dooley staggered to his feet, apparently disoriented from his fall. "Orris, take him down to the cells and make sure he is locked up tight. I want to speak to Siam alone."

Orris pushed past me and gripped Dooley by the collar. Dooley's eyes rolled back and he hung limp in Orris's grasp.

"No, King Aric, he is not an intruder. He is a guest of the Court. I was just bringing him up to meet you," I said quickly.

Aric looked down on me with eyes like daggers. "You think I am a fool? It surprises me, since I had never taken you for one." He ripped the chain from my neck, and the clasp broke. My glamor dissolved, and I fell to my knees.

"Oh, I am sorry. You need this to live, don't you?" Aric swung the amulet back and forth in front of my eyes making me dizzy. "She told me not to trust you. She told me you would ruin everything I sacrificed for."

Who was he talking about?

He walked over to a very large version of the machine Brokk had in his chest. The top of it could not be seen because it rose up to the ceiling of the spire. As I had thought, the spire was itself part of the machine.

Aric's head dropped abruptly, and he clutched his temples between his hands. He muttered something to himself before running over to a table at the edge of the room which contained several vials of what appeared to be the same magic we got from the clinic as well as various tools. He came back to me with a length of copper wire and a vial.

"Here, drink this. You will feel better." I looked up into the stormy eyes of my King. This was the man I had once lived every moment for. I felt the tears escaping down my cheeks before I knew I was crying.

"Never." I choked on the rest of my words as my vision began to fade. "I won't steal from the people of Dell'Aria."

"Don't be silly, Valora. Technically you have already." He swung the amulet in front of me. "This is the only thing that has kept you alive all these cycles. It works by drawing magic from those around you because you are no longer able to produce it yourself. The first wave of the Blight almost killed you, but I was not going to allow that to happen. You see, I love you, Valora."

He knelt down before me, and I noticed that his white silken shirt was missing one of its straps. I pulled the missing strap from my pocket and tossed it at him.

"Brokk knew about what you did. Others have to know as well. You won't get away with this. When I am dead, you will still fail."

Aric shook his head. My legs trembled and collapsed underneath me. My cheek hit the cold stone floor. My face went slack. Sweat pooled at my brow, and I could no longer move my limbs. My vision dimmed. Aric's hands moved about my throat as he fastened the amulet back around my neck using the copper wire. Warmth flowed through me as he tipped the vial and trickled the magic down my throat. He turned me onto my back causing me to involuntarily swallow rather than drown.

Aric took two of the vials and drank them quickly letting the empty vials fall to the ground in front of me. Small driblets of the coppery magic oozed out of the tubes onto the floor. Wasted.

My strength returned to me, but my spirit was broken. I made no effort to rise from the floor and barely moved when Aric swept me up in his arms and carried me out of the spire down one set of stairs and then another. We moved deeper into the bowels of the temple, and the air turned colder as we passed into the crypts below the temple where all the common folk of Dell'Aria were interred. Aric carried me through the crypt, past the fountain in the middle of the room and down one of the side passageways into the room I had seen reflected back in the mirror. And that is where my nightmare truly began.

❧

He laid me down gently onto the silken sheets of the bed and knelt by my side. "I need you to understand why I have done this." He swept my hair away from my eyes.

I couldn't look at him. My whole life had been a lie. I had been fighting to save other fae from my mother's fate. I had been fighting to bring Aric a solution to the problem that he caused. He had tricked me and made me out to be a fool.

"I thought you were sick. In the carriage your face looked yellowed, like those with the Blight." Tears leaked down the side of my face.

Aric knelt beside my bed. "It was necessary to motivate you to leave. I had every intention of coming for you. If you had waited another day on Earth we could have avoided all of this. I told you not to come back here, Valora."

He stood up and paced back and forth in front of the bed. "I know that you know I am not all fae. I am actually surprised that no one else has found out before now. But that doesn't matter anymore."

I pushed myself up to sitting. The amulet beat against my chest, and I could again feel the magic pulling back and forth between us. An invisible connection, but one I could not deny.

"You know I don't care whether you are half-dwarf. But please tell me that this horrible crime was not your doing. Please tell me that the Queen commanded you to steal the magic from Dell'Aria."

"I thought you might understand. No, it was not the Queen. It all began with my father." Aric dropped to his knees before me. "You have to understand." He was pleading with me. "He took me away from my mother. Took me away from all I knew once I began to show the signs of being a fae." Aric made a flippant gesture to his wings.

"I escaped from him. I found a portal, and I was even able to make it back home to my mother." One tear escaped down Aric's cheek as he stared beyond me, reliving some part of his past only he could see. "But she did not know who I was. He had wiped her memory of me, and he sent the Guard to bring me back in chains."

"I saw you that night," I whispered. I could not help but bring my hand to his head to stroke the delicate strands of his white blond hair.

He laid his head in my lap. "After that day I promised that I would find a way to fix my mother's memory and take down this empire he had imprisoned me in."

He reached for the top drawer of the nightstand next to the bed and handed me a photograph. "This was her."

I stared at the picture and couldn't believe my eyes. I blinked back the tears, examining it again to make sure I wasn't seeing things.

He looked up into my eyes. "So I had Brokk build the machine for me to pull the magic from Dell'Aria. I had no idea what it would do when I first turned it on."

I suddenly realized what he was telling me and tried to push him away, but he clamped his strong hands around my waist. I kicked at him as the tears and rage poured from me in waves I couldn't control. I shouted at him, "You killed my mother!"

Aric's strength was double my own as he rode the wave of magic he had downed only moments before. He held onto my hands, reached into a drawer in his nightstand and pulled out a length of cord woven with flecks of iron. He quickly tied it around my wrists and ankles and tossed me back onto the bed. The burning started immediately.

"I never meant to hurt you. I would never have wanted your mother dead, but I had no choice in the matter. My father gave me no choice, can't you see that?" He clutched the amulet. "I contacted a demon to have these forged and to save you. Can't you see how much I care for you? I risked everything for you."

He leaned over me, and I turned my face away from him as he bent to kiss me.

"Then tell me how to undo the connection between us. If you truly care for me, tell me how to make this amulet so it only helps to keep me alive and doesn't bind me to you."

I turned my head back to stare into his eyes. My mother's killer stared right back at me, totally unaware of what he had truly done.

"I won't do that."

He pushed off the bed as shouts carried through the corridor outside. "I will be right back." Before he left he covered me then turned to face me once more. "Valora, I have always loved you since I first saw the light of the moon against your face as you stared at me from your window all those many cycles ago."

And then he was gone and part of me went with him.

❧

It was not too long before I heard the voices die down. The cords around my wrists ached. The amulet pulsed against my chest bringing renewed life to my sore limbs. Somewhere another fae was feeling weakened because the amulet around my neck was drawing away his or her magic to heal me. But I hurt too much to feel guilty.

The pain receded long enough for me to enter a dream state. Images of Dooley being beaten flashed through my mind. I saw Kali alone in a darkened room, crying in the corner. Then the words came through me, "Destrave Segredo Dentro."

The ropes around my wrists and ankles loosened, and my mother's voice shouted at me, "Valora, wake up!"

I didn't know how much time had passed. My jagged breaths were all I could hear. I crawled off the bed and cracked open the door. I continued to crawl partially out of fear and partially because I felt if I stood my legs would give way.

I reached the fountain in the middle of the room. I pressed my parched lips to the cool water, quenching the fire burning in my throat.

As I did so I caught a glimpse of something in the water. Looking down in the water I swore I saw myself as a young fae. Long black hair and dark eyes reflected back at me. My tears started to stream again, and the image blurred even further as I thought again of my mother.

And then my reflection waved at me.

"What the heck?"

I fell backwards onto the stone floor as the water parted and from beneath the surface came Kit. She floated half in and half out of the water.

She giggled, excited to see me, but quickly stopped as she looked at the state I was in. "Valora, are you okay?"

"Kit? What are you doing here? How did you get here?" I feared I had very little time until Aric returned.

"My mother sent me. She wanted me to see if I could do anything to help."

"I thought your mother hated me." I struggled to get myself upright again.

"No, she doesn't hate you. She hates herself for falling for Aric's scheme. She figured out that maybe he hasn't been honest with her all this time."

"She would be right. He hasn't been honest with any of us."

Kit's tail kicked the water up around her.

"Wow, Kit, so you have grown into your fins. How is your father? Is he still with you?"

Kit smiled widely. "Yes, he's very happy now. Mom says he gets to live with us forever."

I smiled. "I am happy you all get to be a family again. I am not sure what else you can do for me now though."

"You can come with me. I can bring you back to Mavrovo. I am sure my mother will know how to help."

I shook my head. "I can't. I need to find Dooley. And I need to stop Aric somehow, but I have no idea what he plans to do next."

"You are in no condition to help anyone, Valora. You can't even stand. Come with me and be safe. You helped me once, let me help you."

"I appreciate it, Kit, I do, but I can't let Aric hurt Dooley or hurt any more fae. He has to be stopped."

"Then you have no choice but to accept the only help I can give you right now."

Kit tipped her head back and her teeth extended into sharpened points. Now she looked every bit as fierce as her mother. She brought her wrist to her mouth and clamped her teeth down. Blood dripped from her arm as she swam as close to the side of the pool as she could, pressing her arm towards me.

"No, Kit, I can't take your blood. I just can't do that."

"You know it is the only way. I don't have a device like Brook did, but you know the magic you need runs through my veins, and the only way you are going to get it from me is this way. My mother told me your amulet can't take magic from me."

The blood dribbled down her arm. "You can either come with me to Mavrovo or you can take what you need to make you strong."

I looked down at my amulet. It was silent in response to the blood. So much blood had been shed because I had failed to accept what was right in front of me. I should have seen Aric for who he was a long time ago.

I took Kit's delicate wrist in my hand and looked into her eyes. "Tell me when to stop."

I closed my lips around her wrist and began to take deep swallows of Kit's salty blood. The infusion of magic was more intense than when Aric had forced me to swallow the vial. Kit was much stronger than I thought. Suddenly she pulled her arm away from me, and I blinked a few times as the room came back into focus.

"I will go back to Mavrovo and tell my mother what's happening. Maybe she will think of a way she can help. You be safe, Valora. May the power of the Selkies bring you strength and good luck."

I nodded. "Thank you, sweet Kit. Say hello to your father for me." Kit gave me a small wave and disappeared down into the fountain. I saw the glow below of another one of the portals. "This must be how Aric spoke to the Selkie Queen. But it doesn't help me now."

I sat with my back against the fountain to give myself a few seconds to contemplate my next move. That was about all the time I figured I had.

The sounds echoing from the stairwell became more agitated. The fae were frantic to come inside the temple. Of course they were unaware that the last place they would want to seek refuge in was this death trap.

I tugged at the amulet. I only hoped that Orris would have followed protocol and brought Dooley down to the cells where they kept the other prisoners. My only problem was that I had no idea where those cells were. "Damn, there is nothing I can do."

I swept my hands through the water in frustration and heard a little yip behind me. I turned to see a soaked ball of fur.

"Pika!" I reached down and scooped the beast into my arms. "What are you doing down here? Can you bring me to your master? Where is Siam, little Pika? Where's Siam?"

Last I had left him he was passed out in the hall, but he would be the one who would know where Orris had taken Dooley.

Pika's tail began to shake furiously, and he tilted his head and stared at me with his large eyes as viscous orange drool oozed out of the sides of his mouth.

"I am not sure why he finds you cute, but hopefully you can find him." I set Pika on the ground. "Find Siam, boy, find Siam."

The pikaki gave a sharp yap and rolled down the hall. I ran after it as fast as I could. We were still on the crypt level, but behind the initial entryway there were mazes of corridors that went on forever beneath the temple. I suspected that Kali had been running down one of these corridors when I had last spoken to her through the mirror. I had no idea how she had managed to talk herself out of being imprisoned.

A wave of relief washed over me as I chased Pika down the corridor. Kali was alive and hopefully had found shelter. One less person I needed to worry about saving.

Pika stopped before a large door and scraped his paw against it. As we entered the room I noticed that it was set up as a storage area. There were several large armoires and stacks of crates. Even in the dim light I could see a dark red trail that led from a pool in the middle of the room to the doors of one of the armoires. Pika ran to the armoire and sat back on his haunches.

I raced to the closet and swung its doors open. Lying at the bottom was Siam. He had been bound, and blood still dripped from an open wound on his head.

"Siam." I bent down and ripped the gag from his mouth. "Siam, are you okay?"

He swung his head towards me as his eyes fluttered up into the top of his head.

"Damn it, Siam."

I took the amulet from around my neck and draped it over his head for a moment until I became woozy and then I slipped it back over my neck.

Siam's eyes came into focus. "How did you do that?"

"Never mind that. Who did this to you?"

"You would not believe me if I told you." I could tell I was losing him again. *He must mean Aric.*

"You would be surprised what I am willing to believe these days. How do I get you some help?"

Siam leveled his gaze at me. "I am bound by my service to the Queen and to the fae of Dell'Aria. Your first priority should not be saving me."

"But, Siam, what am I supposed to do? I think Aric is going to destroy the colony. We need to get everyone out of here."

"I know exactly what is happening, but you need proof. He can still deny any involvement in all this."

I rested Siam's head back to the ground as the reality of the situation hit me. "No one will believe an accused Soulstealer."

Siam nodded and took a heavy breath.

"The scroll!"

I emptied my pockets and quickly found the scroll that Franca had taken from the clinic and the seal breaker that Dooley had brought to me. My heart ached. Where would I be without either of them? And now Franca was dead and Dooley was locked somewhere I could not find him.

I pressed the seal breaker to the scroll, and the seal melted away. I spread out the scroll which contained pages of experiments that were being conducted with the magic stolen from Dell'Aria. It seemed as though the cure for memory loss was easily solved, but there was another experiment that took up most of the resources and took way more magic...wing growth.

Aric was continuing his experiments because he wanted to give me wings.

Pika jumped up into Siam's arms and licked at his face.

"Are you going to be okay?" I asked.

"Valora, I am sorry I so misjudged you. I would have been glad to have you serve next to me in the Royal Court. Know that the only reason you were not offered a spot was because of your father. I am where I need to be. You, however, need to go."

"What? He thought I wasn't good enough."

"No." Siam tilted his head. "I think his exact words to me were that he didn't want you anywhere near King Aric."

"I am sorry I misjudged you, also."

I bent down to kiss the top of Siam's head which was slick with his blood. I had not realized how badly he was injured until I got that close.

"Siam, I need to get you help."

But I was talking to a corpse. The amulet likely gave him the life he needed to tell me what he had, but Siam had already been on the path to death by the time I came into the room. The pikaki whimpered as it bounced about in Siam's lifeless arms.

"Come on, little one, you are coming with me." I scooped up the little fuzzball and stuffed him into the satchel at my side. "We need to find Dooley and my father."

CHAPTER THIRTY-FOUR

I still had no idea where Dooley or Aric was. The machine would be ready again shortly, and I was certain that Aric would use it one last time to bring Dell'Aria down and complete his experiment. But I was hoping that maybe he would be looking for me before he did so.

I pressed my back against the wall of the empty corridor and opened up my satchel. The only thing I had with me was Pika who was now sitting in a pile of his own orangey goop.

"Yuck. Still don't know why Siam loved you." The pikaki tilted his big eyed head at me once more. "But now I know why I love you."

I quickly stripped off my coat, dipped one finger into the pool of orange drool and began to trace the first Reiki symbol across the wall in front of me. I focused on the symbol of power that Dooley had first used to draw me into my memories and to connect with my mind as I tried to focus on Aric and our connection through the amulet which I had been trying to block. Now I completely dropped the mental shields I had erected between us.

In an instant I was transported into his mind's eye and what I saw was not pretty. I saw how he had convinced Brokk that the device needed to be built to help the half-fae transition during their life on Earth and that he had convinced Brokk that he had a higher purpose in mind. Once the machine was built he forced Brokk to either flee the colony or be executed. Brokk left, and Aric turned on the machine. The record, in his mind, of the first wave. Everyone dying and becoming sick. Including me. Aric made a deal with a demon in exchange for the amulet that hung around my neck. Everything was laid out in black and white. The history of his treachery, and it all made sense to him. And the worst was yet to come.

"Valora, didn't anyone ever teach you that it is rude to spy?" Aric forced me out of his thoughts, but not before I was able to see where he was.

I shoved Pika back into the satchel. "Let's go, Pika. We need to find the King's throne room."

∽

I raced through the corridors, twisting and turning in the hopes that eventually I would land upon the right path. I raced past one corridor and came to a dead stop. I had reached the prison cells. Each of the doors had a window covered in iron bars and a slit where food was passed through. I walked along and peered into each cell, and with every step the knot in my stomach tightened further. They were empty. The King likely rid himself of all those he thought were a threat to his secret. He didn't keep them.

"Oh, Dooley, I am so sorry."

"Valora, is that you?" The voice came from the cell at the end of the corridor.

"Kali?" I raced to the last cell, realizing as I did that the rest of them were certainly empty. "Are you okay? What are you doing here?"

"Aric."

Kali's face was streaked with dirt. A large angry gash across her cheek wept blood.

Bile rose in my throat. "I am getting you out of here." I gripped the iron bar that held the door in place, and it burned into my fingers. I lobbed it aside and heard it hit the ground as I did the same thing, clutching my hand in pain.

"Valora!" Kali pushed the door open and knelt down by my side. "Are you okay?" Pika pounced out of the satchel and bounded to my side. "What is Pika doing here?"

The fuzzball sniffed at my ruined hands and began to lick them. Immediately the orange drool calmed the burn. "Siam was smarter than I gave him credit for." I pushed myself up. "Kali, I can explain on our way, but do you think you can make it back to the tunnel you went through to get to the King's chambers?"

"Follow me." I raced behind Kali through the corridors as the sound of thunder roared up ahead. Seconds later we were thrown off balance as Dell'Aria rocked from the effects of another lightning strike. I pushed off the wall and continued on behind Kali.

"We are getting closer now." Kali slowed as we came to the turn that forced us into a dead end. "His chambers are right through that door. I'm sorry Valora. I never wanted you to get mixed up in all of this. If only you had stayed away."

I handed my satchel and the pikaki to Kali. "I would never let you stay imprisoned, Kali. You are my closest friend, like a sister." I wiped the stray tear that fell from her eye. "You need to stay here. I am going to have to face him alone."

Then it all happened at once—Pika's yelp, the door to the throne room swinging open, and Kali pushing me forward into the room before I could even turn around. "We had a deal and I kept my end of the bargain," she shouted at Aric.

"Wait, Kali! No!" I stumbled into the room, and she followed, closing the door behind us. What was happening? Did Kali believe the stories about me? I righted myself and faced her. "I am not a Soulstealer. Everything that Aric has told you is a lie. I can prove it."

My hand tickled the hilt of the blade at my side, but my brain could not wrap around the idea that Kali was a threat to me.

"I know you can. That's the problem." I froze as Kali pulled an arrow taut in her bow, aimed at my chest.

"What are you talking about, Kali?"

"You see, you might be okay with them stubby wings of yours, but I am not okay with mine." Kali gestured to the crooked and ruined wings that stuck out at odd angles from her back. "Aric has promised me some of that magic. It's going to fix my wings. Bring them back to their former glory."

"But, Kali, you can't fix what has happened to you. And you earned your scars in battle for Dell'Aria. Why wouldn't you carry those scars with pride? I know the other fae don't look down upon you for that." I kept my eyes focused on hers, hoping she wouldn't notice as I slowly moved my hand to grasp the hilt of my blade.

"You know nothing. All you know is that you have been ridiculed your entire life because of your stubby wings. You know nothing about what it is like to have them then lose them, what it is like to feel the wind as you glide through the air. What I live now is a half-life, and it is useless. King Aric has promised me wings." The bow that had drifted to the side as Kali began her speech centered back on my chest. "And I won't have you stopping him. Come with me."

Kali lowered her bow and gripped my arm, pushing me further into the King's chamber. I heard a noise and turned. What I saw knocked the wind out of me. Dooley was on his knees in the center of the room. I could barely recognize my lover's face. Beaten and bloody.

Aric moved out of the shadows, his eyes burning with anger. "I will give you some credit. This half-fae you brought to me certainly has stamina. I can't get the bastard to bow before me. Is he as good in bed? As good as I am?"

Aric whipped out the amulet from around his neck, and Dooley's eyes went from it to the one hanging at my throat. His head hung in defeat, and he sat back on his heels.

"Dooley, no."

I started toward him, but Kali latched her hands around my waist. "Not so fast, Valora. We have some business to attend to. Isn't that right, Aric?"

"Yes, but I think I finally found this one's weak spot." He walked over to Dooley and gave him a push. Dooley collapsed to the ground.

Tears tried to force their way into my field of vision, but I pushed them back. If I had any hope of getting both Dooley and me out of this, I needed to stay focused. I tried to remember my training as a Hunter. I tried to remember the day I stared down the dragon and survived. King Aric was just another dragon.

The main door to the King's chamber opened and in stepped Orris wearing the regalia of second in command of the King's Guard.

"Valora, you know Orris? He has recently been in some heroic battle against the Soulstealers who have besieged our colony. I have promoted him to second in command of the King's Guard, and since Siam seems to have disappeared, he is now acting commander of the Royal Guard."

"He knows where your brother is Orris. He killed him!"

Orris flinched. He had once said family meant something to him, maybe he would help me. He looked from me to Aric, but he was not going to question his King directly.

Aric turned to Orris who stood at attention. "Orris, have you gathered the fae? Are they ready to hear my proclamation?"

"Yes, Sire. They are all gathered below." He looked at his feet as he spoke.

Aric walked to the doors that opened up to the pulpit where he gave his mighty speeches to the fae of Dell'Aria and pushed them outwards. The heaving gales outside caught them and slammed them fully open. Wind blew through Aric's hair and ruffled the feathers of his wings. Kali clamped irons on my wrists as Aric took Dooley by the collar and pulled him onto the balcony. I refused to fall to my knees.

Through the shock waves of pain that rolled through my arms and into my legs as the iron chains burned into my skin I heard the chanting from the courtyard below.

"Traitor, traitor, traitor."

Aric turned and gestured to Kali. "Bring her here."

Kali shoved me from behind, and I fell forward onto the balcony. Her face was hardened and without emotion. Aric pressed Dooley's head onto a chopping block that was raised to a height visible to the frantic crowd below.

"Bring me the axe," Aric instructed Kali. Aric faced the crowd below, and as he opened his mouth to speak the fae fell silent. All that could be heard was the wind whistling through the colony and the rain as it pounded down. Aric lifted his voice above it all.

"Fae of Dell'Aria, I come before you today with the one who has brought our colony to this fate. There has been some question as to the loyalty of Valora to our people. But I am here today to tell you that she has brought us the one who has been stealing all the magic from our colony. This half-fae."

Aric kicked at Dooley's side, and he gave a low groan. The blood from his face dripped down the block, and he gave no struggle against the ropes binding his hands behind his back.

"And to prove that she is loyal to the Court and to Dell'Aria she will execute this true traitor to the fae in front of all of us now."

"Kali, undo her chains," instructed Aric.

Kali hesitated. "Are you sure, Aric? I don't think she will do it."

"I think she has no choice. Now do as I say."

Kali slid on the protective gloves and worked with the key to unfasten the irons from my wrists. Aric stared into my eyes and tried to force his power upon me, just as he did weeks ago in his carriage. Through our connection he tried to pry into the part of my brain that still cared for the young half-fae I had seen dragged into the courtyard.

He whispered, "Valora, you know what you have to do. He is all but dead already. I have done the hard part for you. Do this, and I will end it all. I have what I need to restore my mother's memory. I can replace all the rest and bring

Dell'Aria back to its former glory, and you can reign by my side."

"You would have me kill your brother so you can save your mother? How do you think she would feel about that?" I whispered back to him.

I released the wall I had been holding between my mind and his and let him see everything Dooley had revealed to me, the picture of Brokk and their mother, the same woman in the picture Aric had showed me of his mother. I showed him Dooley being taken as a young child from his mother because she had lost her memory. Different fae fathers, one human mother. Dooley and Aric were half-brothers and both half-fae.

"It seems she is not the only one who had their memory tampered with," I said.

Aric stood back with his mouth agape. I took the axe from his hand and held it in my own. Dooley's hair was sodden, and the long strands hung limp on either side of his face which was slack against the stone below his cheek. His eyes were swollen shut from the beating he had received. There was no telling where all of the blood was coming from.

Suddenly the weight of Aric's words came crashing down. The fae of Dell'Aria focused on me, on the axe, on the man that their King said was the cause of their suffering. They expected me to end it all. I was once their burden, and now Aric wanted to make me their savior and their Queen.

I stepped to the edge of the balcony and peered down at the crowd below. I closed my eyes and imagined the face of my mother who would be there to greet me when I died.

I was caught between these two brothers. I was caught between the truth and the fate of the fae of Dell'Aria.

"The wings Valora, they were always for you."

"I sacrificed everything!" A cry rang out behind me as Kali rushed forward, "No!"

My tired muscles strained as Kali fought to free the axe from my grip. She released her hold just as I neared the edge of the balcony and I pitched over the side, the axe falling to balcony floor.

Dooley grabbed my ankle. I thrust my arms around my face as I slammed against the side of the balcony. Hanging there, I heard the locked door to King Aric's chambers slam open with a force so great I knew without seeing that it threw the door off its hinges.

CHAPTER THIRTY-FIVE

I could feel Dooley's grip slipping. He had used the last of his strength to grasp onto me. Another hand gripped my other ankle and assisted Dooley in pulling me back over the railing. I saw that the other fae helping Dooley was Orris, and I also saw my father step through the door. Behind him was Pryn and the Selkie Queen, Elemi.

The Fae Queens had always held more power and magic than the Kings did. You could feel the wave of magic that carried her into the room.

The crowd of fae below had screamed and gasped as I fell over the balcony and now they were shouting and crying in a kind of mass hysteria.

I struggled to my feet. Kali skulked in the corner. Aric ignored me and stood to face the Selkie Queen. I'm not sure he ever believed I was really in danger, but he certainly was now. "How dare you come here uninvited."

"I received an invitation from someone else. You may know her," said Elemi.

From beneath her robes Elemi pulled a brown sack tied at the top with a golden cord. She undid the knot and pulled from the bag the head of the Queen of Dell'Aria. She tossed it to Aric's feet.

"I would appreciate it if you stopped disposing of your bodies through the portals. They have a tendency to end up on my doorstep, and I am starting to tire of your little games."

Orris picked up the axe from the ground where I had dropped it.

"In the name of the Queen and by the power of the Royal Court Guard I hereby proclaim King Aric guilty of treason, for the murder of the Queen and the head of the Royal Guard, my brother Siam. I sentence him to immediate death," said Orris.

The crowd below was getting only half of what was being said, but they heard enough that they suddenly became silent. Orris held the axe aloft. I grabbed Dooley away from the chopping block and cradled him in my arms. My father stared at the head of the Queen laid out at the feet of the King.

"What is this treachery?" my father shouted. I had never heard him speak with such vigor. "By the power of the second in command, I hereby relieve you of your duties as King and side with the Queen's Court in ordering your execution."

Aric turned to face me as I clutched Dooley to my chest.

"Valora, this was not all my doing. You must believe me. You will see me again. I will not let go of you that easily."

Above the pounding of the rain I heard the familiar sound of the cogs and gears of the Peixes which appeared suddenly about fifteen feet off the side of the balcony. Orris swung the axe in Aric's direction. The King ducked and grabbed Kali around the waist as he jumped off the edge of the balcony and spread his wings, landing on the deck of the Peixes.

"Arrows!" called Orris. But it was too late. The Peixes turned and flew away. I watched as it did. Aric stood resolutely at the edge of the deck, never taking his eyes off me.

He lifted from his neck the amulet and mouthed to me, "Forever and always."

He dropped the amulet to his chest and clutched on the railing as the Peixes took a sharp turn and disappeared off the easternmost edge of Dell'Aria. The dark storm clouds quickly enveloped the ship, and then it was gone.

☙◦❧

The remainder of that evening passed in a blur. My father and the Selkie Queen addressed the people of Dell'Aria. Every citizen was invited to view the scrolls which showed the experiments which were being done with the magic of Dell'Aria and then to pay their respects to the Queen. Everyone believed that Aric had killed her to keep her quiet, but with Kali's involvement I still wasn't sure which one of them had done it.

Kali had gone to great lengths to deceive me. Despite his treachery I believed that Aric had wanted me safe. Kali only seemed to want me out of the way. I think Aric had likely put her in the prison cell to keep her from interfering and then I went and freed her.

Honor was restored to many families after everyone found out that the only Soulstealer that had existed was the King himself.

The storm passed and, although weakened, the fae of Dell'Aria had a renewed sense of purpose. They no longer believed that their own brethren might be the ones causing the colony to fall into ruin.

Kali's treachery stabbed at my heart. I wasn't sure how I was going to recover from her betrayal which felt ten times more painful than that of the King. Time may or may not ever heal that wound.

The last thing I remembered was Orris and my father begging me to release my hold on Dooley.

Pryn had knelt down to me and whispered in my ear, "Your mother would have been proud."

He put his hand on my shoulder, and then I passed into darkness.

I awoke to the familiar blue canopy of the bed I had slept in every night of my life as a young fae. My mother had secretly stitched the pattern of the night sky into the underside so that I could pretend I was able to fly amongst the stars like the other fae. The bed depressed with the weight of another, and I half expected to see my mother sitting at my bedside.

"Are you feeling better?" My father sat next to me. Through the window I could see blue sky. Something soft brushed against me. Pika pushed his way under my hand, looking for a scratch.

"The pikaki seems to have taken to you. And since his kind seems to have some medicinal properties to the fae, I didn't think it would be bad if he snuggled up to you for a while."

I turned onto my side. My father had been silent on the one topic I was dreading to ask him about. "Is Dooley gone?"

"Don't worry. We were able to get to him in time. He will be fine. He is resting in one of the rooms down the hall. You have Pryn and Queen Elemi to thank for that."

"Why did Queen Elemi help us?"

"It seems that you befriended her daughter and her lover, both of whom consider you and the fae of Dell'Aria friends. Elemi was ready to let us fall into Underworld after what she learned about King Aric. But when she realized you were not on his side, she changed her mind."

I noticed that my father was wearing the official robe of the King, but not King Aric's robe; he was wearing the colors chosen by the King before King Aric's father.

"What is this for?" I ran my fingers through the velvet edging.

"This would be Orris's doing. Orris was put in charge of the Royal Guard, and since Aric is no longer King he decided to appoint me in his stead."

"Does that mean you will be taking a Queen?" I thought of my mother. How simple a woman she had been. I could never imagine her wielding the power that most fae Queens had to.

"No. Your mother was my only Queen." He pointed at the stars on the canopy above my bed. "And I know she is watching from her throne next to the Goddess Varuna and will approve of the decree I have made. When I pass, you are to be named Queen of Dell'Aria. And then it will be up to you to decide who your King will be."

"But what about Dell'Aria and the magic?"

"We were able to destroy the machine in the temple. It will take time, but Dell'Aria will replenish its magic."

"Do you really think I can be Queen? That the fae of Dell'Aria will accept me?"

"My dear Valora. It has never been about the fae of Dell'Aria accepting you. It has always been about you accepting yourself. Do that, and there is no one that can deny you your rightful place. And, yes, I do think you would make an excellent Queen, my daughter."

My father reached down and kissed me on the forehead. "Now rest. There will be many cycles before you will need to think of any of it, and you need more time to heal. I have drawn up the treaty you proposed between the dwarves and the fae of Dell'Aria, and I need you to be rested enough to help me finalize it."

For the first time since my mother died I passed into a deep sleep with the knowledge that all of those I cared about were taken care of.

❦

The next time I awoke it was dark, and the real stars were out. The clouds had all moved on, and Dell'Aria was silent in its peaceful slumber. I saw a shadow move from the corner of my eye and sat up, wrapping my robe tighter around me. Dooley stood up from a small stool he had been sitting on.

"How long have you been there?" I could barely see his face in the dark. The only light in the room was from a moonbeam that broke through the open window and created a divide in the room between Dooley and me.

Dooley stepped closer to the light, but stayed just out of its reach. He had bandages on his arms, legs, his face, almost everywhere, but through it all I could see his smile.

"I woke up a little while ago. I wanted to see you. But you seemed so peaceful sleeping I didn't want to disturb you."

He reached out and gave a little tug on my nightshirt, bringing me closer to him and into the light.

"This white gown and your wings. You certainly are my angel," he said.

"Fae. Very different than an angel."

Dooley laughed and wrapped his arms around my waist.

"I will remember that. You are no angel." His lips danced over the top of mine, and I felt the warmth of his breath against my face. His hands moved up my back, hooked around the base of my wings and pulled me into a deep kiss. Intensely urgent.

He drew back quickly. "I thought I was going to lose you."

"And I thought I was going to lose you."

Dooley looked down at the amulet around my neck. "They have found no way to remove it from you?"

I could do nothing but shake my head. How would I ever be able to be with Dooley as long as I had this connection to Aric? I couldn't imagine that he would be okay with it, especially since there was no real way to know how far that bond connected us. It was demon magic, and the details of the deal Aric made were between him and the demon, only known to them.

Dooley started to remove the amulet from my neck, and I closed my hand around it. "No, I can't take it off."

"Trust me."

A pause and I knew in that moment that I did trust him. I knew that Dooley would never harm me. I let go of the chain, and Dooley laid me down on the bed. He wrapped the chain of the amulet around my wrists and placed the amulet into my hands.

"Now don't let go." There was a flicker behind Dooley's eyes that sent trembles of pleasure down my spine.

Dooley turned me over onto my stomach and loosened the neck of my gown. His hands lovingly stroked my wings from tip to tip and relaxed every muscle in my back.

"Dooley, you still need to heal," I mumbled into my pillow. I was concerned about his health, but I didn't want him to stop.

His hands trailed the length of my legs, up and under my gown. I pushed myself into the bed trying to relieve some of the tension that was building between my legs. He pushed my gown up over my back to reveal my naked backside and traced his fingers in deliberate patterns over my back. My buttocks. My thighs. There was a tingling through my whole body.

Dooley laid his body, now free of any clothes, against me as I gripped the amulet in my hand. I could feel his hardness pushing up against me, and I wanted nothing more than to flip myself over and welcome him inside. But with one hand he encircled my waist and pulled me against him as he lay by my side and spooned his legs around mine. His hand snaked about my hip, dipped into the wet cleft between my legs and centered on the swollen mound of flesh that cried out for his caress.

He pressed his face into the down of my wings and penetrated my mind with the magic of the symbols he had traced over my body. As he entered my thoughts and combined them with his own he continued to ply my body with his fingers until I came to a shivering climax. My body burst with pleasure, and I eased back onto the firm length of him, no longer able to contain my need.

Then he thrust inside me, deeper and deeper. I could hear his thoughts in my mind, swirling with desire. I pushed back against him, burying him further inside and allowing him access to a corner of my mind I had kept closed to him until now. "I love you, Dooley. I want you. I don't need you. I want you. My King."

ভ∽৯

The next morning I awoke to a pure burst of sunshine. No longer did the copper plating that had once colored everything a dusky brown litter the skyline. Dell'Aria was slowly returning to its former glory. From my window perch I could make out the ice fruit fields on the other side of the city and the small roof of the hut I had once shared with Kali. The trees were starting to bounce back to life. Everything in Dell'Aria was. Fae bustled about, no longer needing every minute of their day focused on keeping out the Blight.

Clumps of bright blue ice fruits dotted the field, but all I could see were Aric's eyes staring back at me. Dell'Aria was safe, but only for now.

ABOUT THE AUTHOR

Photo by Phil Holden

Nicolette is a mother, wife, paralegal, writer, knitter, traveler, violinist and anything else she can get her hands on. She turned to writing stories at an early age, when filling out Mad Libs just wasn't enough.

She enjoys watching dark comedies, warped fairytales, and cheesy 80s comedies. Her interest in music spans from George Winston to Thrill Kill Cult to Bel Canto and U2. She loves to travel, and plans to do more as her son grows older. In her younger days she loved to go out dancing, and you may still, on occasion find her shaking her booty during 80s or goth rock nights at the few clubs they still exist at. She is constantly picking up new hobbies and interests. She knits socks, grows mini cucumbers in her garden, and played the violin for 5 years. She has a pug dog with a nervous temperament and speaks a little Spanish. She's eclectic.

Please come visit Nicolette Reed at: www.nicolettereed.com